The Witness

The WITNESS

A novel by Josh McDowell

Tyndale House Publishers, Inc.
Carol Stream, Illinois

Visit Tyndale's exciting Web site at www.tyndale.com.

Visit Josh McDowell's Web site at www.josh.org.

The Witness

Previously published by IMprint Edition of Campus Crusade in 2008 under
ISBN 978-981-08-0788-7.

First printing by Tyndale House Publishers, Inc., in 2010.

Designed by Andrew Milne Design Limited

Library of Congress Cataloging-in-Publication Data

McDowell, Josh.
The witness / Josh McDowell.
p. cm.
ISBN 978-1-4143-3412-7 (pbk.)
I. Title.
PS3613.C395W58 2010
813′.6—dc22 2010017410

Printed in the United States of America

16 15 14 13 12 11 10
7 6 5 4 3

PART ONE

1

His daughter was dead. His wife was missing. And now Rafeeq Ramsey clearly feared for his own life.

"We have only two more days," the old man said, pacing the sumptuous living room of his palatial flat on the shores of Monte Carlo and chain-smoking like a man who might rather die of lung cancer than a car bomb or an assassin's bullet. "I received a new note just before you arrived. If I don't wire them more money by Friday, they say they'll kill Claudette and come after me. So please, Mr. Accad, I beg of you—tell me you have good news, because I don't think I can take much more of this."

"How much are they asking for now?"

"Twenty-five million," Ramsey said. "On top of the 11 million euros I've already paid."

It was an enormous sum of money—at least it would be for a mere mortal. But the seventy-nine-year-old Ramsey was no mere mortal. Six months earlier, he had sold his company—Blue Nile Holdings, founded with his late brother back in 1963—to a French conglomerate for a cool €563 million. He was now one of the wealthiest men in Egypt and a living legend among the business elite throughout North Africa and the Middle East.

Marwan Accad sat a few meters away on a long couch made of rich Italian leather and took in the moment. In so many ways, Ramsey was the perfect client—old, rich, and terrified. It was men like this for whom Marwan had launched his executive security business in the first place.

But this case had left the vilest taste in his mouth. Greed. Corruption. Blackmail. Murder. Everywhere he looked, every stone he turned over, he found himself face-to-face with the depravity of men's souls. He certainly did not have any words of solace for this wretched old man, now bereft of the two women he loved most in the world, and he began to wonder if it was time to get out of this business once and for all.

Marwan finished his espresso and stared out over the glistening Mediterranean and at the reflection of the late-afternoon sun in the windows of the other luxury apartments nearby. He wondered what his parents would have thought of the life he now lived—the jet helicopters and the Humvees, the Armani suits and the Kevlar vests. The more risks he took, the more money he made. Wasn't that just good business?

He knew what his mother would say. She had begged him to get out of Beirut after his army service and become a doctor or an engineer and move to Paris. She had longed for him to live a safe and quiet life, to have sons and raise them to be men of peace, men of science, men of accomplishment. But like a fool, he had not listened. Could she see him now? Did she know how much time he spent helping the rich buy their trophy wives back from blackmailers and drug lords? Did she see how much time he spent jetting clients in and out of Baghdad and Mosul and Fallujah? Did the dead cry themselves to sleep?

"I do have news," Marwan Accad said at last. "But I'm afraid it is not good."

"What have those animals done to Claudette?" Ramsey demanded. "I'll kill them. I swear to you, Mr. Accad. I will not rest until I hunt them down and make them suffer."

Marwan shook his head.

"It is about Claudette, but it's not what you think. Please, have a seat."

"Just tell me what you know."

"I will, Mr. Ramsey. But please, sit, and then I will tell you everything."

A corpulent man whose health had been slipping fast over the past two weeks, Ramsey slumped down in a large overstuffed chair and nervously lit another cigarette. His eyes were red and moist and filled with anxious expectation. He leaned forward. "Please, Mr. Accad, don't toy with me."

Marwan nodded. "Mr. Ramsey, what does São Paulo mean to you?"

The old man looked confused. "You mean the city, in Brazil?"

"Right."

Ramsey shrugged. "Nothing; why?"

"Nothing?" Marwan insisted.

"No. Should it?"

"Did Blue Nile Holdings have any offices or factories there?"

"No."

"Were any of your senior management team from there?"

"No."

"Were any of your employees from there?"

"I don't think so."

"Have you ever been to São Paulo on business?"

"No, I tell you."

"Have you ever been there on vacation with your wife?"

"Who has time for vacations?" Ramsey sniffed. "I am a busy man."

"Has Mrs. Ramsey ever been to São Paulo alone for any other reason?"

"No, of course not."

"You're absolutely sure?"

"I don't see what you're trying to—"

"Are you sure, Mr. Ramsey?" Marwan pressed. *"Think."*

Rafeeq Ramsey got up from the chair and began pacing around the room again, taking long drags on his cigarette.

"Well, actually, come to think of it, I think she did," he said after a moment.

"Tell me about it."

"There's not much to tell," Ramsey said. "Claudette's second cousin once married a Brazilian. It lasted about six months before they got divorced."

"Did you go to the wedding?" Marwan asked.

"No, but Claudette did. She hated it—São Paulo, that is.

Too crowded. Too noisy. New York without the charm, she said."

"When was the wedding?"

"I don't know, maybe three or four years ago," Ramsey said, mixing himself a drink at the bar by the windows. "Why? Where are you going with all this?"

Marwan reached down, opened his briefcase, pulled out a large manila envelope, and held it out to Ramsey.

"What is that?" the old man asked. He sipped his martini.

"Open it," Marwan said. "You'll see."

Ramsey stared at Marwan for a moment, then set down his drink, walked over, took the envelope, and opened it slowly.

As he pulled out an eight-by-ten black-and-white photograph, all color drained from his face, and a look of profound confusion filled his eyes.

In Ramsey's hands was a photograph of his wife, date-stamped less than forty-eight hours earlier. Unlike the previous photos that had come with the ransom notes, in this one she was not bound. She was not gagged. Instead, she appeared to be sitting in an office, in front of a desk, talking to a clerk or manager of some kind.

"I don't . . . I don't understand," Ramsey finally managed to say, though his voice was weak and his hands were trembling. "What is this? Where was this taken?"

"It was taken by a surveillance camera inside a bank in São Paulo," Marwan explained. "Your wife withdrew funds from the money you wired for her ransom."

Ramsey was clearly having trouble processing the image in his hands.

"What are you saying, Mr. Accad?" the old man said at last.

"That my wife . . . you think she planned this whole thing? You're saying this is proof that she betrayed me?"

Marwan said nothing. He waited for the painful truth to sink in before he offered his client a plan of action. But he never got the chance. The plate-glass windows suddenly exploded around them. The noise of two shots filled the room. The old man crashed to the floor. His blood formed a slowly growing pool on the carpet.

Rafeeq Ramsey was dead, and Marwan Accad feared he might be next.

2

MARWAN DOVE FOR COVER behind Ramsey's massive oak desk as more gunfire filled the suite, shattering dishes and picture frames and sending shards of glass flying everywhere.

Two of Ramsey's bodyguards burst into the room, guns drawn, but they were shot dead before they could identify the sniper, much less return fire.

Marwan grabbed the phone, but the line had been cut. He reached for his gun before remembering it had been taken from him by the security guards at the front desk. A collection of ancient vases exploded over his head. Multiple rounds ripped up the furniture all around him.

He couldn't stay there. Whoever had just killed Ramsey was obviously using a scope. They knew Marwan was in the room, and they knew where.

Marwan rolled left and scrambled to the slain bodyguards. The gunfire intensified. He grabbed the men's sidearms and doubled back to grab the photo of Ramsey's wife, then dove out the open door into the main hallway.

Two more guards were coming off the elevator.

"Get down! Get down!" Marwan shouted as the hallway filled with gunfire.

The first guard hit the deck instantly. The second wasn't fast enough. As the glass of the hallway windows exploded inward, he took two rounds in the back and began shrieking in pain.

"Quick, Mr. Accad, take the stairs," the first guard yelled, trying desperately to help his colleague, though his efforts appeared to be in vain.

Marwan took the advice and moved quickly into the stairwell, guns drawn in case anyone was waiting for him. The stairs were clear. He raced down ten flights, his mind reeling.

Moments later he burst into the lobby, wondering if there was any hope that his driver was still waiting for him. He scanned the growing crowd but didn't see anyone he recognized. He could hear sirens in the distance. A fire alarm was going off. People were screaming. It was pandemonium. But the gunfire had stopped, at least for now.

"Mr. Accad?" someone yelled through the crowd.

Private security guards and plainclothes agents were racing in from all directions. Residents of the building flooded out of the elevators, panic on their faces. He saw no one he knew, but he heard the voice again.

"Mr. Accad, over here."

He turned and looked again and this time saw his driver, a small, kindly-looking man, running toward him.

"Mr. Accad, please," the man said, trying to catch his breath, "we need to get you out of here. Wait here, and I'll bring the car to the door."

"I'll go with you," Marwan said.

"No, no, monsieur," the driver insisted. "I will only be a moment."

The driver was already heading toward the door, weaving his way through the crush of people trying to flee Sovereign Plaza and the adjacent Seaside Plaza, two of the most luxurious and sought-after apartment complexes in Monaco.

Marwan had no interest in arguing with the man. There was too much else to think about. Had Claudette Ramsey and her accomplices known Marwan was tracing their money transfers? Did they know he'd tracked them to São Paulo? Is that why they had killed Rafeeq Ramsey today, before he could act on these new leads? How was that possible? He had only told Ramsey himself moments before he died.

Accad & Associates had been working for Ramsey for just the past ten days. Ramsey had employed a Paris-based security firm for years; Accad's company had been brought in to investigate the death of Ramsey's daughter and the disappearance of his wife, nothing else. Marwan had offered to supplement or even replace the French bodyguards with his own men, but Ramsey had said no. He didn't want to implement any obvious changes that might upset the blackmailers or push them toward mistreating his beloved wife in any way. It had been a fatal mistake.

Marwan watched police cars and other emergency vehicles converge on the area from every direction and knew the media wouldn't be far behind. That was the last thing he needed—his face plastered all over newspapers throughout Europe and the Middle East. It was not exactly the kind of publicity the CEO of a thriving executive security company craved.

He checked his watch and scanned the crowd outside. He finally spotted his driver crossing the street, getting into the gleaming new Range Rover, and starting the engine.

Marwan moved for the front door. He wanted to get out of there as quickly as he possibly could. But just as he exited the building and began making his way across the plaza, the SUV suddenly erupted in a tremendous explosion, the force of which sent Marwan crashing to the ground. Flames and smoke shot into the air. Glass and pieces of burning metal rained down from the sky. And in that horrifying moment, Marwan suddenly realized that he, too, was being hunted.

3

Bodies littered the street and grounds. The wounded screamed for help. Others stumbled around in silence and in shock, looking for friends and loved ones or wondering what had just happened and why.

Marwan got up and wiped the blood from his face, wincing as the handkerchief passed across the tiny gashes spotting his cheeks and forehead. He removed the ammo clip from one of the guard's pistols he had taken, emptied the chamber, wiped his prints off the gun, and threw it in a nearby trash can. Then he stuffed the other in his belt, covered it with his jacket, and began running north for the main business district, just a few blocks away.

He needed to get back to his hotel, gather his things, and get out of town. No one stopped him. Everyone seemed frantic or too shell-shocked to care who he was or why he was in such a hurry.

He flagged down a passing cab.

"Le Méridien," Marwan told the driver.

"Yes, sir," the man replied in a heavy accent. A moment later the two sped off.

The sun was slowly approaching the mountains. The lights of the city were coming on. The casinos and cafés were open for business. Monte Carlo, the playground of the rich and famous, was coming alive, though news of the attacks would be spreading soon.

Marwan watched the yachts in the harbor blur by as he made a mental checklist. He needed to call his brother. He needed more cash. He needed a flight—reservations, tickets. But to where? from where? Was he headed to Italy or France?

Running would make him look guilty, he knew. But given all that had just happened, he wasn't sure he had a choice. Staying could be a death sentence. He would be questioned at length by the police, of course. *Who had first introduced him to Rafeeq Ramsey? Why had Marwan come to Monte Carlo when he knew full well that Ramsey already had a French security firm working for him? How could he explain that his second meeting with Ramsey had ended in the man's death? Why had he taken the security guards' weapons? Why had he not claimed his own pistol from the front desk?* On and on it would go, and those were the easy questions. What really concerned him was something Ramsey had said the first time they had met.

The taxi pulled up to the hotel. Marwan paid the driver and asked him to wait. He wouldn't be long. Then he raced inside and took an elevator to the fifth floor.

An attractive young woman in her early twenties rode up with him. She reminded him vaguely of a woman he used to date. Long dark hair. Soulful brown eyes. White silk blouse, black skirt, black stockings, pearl necklace. Red painted nails and red lipstick, with a bit too much eye shadow. *That was a long time ago,* he thought. She smiled shyly. Normally Marwan would have smiled back, struck up a conversation. But not tonight.

He looked down at his feet and forced himself to refocus. He tried to reconstruct his first conversation with Ramsey, a week and a half earlier. The broad strokes were easy. Ramsey had recounted the events leading up to the simultaneous abduction of his wife and daughter, one from the beauty salon, the other on her way home from school; one leading to blackmail, the other to murder.

But it was the names of suspects that Marwan kept running through in his mind. Ramsey had suggested no less than a dozen ex-employees and business rivals who he believed might have the motive, the means, and the opportunity to attack his family. But there was one scenario that concerned him above all others.

The elevator bell rang. The door opened on the third floor. The woman beside him pulled out a cell phone and began dialing as she stepped off. He took one last look at her. *Missed opportunities,* he mused as she strutted away.

The door closed again.

Marwan's thoughts returned to his conversation with Ramsey. The old man had told him that several years earlier, two French intelligence operatives had tried to blackmail him, claiming that if he did not pay them two hundred and fifty thousand euros, they would get their friends in the tax bureau to launch an investigation into Blue Nile Holdings for tax evasion and accounting irregularities. They said they would leak stories to the newspapers designed to embarrass him and his company.

At the time, Ramsey had been trying to sell his company to a Paris-based multinational. He didn't want the deal scuttled by some long and public government investigation, even if the allegations were false. He told Marwan that he had paid the men, writing it off as "consulting fees." But when they had demanded more—this time, one million euros—Ramsey had contacted Interpol, which had set up a sting operation. The agents were soon caught and faced twenty-five years to life in prison. But when they cut a deal with prosecutors and promised to name several coconspirators, they were found dead in their jail cells. The murders were never solved, and the case went cold.

The French government officially apologized to Ramsey, and—though he never blamed them—they seemed to go out of their way to assure him and his wife that those responsible were rogue agents who had been acting on their own and that they in no way represented the intelligence services or the administration in Paris.

Still, Ramsey had confided in Marwan that he also believed there was at least one more rogue agent deep inside French intelligence who had planned the blackmail operation from the beginning. Furthermore, he believed this rogue agent had had his coconspirators killed in prison to keep them from talking and was once again trying to shake him down.

That, Ramsey had said, was why he had contacted Marwan—

because he wasn't sure whom else he could trust. If some higher-up in French intelligence, acting on his own, was coming after him, how could he trust some low-level homicide detective in the Parisian police force to solve the case and bring the guilty party or parties to justice?

The elevator bell rang again.

The door opened on the fifth floor. But Marwan, lost in thought, barely noticed. Could Ramsey have been right? What's more, could Ramsey's wife have been working with this unnamed, unknown French operative from the beginning? Why? What would have been her motive? From all appearances, Rafeeq and Claudette Ramsey seemed a happy couple—rich, amorous, and about to enjoy his long-overdue retirement. What had gone wrong?

The elevator door began to close.

Marwan suddenly snapped back to the reality of the moment. There would be time to figure this all out later. Right now, he needed to get his things and get out of there. If the police wanted an interview, he would let them know where to find him. But he wouldn't hang around to get picked off by a sniper or another car bomb.

He reached out his hand and triggered the doors back open. Then, stepping off the elevator, he turned right and headed down the hallway. Something seemed odd, different in some way, and it wasn't until he was five steps out of the elevator that he realized how dim the light was, as if some of the lights had blown out or the bulbs had been removed.

At the end of the hallway, a figure moved in the shadows. Marwan heard the distinctive sound of a hammer being pulled back. And he knew instantly that he'd been found.

because he wasn't [illegible] enough [illegible].

The dream returned again.

The dream started in the [illegible] [illegible], but Marcus [illegible] in thought [illegible] [illegible] [illegible] Manning [illegible] [illegible] [illegible]. [illegible] [illegible] [illegible] [illegible] [illegible] with [illegible] [illegible] [illegible] [illegible] [illegible] [illegible] [illegible]. What [illegible]?

[illegible] was going to pay.

Marcus suddenly snapped back to the reality of the moment. There would be time to figure this all out later. Right now, he needed to get the things [illegible] out of there. If the police [illegible] [illegible] [illegible], he would [illegible] [illegible] [illegible] [illegible] [illegible] [illegible] [illegible] [illegible] [illegible] [illegible] [illegible] [illegible] [illegible].

He [illegible] [illegible] the [illegible], [illegible] the door, back [illegible].

At the end of the hallway, [illegible] [illegible] in the shadows. Marcus [illegible] [illegible] [illegible] [illegible] [illegible] [illegible] [illegible] [illegible] [illegible] [illegible] [illegible] [illegible].

4

Marwan broke left as the gun fired, and the blast echoed through the hallway. The shot ripped a hole in the wall beside him, sending chunks of Sheetrock into the air.

He quickly drew the gun from his belt and returned fire. As he did, the exit door at the other end of the hall flew open. Marwan turned in time to see another figure emerge from the shadows—the woman from the elevator.

Marwan dropped to the floor just as another round exploded in the wall over his head. He aimed for the woman's head and squeezed off two shots, then pivoted back and fired two more rounds at the man in the shadows ahead of him. None of the shots hit their intended targets, but they bought him a few precious seconds.

Just ahead several meters was a tiny side hallway on the

right—a vestibule, almost—leading to a large suite. It didn't offer much protection, but it was all he was going to get for now. He fired again—twice in both directions—then dashed to the side hallway, turning the corner just as the return fire began. For the moment, neither hunter had a clear shot at him. But that wouldn't last for long.

Again the hallway filled with the sounds of gunfire.

They were already closing in. Meter by meter. Door by door.

He had only a few seconds to make his move.

Marwan fired two more shots around the corner to the left and two more to the right; then he wheeled around and fired into the Do Not Disturb sign hanging from the door handle. Smashing the door with both feet halfway down from the plaque declaring this the honeymoon suite, he knocked it off its hinges. Marwan dove forward as more gunfire erupted behind him.

Inside the room, a young couple huddled in the corner behind their room service trays, shivering with fear.

"Get down," Marwan ordered in a voice not much louder than a whisper. "Under the bed—quick!"

He had no time to explain he wasn't the villain in this nightmare. All he wanted to do was try to keep them as safe as possible for as long as possible. The two lovers scrambled to the floor and crawled under the large canopy bed, staring back at him as he ejected the spent magazine from his pistol and reloaded. Then Marwan moved to the sliding glass door and stepped onto the balcony.

He felt the bullet slice into his right shoulder before he heard the gun go off.

The impact sent him reeling. He crashed into a small glass table on the balcony, which collapsed beneath him. Still, he had the presence of mind to roll over, firing back into the room with one hand while shielding his face with the other.

One round went wild, and the partly open sliding door exploded into a thousand shards of glass, but the other rounds hit their mark. The woman with the pearls took two bullets in the chest. She screamed in agony and collapsed to the floor.

One down, but there was still one to go.

Marwan moved with as much speed as he could muster, fighting his pain. He shook off the glass, scrambled to his feet, and staggered back inside the hotel room, his gun still aimed at the door to the hallway, waiting for the partner to show his face. To his right, the young bride was hyperventilating. Her husband of probably only a few hours tried in vain to comfort her.

Marwan bristled with a murderous rage. He reached down and felt the pulse of the woman with the pearls. She was dying but was not yet dead. Her pulse was slow and erratic. He kicked her pistol out of her reach and turned her over, only to find her blouse turning crimson.

He fired a shot through the hallway door, buying himself a few more seconds. Then he thrust his pistol in the woman's throat.

"Who sent you?" Marwan said through gritted teeth.

The woman, nearly unconscious, smiled weakly but said nothing.

Marwan repeated himself in French, but still the woman kept silent.

"Claudette Ramsey? Did she send you from São Paulo?" he demanded.

The woman's face suddenly registered real fear—and surprise. It was clear she knew that name. She knew that city. He pressed the gun deeper into her neck, but she still refused to talk, and then suddenly her eyes rolled back in her head and her faint breathing stopped altogether.

Marwan's heart was still racing. A nearly toxic combination of adrenaline and revenge coursed through his veins. He grabbed the woman's pistol, checked the magazine, and stormed into the hallway, both guns blazing. The man in the shadows never had a chance. Marwan tossed his guns onto the man's crumpled body, then pried the pistol from the man's left hand and the spare magazine from his suit pocket.

The man had no identification on him whatsoever—no wallet, no passport, nothing. Marwan doubled back to the honeymoon suite. The woman with the pearls had no ID either. These were professionals—trained to be invisible, anonymous; trained to stalk their prey in the shadows and then strike without warning. What if Ramsey had been right? What if they were French intelligence?

For now, one thing was certain: they had picked the wrong fight.

As his heart rate finally slowed, the burning in his right shoulder intensified. He felt blood streaking down his cheeks from the multiple glass cuts on his head.

And then he heard the sirens.

5

Should he stay or run?

He had only seconds to decide. The police would be there any moment. The thought should have made him feel safer, but it only increased his anxiety.

Yes, he had an airtight case of self-defense. But would it matter? He was being hunted. And whoever was after him apparently knew his every move. They had known he was in Monaco. They had known he was staying at the Méridien, despite the fact that he had registered under an assumed name. They had known he would meet with Ramsey. They had known when. They had known where. They had known what car he'd be in, what elevator he'd be in. How was that possible? How could they have known?

He supposed it was possible that his pursuers had no

connection to a European or Middle Eastern police force or intelligence service. But the odds were dropping quickly. Who else could be tracking him so closely? Only the tiniest handful of people had even known about this trip, and it had been arranged less than forty-eight hours earlier.

Marwan decided he would try to find the taxi that had brought him to the hotel. If it was still out front—if the driver had not yet been scared off by the commotion or forced to leave by the police, or if he had not gotten sick of waiting—Marwan would consider it a sign that he should run. He would head to Milan, then to Rome, and then get back to his brother in Beirut as soon as he could.

But if the taxi was not there, if there was no way to escape, Marwan would accept this as a sign that he should remain, that his fate was sealed, that he must go to the police and take his chances.

Perhaps if there had been more time, he would have devised a more clever plan. But there were only precious seconds now.

"Don't you move from under that bed," Marwan commanded the couple, who continued to cower under the box springs.

Marwan stuffed the pistol into his belt and ran into the bathroom. He splashed water on his face and hands. He washed as much blood out of his hair as he could.

Gently, he slid off his jacket and pulled his shirt over his head, realizing for the first time just how badly he was hurt. He used a warm washcloth to clean the excruciating gash in his shoulder. The entry wound was not large, but the area around it was discolored. There was no exit wound in the back, which meant that the bullet was still in there. He desperately needed to get the bullet out and the wound cleaned. And even then, he knew he still ran a serious risk of an infection.

But there was nothing he could do about it now except swallow a handful of pain relievers, which he did, taking them from a plastic bottle beside the sink. A black T-shirt lay crumpled in a ball next to the tub. He snatched it up and slid it over his head. It smelled of American cigarettes and cheap champagne.

Next, he stuffed a dry washcloth under the shirt as a dressing for his shoulder wound and ditched the rest of the bloody towels in the tub. He wished he had some alcohol or other antiseptic to soak the washcloth with, but at least for now, this would have to do. After sliding his jacket back on, he grabbed one of the couple's garment bags from the closet by the bathroom, bolted out the door, and ran toward the emergency exit.

He raced down the stairwell and peeked out the hotel's side door. The first police car had reached the hotel. He saw two officers jump out and run into the lobby. He also saw his taxi still waiting for him, just a few yards away. He made a dash for it and climbed into the backseat.

"The airport," he said in French.

But the man did not move.

Marwan repeated himself in English, but still nothing.

He leaned forward to shake the man awake and saw blood on the dashboard and the passenger seat. The driver was dead—shot in the left temple.

Marwan spun around and drew his pistol again. He scanned the parking lot, the road, the front entrance. He saw no one. But he heard more sirens approaching.

What kind of sign is this? he wondered. He had a car but no driver.

And then a terrible thought came over him. His fingerprints were all over the door and interior of the taxi. If he ran now, he would be suspected of murder. A warrant would be issued for his arrest. His career would be finished. His company would be ruined. Rich men didn't hire bodyguards who were wanted for murder, no matter how loudly they insisted upon their innocence.

But running offered one benefit that staying might not—the chance to live.

With all that had just happened, Marwan was convinced that staying in Monte Carlo was a death sentence. The people hunting him knew too much about him, and they had the initiative. Running at least gave him the hope of getting out of Monaco, out of Europe, and slipping off the grid until he could figure out who was after him—and why—and plot his next move.

It was decided. He would run.

Marwan glanced behind him and from side to side. For the moment, there was no one around. He reached over the dead man and found a switch to lower the driver's seat all the way back. When that was done, he dragged the man's body into the backseat. Then he got out, went around the car, opened the front door, and popped the trunk.

In the trunk he found a blanket and some maps. He quickly laid the blanket over the body and tossed the maps into the passenger seat. Marwan reached into the glove compartment. Beside the owner's manual, the registration, an insurance card, and several pads of blank receipts, there was a small stack of napkins and some ketchup packets. The napkins would have to do. Marwan glanced around again, then cleaned up as much of the blood and bits of the driver's head from the interior of the car as he could, as rapidly as he could. He felt his gag reflex triggering at what his hand felt through the napkins, but still he pressed on.

Fortunately—at least for Marwan—the driver's side window had been open when the man had been shot. The window itself was still intact. Marwan got into the car, rolled up the window, turned the key, and checked his rearview mirror. His shoulder was throbbing, but he had no time to think about that.

Flashing lights were coming up fast.

The manager of the hotel ran out the front door and waved the police in. He yelled something that Marwan couldn't hear but took to mean "move."

Marwan complied, cautiously pulling out of the hotel driveway and heading west.

Italy was a mistake, he decided. France was better. He had some cash, clothes, and half a dozen fake passports stashed in Marseille, as he did in several cities throughout Europe and the Middle East, a necessary precaution in his business. Depending on traffic, he could be in Marseille in just a couple of hours. There, he could ditch the car and body and catch a plane for Casablanca.

It had been years since he'd been in Morocco, and he had vowed to never go back. The scar from the knife wound on his side gently tingled as he thought about what had happened there. However, Casa was also where one of his closest friends lived—a man who had been on many missions with him a lifetime ago; the one man, besides his brother, whom Marwan knew he could trust—Kadeen al-Wadhi.

6

Marwan wound through the streets, passing from Monte Carlo into the neighboring residential ward of Saint Michel. He was anxious to get onto La Provençale, the freeway that would take him to Marseille. There was something that was keeping him from heading that way, though—a black Peugeot about a block and a half back.

He wasn't sure how long it had been there. In the craziness of leaving the hotel with a dead body in the backseat and a bullet in his shoulder, he had forgotten one of the key tenets of being a security man—always watch your back. *Stupid, stupid, stupid!* Marwan didn't want to tip his hand about heading to Marseille, but he also couldn't afford to spend all evening on a tour of Monaco's ten wards.

Keeping one eye on the rearview mirror and one eye

toward the front, he made a right turn. Sure enough, the Peugeot turned after him. Two blocks up, he turned right again. Ten seconds later, his shadow followed. After two more right turns, he had completed a circle. Now there was no doubt in his mind that he was being followed. He needed to lose them, but where? The last thing he wanted was to attract the attention of the police with some insane high-speed chase. *If I could just—*

A car pulled from a side street right in front of Marwan. He slammed on the brakes, but not quickly enough. The taxi plowed into the side of the car. The air bag exploded in his face, then deflated. The shock of the slam to the face was quickly replaced by excruciating pain from his shoulder. He cried out, but the cry quickly turned into coughing from the air bag's powder.

Suddenly, his head was thrown backward as the car that had been trailing him hit the cab from behind.

Instinctively, he dropped flat along the front bench seat. Half a second later, the rear window shattered. The pistol that had been on the seat next to him lay on the floorboard. He reached for it, pointed it over the back of the seat, and fired off two rounds.

Pushing open the passenger door, he slid across the seat and out onto the street. The agony from the collision with the pavement caused his vision to momentarily gray, but he shook himself alert. He rolled to give himself a view of the car behind. As he did, a man with a gun stepped out. Marwan fired two shots, both connecting with the gunman and dropping him to the ground.

Bullets thunked into the door Marwan had just pushed

open. He swiveled back around and connected one of two shots directed at a man who was firing over the hood of the car he had hit. One shot was enough. *Two down. How many more to go?*

He heard yelling but couldn't make out the words. *Still more than one.* He rolled so he could see under the car. A pair of feet was slowly making its way along the other side. He fired one shot into the right ankle. A man cried out and fell.

His head cracked on the pavement, then turned. His eyes locked with Marwan's for what seemed like a minute, though it was less than a second. *I hate seeing their faces,* Marwan thought as he fired his weapon. One of the man's eyes disappeared; the other went lifeless.

There's at least one more around here somewhere, he thought as he scanned under the car one last time. He pushed himself into a squat. Looking around, he didn't like what he saw. Although this was a quiet residential street, the battle was beginning to draw spectators. He knew he had only a matter of minutes before the police arrived.

Marwan glanced up through the taxi's windows, but the other side of the car was clear. He dropped back down. *Where is he?* He listened for any signs of movement, any breathing or coughing that would indicate he was close.

"Mon dieu," cried a woman's voice from the house in front of him. Marwan twisted to his left and fired, a lucky guess that saved his life. The fourth man buckled forward, then collapsed toward the curb.

In a squat, Marwan made a circuit of the cars, making sure that no attackers were left. He heard voices and looked out. People were beginning to come out of their houses.

"Are you okay?" one man called out. "I saw the whole thing. Who were those men?"

Instead of answering, Marwan quickly assessed the situation. His car and the car that he hit were clearly undrivable. But the Peugeot . . .

"I called the police. They're on their—"

Marwan pushed past the first man who had arrived at the scene. The man called out to him, but he ignored him. He reached into the taxi and pulled out the bag he had taken from the couple at the hotel.

Then, amid the angry curses of the neighbors who had come to help, he slid into the front seat of the Peugeot. He twisted the key, threw the car into reverse, and backed down the street, hoping that no one had written down the license plate number from the back bumper.

When he got to the next intersection, he slammed on the brakes, pulled the car into a one-eighty, then raced off the way he had come.

7

Soon Marwan was heading west again. He kept a close watch on his mirrors but this time didn't see anything. Keeping his right hand loosely on the wheel, he reached up and gently touched his shoulder.

He sucked in air through his teeth. The pain, although extreme, he had expected. The dampness from his blood soaking through the hotel washcloth, he had not. His jacket and the black T-shirt would hide the spreading stain for a while, but not long enough.

Pulling to the side of the road, he took out a small pocketknife and used it to cut a large swatch out of the fabric of the passenger seat. He folded the square twice over.

Gritting his teeth, he reached under his shirt and tugged at the washcloth. When it finally gave, he quickly tossed it to the ground. He threw his head back against the headrest and rode the wave of pain. When it finally subsided enough, he slid the fabric square under his shirt and over the wound.

His head spun as he slowly pulled out into the street. *Keep it together!* he told himself. *You're still a long way from safe.* He needed to get to Marseille. But first he had to get rid of the car.

He was still trying to come up with a plan when he crossed from Monaco into France—a border that was rarely, if ever, monitored. Soon after, he saw a sign for the town of La Turbie. A plan began forming in his mind.

Upon entering the town, he followed the signs to the Trophy of Augustus. This stone monument that towered more than thirty meters into the sky was built in 6 BC by the Romans to celebrate Emperor Augustus's victory over the tribes that once ruled the Alps. The monument and the surrounding ruins drew tens of thousands of visitors each year.

But Marwan wasn't going there for the history. In fact, he wasn't planning on getting beyond the parking lot.

He drove past the line of tourist buses and in among the cars. Finding an open space, he pulled in and waited. He drummed his fingers on the Peugeot's steering wheel out of nervousness and impatience.

Once he saw that the lot was clear of people, he quickly got out of the car. Using the butt of his gun, he smashed the rear driver's side window of an Avis rental Citroën C3. Reaching in, he opened the rear door. Then he transferred his bag over and popped the lock for the front door.

Once in, he reached under the dash and got the car started—a skill that he and his brother, Ramy, had practiced often but never really thought they'd use. As he pulled out, he looked to the great stone structure that towered over the city. *I wonder if life was as complicated back then as it is now. It couldn't have been. You either worked a farm and waited to be raided by a conquering army or a wandering horde of barbarians, or you fought with a conquering army or a horde of barbarians. Either way, you knew that whatever you started out as in life, that's probably how you would live, and that's probably how you would die.*

We travel all over the world. We go places we have no business being. We have weapons to kill each other at long distances. And it's not always easy to tell the good guys from the bad ones.

Despite himself, he started laughing—a dark, brooding sound. *Look who's talking! You think of yourself as a good guy. Yet you've killed how many people today? And now, here you are making your escape in a stolen car. Face it, Accad, no matter what you tell yourself, ultimately, you're not a good man. The only difference between you and the people you killed today is who's paying you.*

A dark cloud came over Marwan as he drove. The thought that he was no different from those he had always considered "the bad guys" weighed heavily on him. Finally he turned on the radio to try to distract his thoughts, but it didn't help.

By the time he finally reached La Provençale and began his run to Marseille, the darkness had settled into his heart. He was desperate to hunt down whoever was behind all this, and he was ready to kill whoever got in his way. *And if I should die in the process, so be it! Whatever I get, I deserve—both here and now and in whatever happens once this sorry life of mine is over.*

8

Inspector Jean-Claude Goddard eased his aging, two-door Renault through a maze of emergency vehicles and TV satellite trucks (already beaming the sensational story to millions) and found a place to park outside Ramsey's building. He grabbed his sidearm and badge out of the glove compartment and stepped outside into the November chill.

He had been a detective in Monaco for almost twenty years, chief of detectives for the last five. But in all his years, he had never seen a crime like this.

With a population of only thirty-three thousand people, the principality was the second-smallest sovereign territory in the world, after the Vatican. Nestled between Italy and France, along less than two square kilometers of rugged mountains sloping down to gorgeous and high-priced beachfront property, Monaco certainly had its share of petty crimes and burglaries and other assorted troubles. And with more millionaires per capita than any other place in Europe, one could expect it to be a natural target for those driven by envy and greed. But car bombings? Assassinations? Multiple homicides in multiple locations—all on the same day, no less? Never. It was unheard of. Until now.

He passed the charred remains of the Range Rover, still smoldering in the street, and entered the lobby of Ramsey's building. Then he took the elevator up to the central crime scene.

His assistant, a twenty-eight-year-old brunette named Colette DuVall, met him in the living room as Goddard's small but professional team of investigators gathered clues throughout the flat. "Brace yourself, boss," DuVall said. "This one's pretty bad."

Goddard found himself stepping over bodies and bullets from the moment he walked through the front door. "What do we know so far?" he asked, trying to maintain his cool as he surveyed the carnage in one of the most lavish apartments into which he had ever set foot.

"You got the basic overview from the chief, right?" DuVall asked.

"I did."

"Then let's start over here." DuVall walked him to the portly corpse at the center of the room. "Meet the late Rafeeq Ramsey."

"So this is definitely him—*the* Rafeeq Ramsey?" Goddard asked. "The Egyptian millionaire?"

"I'm afraid so," DuVall said. "Why, do you know him?"

"I met him and his wife at the Grand Prix a few years ago," Goddard recalled, "but he's definitely aged since then. We talked for a while. Fascinating man, really. He and his brother grew up penniless in Aswan or Luxor or somewhere and went on to become richer than the pharaohs. Mining, at first—iron ore, steel, gold, phosphates, that kind of thing. After his brother passed away, he got into the natural gas business, mostly in the Nile Delta. Made a fortune. Seemed like a decent guy, actually—charming, unassuming, down-to-earth. His wife, on the other hand, she was a real . . ."

Goddard suddenly lowered his voice and asked, "Is she here?"

DuVall shook her head. "Not exactly."

"What do you mean, not exactly?"

"She was kidnapped two weeks ago in Paris."

"Oh," Goddard said, feeling a twinge of guilt.

"It gets worse," DuVall said.

"How?"

"Ramsey's daughter—his only daughter, from his first marriage—she was murdered the same day that her stepmother disappeared."

Goddard winced. How was that possible? The father was dead, the daughter was dead, and the wife was kidnapped. What curse had fallen on this poor family?

"How old was she?"

"Forty-two."

"No, not the wife," Goddard said. "The daughter."

"Oh, sorry." DuVall checked her notes. "Brigitte was only twelve."

Goddard shook his head. His own daughter was about to

turn ten. "Any suspects yet?" he asked, vowing in his heart to find whoever had done these horrible crimes and bring them to justice.

"No, not yet," DuVall said.

"Any witnesses?"

"There may be one."

"Who?"

"A man named Marwan Accad," DuVall said.

"Find him," Goddard ordered. "And bring him to me."

9

Marwan knew he was in trouble the moment he walked in the door. He was an hour and a half late coming home from school on a day that his parents had made him promise that he would be home on time. His mind raced through excuses.

I could say that I was in a study group. Or better yet, I was meeting with a teacher—Mr. Chehab—getting help with my physics. They've already told me I should try to spend some time with him to bring my grade up.

But in the end, when his father confronted him, he simply admitted to the truth. He and Kadeen al-Wadhi had gotten caught up in a football game, and he had lost track of time.

The next three minutes were spent enduring a typical chewing-out by his dad. Words like *selfish*, *irresponsible*, and *child* were used multiple times. Finally he was saved by his mother, who stepped in the doorway and tapped her watch.

Taking Marwan by the shoulders, his father said, "Son, you're nearly fifteen now. You're almost a man. I'm very proud of much that I see in you. You are everything that I hoped for when I first held you in my hands so long ago. The only thing lacking is that I need to be able to trust you. Do you understand what I'm saying to you?"

Marwan knew his dad was unique. So many of his friends would have just received a slap across the face from their fathers. He wanted to do right for him. Sometimes it was just so hard.

"I do understand. Again, I'm sorry. I really am."

"I know you are. And you're forgiven," his dad said, pulling him into a hug. "Mom and I will be gone at the banquet until late tonight. It's a school night, so you make sure that Ramy is in bed by nine. If he gives you trouble, remember, 'A firm hand . . .'"

"'. . . and a soft heart.' I got it, Dad."

Marwan's mother stepped back into the room. "Adib," she said impatiently.

"I'm coming, Sarah," Marwan's father answered. Then, to Marwan, he said with a smile, "I guess you're not the only one running late today."

Sarah gave her husband a light slap on the shoulder as she passed him. After giving Marwan a hug and a kiss on the cheek, she said, "Have Ramy—"

"In bed by nine. Dad already told me."

After saying their good-byes to Ramy, they left the apartment. Ramy and Marwan went to the balcony of their flat to wave to their parents as they walked to their car. It was a tradition that they had kept for countless years and one that Marwan was feeling a little old for. But it was still important to Ramy, so Marwan kept up the ritual for his sake.

Soon, Adib and Sarah Accad exited the building. Automatically, upon reaching the street, they turned and waved at the boys they knew would be there. The brothers returned the wave, and when their mom blew them a kiss, Ramy returned that also.

Suddenly a sound like a lightning strike crashed through the air, and the two brothers were thrown back into their flat. Heat and flames poured through the balcony doorway and caught the gauzy drapes on fire.

As he lay on the ground, Marwan heard a voice. It sounded like it was echoing down a long tunnel. He shook his head to clear it, and the pain that caused made him vow not to do it again. Gradually, as he began to regain his senses, he realized that the voice he heard was Ramy screaming next to him.

Movement caught his eye, and he saw that the curtains were burning. He jumped up and staggered to the doorway, then snatched a pillow from a couch and began trying to beat the flames out. Moments later, he saw Ramy doing the same thing on the other side of the door.

Once the flames were out, the brothers locked eyes. At once, the same thought came into both their minds.

"Mom," Ramy cried out, running toward the doorway to where the balcony used to be. Marwan just had time to catch him by the collar of his shirt. He yanked him back with all of his might. Both brothers tumbled to the floor.

"Wait here," Marwan ordered his little brother. He could

see that all of Ramy's feelings had settled into one overwhelming emotion—terror.

On his hands and knees, Marwan crawled to the balcony door. When he looked out, he could see it was now a sheer drop down the three stories to the ground below. Rubble was strewn all about the place. A car burned across the street. All around, people were screaming, and Marwan could hear the first of the sirens coming from a distance.

Where are they? Marwan frantically searched the dazed people wandering below. *Come on, Mom, Dad, let me see where you are!*

Deep inside, he knew where he needed to look, but he couldn't bring himself to do it.

Then, from next to him, a hand pointed down, and a voice screamed, *"Mom!"*

Marwan followed Ramy's finger to the center of the street. It was impossible to make out any facial features, but the clothing was familiar. What sealed it was the purse ten feet from the bodies. It was a Parisian purse, one that their mom was so proud of. One that she loved so much that her hand still held it, even in death.

10

Marwan woke from his daydream with a start. He wiped a tear from his eye, then pinched himself hard on the forearm to help himself focus. He had been on the road for almost an hour. It had all been a blur. A debilitating cocktail of fear and fatigue and burning pain ran through his veins, blurring his thoughts, dulling his senses.

At every toll station he expected to be stopped. With every sighting of a police car, he expected to be pulled over. But so far, the drive had been quiet. Too quiet.

The clock was ticking. The authorities in Monaco had to be looking for him. Which meant the French and Italians were looking for him. Which meant even if he wanted to hide out in Europe, he could not. He had to get to North Africa. But he couldn't take a ferry. That would take too long. He had to go by air. But he couldn't fly under his own name. Which meant he had to get those fake passports he had stashed away for such a time as this. Which meant his only shot at freedom was catching the last flight out of Marseille.

If he remembered correctly, Royal Air Maroc had a flight that left at ten, which would put him in Casablanca sometime around midnight. It was a gamble, to be sure. He'd run the risk of being arrested at either airport, but he didn't see any other choice. He had to try.

A road sign whizzed by. He still had more than a hundred kilometers to go. He cursed under his breath and tromped on the accelerator.

As Marwan sped west on Highway A8, he knew all too well that he was dangerously exposed on a main thoroughfare like this. But he wouldn't be much safer even if he took the coastal road or back roads or zigzagged his way in. And even after he made it to the airport, what was he going to do with the stolen car? And how was he supposed to board the flight? He didn't even have a reservation, much less a ticket.

He dialed Beirut. A familiar voice answered at the other end.

"Hello?"

"Ramy, it's Marwan."

"Marwan! Is that really you? Are you okay? I just heard a report on the radio. . . . Something terrible has happened in Monte Carlo—a shooting, a bombing, but they didn't have many details."

"I'm fine, really," Marwan said. "Just a little shaken up."

In truth, the pain from the wound in his shoulder was

almost unbearable, but there was no point in worrying his only brother. Not about this, anyway. There was so much more.

"Are you alone?" he asked.

"Of course," Ramy said. "Everyone else has gone home for the day."

"Good. I need your help."

"Anything, Marwan. Just tell me what happened."

"In a minute," Marwan said. "First, I need you to book me a flight."

"When?"

"Tonight."

"Where to?"

"Marseille to Casa."

"Marseille?" Ramy asked. "I thought you were in—"

"Ramy, please, I'll explain in a moment. Marseille to Casa. When's the last flight leave tonight?"

"Eight thirty, but I don't—"

"No, no," Marwan said. "I thought the last flight left at ten or thereabouts." Marwan suddenly spotted what looked to be a patrol car coming up on his left. He eased off the accelerator ever so slightly as Ramy corrected him.

"Trust me, Marwan. I've taken it a hundred times. Flight 256. Royal Air Maroc. It's a code-share with Air France. Departs at eight thirty. Lands in Casa at ten."

The patrol car turned on its lights. Marwan cursed aloud.

"What is it?" Ramy asked.

"Nothing," Marwan insisted. "Isn't there anything else?"

Should he pull over? What then? How would he explain the busted-out window? or the fact that his name didn't match the one on the rental agreement? He could hear his brother typing away feverishly on his laptop. He could picture him checking all the travel search engines.

"Sorry, Marwan," Ramy said finally. "If you want to get to Casa tonight, 256 is your only hope. Can't you stay overnight and catch something in the morning?"

Marwan was beginning to panic. The patrol car was coming up fast.

"No," he told his brother. "I need to get out tonight."

"Then we need to get you on the eight thirty. Where are you?"

He slowed the car and pulled onto the shoulder.

"Book it," Marwan ordered.

"One-way?"

"No, round-trip."

"Returning when?"

"God only knows."

"Okay," Ramy said. "I'll make something up. You still have that locker at the airport, right?"

Marwan didn't respond. His eyes were fixed on the approaching patrol car.

"Marwan?" Ramy asked again. "The locker in Marseille? Do you still have it?"

"Of course," Marwan snapped. "Why else would I go to Marseille?"

"Hey, hey, relax," Ramy said. "I'm just trying to help."

His brother had to be joking. Relax? Now?

"I'm just saying," Ramy continued. "Who are you going to be tonight?"

"Make me Cardell," Marwan said.

"Jack Cardell?"

"Right."

Marwan rolled to a complete stop and turned on his flashers.

"Fine," Ramy said. "Aisle or window?"

Marwan glanced at the pistol on the seat beside him and held his breath.

"Marwan—aisle or window?"

Marwan said nothing. He slowly set down the phone and began reaching for the pistol. He could still hear his brother shouting through the phone; he felt the cold steel and tightened his grip on the handle.

"Marwan? Are you there?"

His palms were sweaty. His heart was racing.

"Marwan?"

The patrol car rushed by.

It was not after him. It pulled over another car—a red Porsche Turbo—half a kilometer ahead, and a shudder ran through Marwan's body. But it was not relief. It was revulsion. He couldn't believe what he had just done. Or almost done. He hadn't just considered killing an innocent police officer in cold blood, had he? Had he actually been preparing himself to pull the trigger? What was wrong with him? What was he becoming?

For a split second, it was as if Marwan could stare into his own soul, and as he did, he found it darker than the night through which he drove.

"Marwan?" Ramy shouted again. "What in the world is going on?"

Marwan set down the pistol, wiped his hands on his suit pants, and tried to breathe. Then he picked up the phone and said, "Yes, Ramy, I'm still here. Sorry."

"What happened? Are you all right?"

"No," Marwan said. "Actually, I'm not."

He gunned the engine and raced onward toward Marseille. But as he did, a dam broke deep within Marwan's heart. He began telling his brother all that had happened. His conversation with Ramsey. The assassination. The car bombing. The gunfight at Le Méridien. The taxi driver. The residential shoot-out. The stolen car. His decision to run. And how close he had just come to murder.

It was a confession borne partly of anxiety but mostly of guilt. But it was also information Ramy had to have. He was, after all, the number two man in Marwan's company, and everything that had just happened was about to dramatically affect that company. Perhaps more importantly for the moment, Marwan needed from his brother a level of clarity and emotional distance from the events of the last few hours that he himself could not muster.

"You think I made a mistake?" Marwan asked when he had finished the story.

"What, you mean leaving Monte Carlo after all that?" Ramy asked.

"Right."

"Not at all," Ramy said without hesitation. "I would have done the exact same thing."

"Really?"

"Absolutely," Ramy insisted. "You had no choice."

"And if the patrol car had stopped you?" Marwan pressed. "What would you have done then?"

"Just thank God it didn't come to that," Ramy replied.

The truth was Marwan was in no mood to thank God.

He had been angry with God for years. His prayers seemed to count for nothing. Every day they seemed to evaporate like the morning dew. He had questions that were never answered. He had wounds that were never healed. He had lost everyone he had ever loved, except for Ramy. And now all that he had worked for was about to slip away.

"This thing could sink us, Ramy," Marwan said after a pause.

"Or kill us," his brother noted.

Marwan's stomach tightened. Ramy was right, and Marwan felt terrible for putting him in this situation. He had always been Ramy's protector. Now he had exposed them both to great danger.

"I'm so sorry," Marwan said. "I didn't mean for any of this to happen."

But Ramy wouldn't hear of it. "Hey, don't worry about me," he said.

"But I do worry about you," Marwan replied.

"Marwan, really, I'll be fine," Ramy insisted. "So will you. We've been through worse, right?"

"I'm not so sure, little brother," Marwan sighed. "I'm not so sure."

11

Police helicopters buzzed over the city. Checkpoints were up on all roads leading in and out of Monte Carlo. Cars, taxis, buses, and trains were being checked, as were hospitals and hotels. The harbor had been shut down; so had the private heliports. Officials at the airport in Nice, the closest airport serving Monaco, had been notified and were on the lookout.

But thus far, there had been no sighting of Marwan Accad, the only witness to a crime that had rocked the tiny coastal city, much less a serious lead to whoever had pulled the trigger and killed Rafeeq Ramsey in the first place. Inspector Jean-Claude Goddard shook his head and stepped out on the balcony. He breathed in the brisk night air and stared at the waves lapping against the cement piers, waiting for the ulcer to start forming in his stomach.

"Here's the photograph you requested," Colette DuVall said, handing Goddard an 8½-by-11 glossy, fresh out of the printer.

"This is from the surveillance footage?" Goddard asked.

"Yes, sir," DuVall said. "And the video's all cued up for you when you're ready."

"In a moment," Goddard said.

For now he stared at the image of Marwan Accad in his hands. He was a good-looking young man, but not a standout, not the model or movie-star type. He had light olive skin, jet-black hair that was closely cropped, and in this photo at least, he was clean shaven. No mustache. No beard. No sideburns. No hint of stubble. He had a small nose and a strong chin and appeared to be in excellent physical condition, but as far as Goddard could tell, he had no other distinguishing features. No scars. No blemishes. Nothing that would make him stand out in a crowd. The perfect bodyguard.

What really struck Goddard were Accad's eyes. They were large and brown and warmer somehow than he had expected. To Goddard they communicated a sharp, ambitious mind but also a sense of decency, a sense of honor. And there was something else. Goddard could not put his finger on it just now, but there was something in those eyes that intrigued him, that made him curious. A hint of sadness, perhaps?

"Get this to all our men in the field," Goddard ordered. "And get it out to the TV stations, saying he's wanted for questioning."

"Yes, sir."

"And issue a reward."

"How much?" DuVall asked.

"How much is left in the account?"

"A hundred, I think."

"Fine, use it all," Goddard said. "A hundred thousand euros for information leading to the arrest and conviction of those responsible for this hideous crime. And make sure you get everything we have to Interpol. See what they can send you on this Marwan Accad."

"Right away, sir."

"And expand the search grid," Goddard added, his worries growing.

"You don't think Accad is in Monte Carlo any longer?"

"I don't know," Goddard conceded. "Put fax bulletins out to the airports in Cannes, Marseille, and Hyères, as well as to Albenga and Genoa in Italy."

"That far?" DuVall asked.

Goddard nodded. "We can't take any chances, Colette. We have no idea who the killer is. Or killers, for all we know. We don't know whom to look for. The only real lead we have at the moment is Accad. He's probably still here, but we certainly don't know that for sure."

"Yes, sir."

"Contact the train stations and ferry services in the smaller towns as well. And check back with me every thirty minutes. I want constant updates."

"And the other thing?" DuVall asked. "Have you called him yet?"

Goddard said nothing. He just shook his head.

"Don't you really have to?" DuVall pressed gingerly.

Goddard sighed. "I suppose you're right."

"Would you like me to take care of it for you?"

Goddard wished. But as the chief of detectives, the task—however distasteful—fell to him, and he couldn't postpone it any longer.

"No," he said at last. "I'll do it. Just get him on the phone. Tell him it's urgent. Then bring the phone to me."

"Right away, sir," DuVall said.

Goddard retired to a small office off the master bedroom, where another of his detectives showed him the surveillance videos. He was struck by the worry in Ramsey's eyes throughout the conversation, and by how relaxed Accad looked.

"Wait, stop the tape," Goddard said abruptly, leaning forward in his chair. "Right—there. Okay, play that part again."

Accad was handing Ramsey an envelope. The expression on Ramsey's face was first one of shock and then—what was that next? Anger? Indignation?

"What is that?" Goddard asked the detective. "What did he just take out of the envelope?"

"I can't tell," the detective said. "The angle is partially blocked by Monsieur Accad."

"Do you have another angle?" Goddard asked.

"No, sir, I'm afraid this is all we have."

"Is that a photo of some kind?"

"It might be."

"Can you zoom in on it, clarify it a bit?"

"Not here, sir," the detective said. "But I might be able to enhance it digitally back at headquarters."

"Do it," Goddard ordered. "And get back to me as soon as you have something."

12

The simple fact was that he couldn't stand Inspector Marcel Lemieux.

There was no other way to put it. The idea of having to talk to him again, much less work with him, turned Goddard's stomach. But what could he do? Lemieux was leading the investigation of the kidnapping of Claudette Ramsey and the murder of Brigitte Ramsey. The man had to be told. He would want to see the crime scene and the video from the surveillance cameras inside Ramsey's flat. He would have to know about this Accad fellow, who could turn out to be the best witness they had, if they could only find him.

Lemieux was something of a living legend throughout the police forces of Europe. He had solved some of the continent's biggest cases—murder, kidnapping, bank robbery; the kind of cases that involved the rich and famous and those with very powerful friends in very high places.

But Goddard still couldn't stand him. They had worked together on two previous cases, and both experiences had left nothing but a bad taste in Goddard's mouth.

The first time was when a French diplomat on holiday in Monte Carlo had gone missing for three days. The wife had received a ransom note but was warned not to pay. A week later, Goddard and his men found the diplomat's body washed up onshore. The same day, a waitress at one of the casinos was found dead, an apparent suicide. Was there a connection? Goddard began interviewing all of the woman's friends and relatives. Within forty-eight hours, he had compiled circumstantial evidence that the two cases were connected and had even been able to put together a rather compelling list of three suspects, none of whom had convincing alibis for the days in question.

But then Lemieux swooped in and essentially yanked the case away from him. Not to solve it more quickly, Goddard would later note to colleagues. Indeed, the case was never solved at all. Instead, leads went cold. Suspects walked. Key evidence was mishandled or disappeared. And Lemieux couldn't have been more pompous or rude during the entire "investigation," if that is what it could be called. In time, Lemieux declared the case "virtually unsolvable" and went back to Paris, leaving resentment and ill will in his wake.

Goddard's second run-in with Lemieux occurred in the late summer of 2003 when a wealthy French shipping magnate and his sons disappeared after taking his gleaming new $25-million yacht out of Monte Carlo's harbor for a quick spin around the Mediterranean.

Goddard remembered it like it was yesterday. The urgent phone call from headquarters just after 6 a.m. The hysterical wife. The media feeding frenzy. The sensational headlines.

It wasn't every day a man of such prominence—a close friend of the French prime minister—vanished into thin air. But he and his sons were nowhere to be found. No bodies. No blood. No clues of any kind. Everyone demanded immediate answers. For days, the Parisian press hammered away at the Monte Carlo authorities, accusing them of dragging their feet. Goddard was under tremendous pressure to produce results—a fingerprint, a witness, anything to show progress. He didn't eat. He barely slept. He ran his men ragged and almost had to be hospitalized himself for exhaustion.

And then it came. The break they had been working for, praying for. Goddard discovered that the shipping magnate's sons owed money to a man they thought was a Russian banker but who in fact worked for the Russian mafia. Goddard then discovered that the Russian owned a flat in Monte Carlo and had been spotted in town just days earlier. What's more, two of the Russian's associates had been seen wandering around the harbor on the morning of the men's disappearance, asking about renting a speedboat.

Momentum began building. Goddard had a suspect, a motive. He requested permission from his superiors to fly to Moscow to follow the trail. But to his shock, he was denied.

Forty-five minutes later, Lemieux walked into his office, claimed jurisdiction of the case, and demanded copies of the case files. Goddard protested but was overruled by his superiors.

The next day it was Lemieux, rather than Goddard, who

flew to Moscow. Once again the case quickly ran aground. The Russian "banker's" associates mysteriously vanished. The man himself offered up the most pathetic of alibis. But Lemieux barely pressed. Instead, Lemieux soon cleared the Russian and went back to Paris, promising to keep the case open but offering little hope of ever seeing it solved. Worse, the suspect actually received official apologies from several governments, including Goddard's own, and Goddard was suspended for a week without pay for "unfairly impugning the reputation of a valued friend of Monaco."

And now he was coming back, Marcel Maurice Lemieux, the most arrogant detective in Europe.

DuVall joined Goddard on the balcony and held the phone toward him.

"It's him," she whispered.

Goddard rubbed his eyes and then took the phone.

"Inspector Lemieux, what a pleasure to speak with you again," he lied.

"You are interrupting my day off," Lemieux replied.

"I am very sorry, monsieur, but it could not be helped. I'm afraid I have some very bad news."

"And I thought hearing from you was bad enough," Lemieux groaned.

Goddard bit his tongue. "I regret to inform you that Monsieur Ramsey has been murdered."

There was silence at the other end of the line.

"Rafeeq Ramsey?" Lemieux asked at last.

"I'm afraid so, sir," Goddard confirmed and then briefly explained the circumstances of the death, so far as he knew them.

"Any suspects?" Lemieux asked.

"Not yet," Goddard said. "But we've just begun our investigation, and I thought you might be able to help us on that front."

"Any witnesses?" Lemieux asked.

"We're still canvassing the area for them, but there is one man, Marwan Accad," Goddard said. "He's the CEO of an executive security company. He was with Ramsey at the time of the shooting. Ramsey may have been trying to hire him. We're hoping Ramsey may have told him something that will shed light on who killed him and why."

"What do you mean you're *hoping*?" Lemieux wanted to know. "Haven't you asked him yet?"

"Well, no," Goddard said, "not exactly."

"Fine," Lemieux said with disgust, "I will ask him myself. I'm heading to the airport now. Have someone meet me at the helipad in twenty minutes."

"Twenty minutes?" Goddard asked, caught off guard. "Aren't you in Paris?"

"No, I'm in Nice."

Lemieux said it as if Goddard should have known. And he probably should have. Why hadn't DuVall warned him? She knew Goddard hated surprises.

"Well, Monsieur Lemieux, I will certainly have one of my men meet you and bring you up to the Ramsey flat. But I'm afraid I won't be able to put you in front of Marwan Accad quite yet."

"Why not?" Lemieux demanded.

"Accad seems to have disappeared."

"Disappeared?"

Goddard took a deep breath. It was the last thing he wanted to admit, and to Lemieux of all people. "Yes, I'm afraid so. He slipped away in all the chaos, the commotion. But we've sealed off the city. We'll find him soon and bring him in for questioning. He may be the best witness we have. Indeed, he may be our only witness."

"No, Monsieur Goddard," Lemieux shot back. "That, I am afraid, is where you are wrong. Marwan Accad is no witness. He has just become my prime suspect."

"Suspect?" Goddard asked. "We don't know anything about him yet—who he really is, why he was here, nothing."

"Then find out," Lemieux insisted. "Issue a warrant for Accad's arrest and alert the authorities from Milan to Marseille. I don't want this guy getting away. Or I promise you, Monsieur Goddard, heads will roll, starting with yours."

13

It began to rain. Marwan turned on the windshield wipers and prayed, to a God he didn't believe in, that he wouldn't suddenly go sliding off the highway. *And why should I believe in you,* he thought angrily. *What have you given me other than loneliness and pain? And now this! When I was trying to help a man who had just lost his daughter and whose wife was missing? This is what you give me?*

The cell phone rang, shattering the silence and rattling his nerves.

"Hello?"

"Marwan, it's Ramy. Are you there yet?"

"No, not yet."

Marwan checked his watch and his map, and the knot in

his stomach tightened. It was almost seven thirty, and he was only now approaching the outskirts of Marseille.

"Ramy, I don't think I can make it."

"You have to," Ramy insisted. "You don't have a choice. I can get you out of North Africa. But I can't get you out of a French prison. How much farther?"

"Five kilometers, maybe ten, but look at the time."

"I know, I know," Ramy said. "But look, we have to go over some things before you get to the airport."

"Like what?"

"Your phone, for starters. You said it was originally the taxi driver's."

"Correct."

"But you called through our scrambler system in Prague, right?"

"Of course."

"Then the cops probably can't trace it back to me. But they're going to try, so you can't keep it, and you can't use it again. As soon as you hang up with me, you need to ditch it immediately. You got it?"

"I got it."

"When you get to Casa, buy a satellite phone," Ramy continued. "Use cash. And don't skimp. Get a good one. Something nobody can trace or tap."

"Right."

"But only use it to call me. No one else."

"Right, no one else."

"Marwan, I'm not kidding," Ramy said. "You're tired. You're fighting off shock. You're not yourself tonight. You've got to be extra careful. You can't afford to make a single mistake. And until we figure this thing out, you need to get low, stay low. No friends. No old hangouts. Nothing familiar."

"That should be easy," Marwan lied. "I don't know anyone in Morocco."

"Good," Ramy said. "Keep it that way."

Marwan knew Ramy had never liked Kadeen al-Wadhi, and with good reason. When they were all kids, Kadeen, Marwan's best friend, seemed to feel an obligation to make the younger boy miserable. Sometimes, when things got out of hand, Marwan would step in. But mostly he just stood by and laughed as Ramy cried or tried to fight back.

Age had changed everything. Kadeen moved away and found religion, and Ramy moved into that best friend position in Marwan's life. Still, because of that history, although Marwan kept in regular contact with Kadeen, he never mentioned him to his younger brother. Those were wounds that he knew might never heal.

"Now look," Ramy continued, "one thing seems certain. Your instincts about Claudette Ramsey were right on the money. She's alive. She's in São Paulo. She's making wire transfers. Which means she's probably behind this whole thing. That's the good news—we know that much already."

"And the bad news?" Marwan asked as the rain began to fall harder over Marseille and the throbbing in his shoulder worsened by the minute.

"She and whoever she's working with know you're onto them."

"But that still doesn't make sense," Marwan said. "I'm the only person who could have known, plus my sources in Zurich and São Paulo."

"Might they have double-crossed you?"

"I don't see how," Marwan said. "I've known those guys for fifteen years, at least."

"What if the phone in Ramsey's place was bugged?" Ramy asked.

"The one in Monte Carlo?"

"No, the one in Paris," Ramy said.

"It's possible," Marwan said. "But by whom? The security company?"

"Or the police," Ramy said. "Didn't you say he suspected someone in French intelligence was after him?"

"Yeah."

"Well?"

Marwan considered that for a moment. Perhaps Ramy was right.

"What did you say when you called Ramsey the other day?" his brother asked. "Did you tell him about the photo? Did you mention São Paulo?"

"No, no, of course not," Marwan said. "I just said I had urgent news that couldn't wait. I told him I needed to see him in person, but not in Paris."

"Did you suggest Monte Carlo?"

"No, he did."

"And he gave you all the details of where and when to meet over the phone right then?"

"Right."

"Then that's got to be it," Ramy said. "That phone was bugged."

"Whoever was listening in didn't have to know what I had," Marwan realized aloud. "They just knew I had something big, and whatever it was, it couldn't be good for them. Claudette and her people must have panicked. They must have decided to shut down the whole operation."

"Exactly," Ramy said. "Which meant not only taking out Ramsey, but taking out you, as well."

"Then they have to know I'm still alive," Marwan said, "that all their attacks in Monte Carlo failed."

"Which means they've got to be scared," Ramy added. "They won't give up until they find you and kill you."

"Then we'd better find them before they find us."

"How?" Ramy asked.

"First, put a team on the next plane to São Paulo," Marwan said. "We need to find Claudette before she runs. If we find her, she'll lead us to the others."

"I'm on it," Ramy said.

"Second, find out who's doing the investigation back in Monte Carlo. Find out if he's in on this thing or if he's somebody we can trust."

"Got it. What else?"

"Who do you know in Paris?"

"I've got a good friend in French intelligence," Ramy said. "I met him when you sent me to open the Paris office, before you moved up there. He's pretty high up. Knows everybody. And he owes me a favor."

"Good, see if he's heard anything," Marwan ordered. "But be careful, Ramy. We still don't know exactly what we're up against."

"Don't worry. My friend will be discreet."

"He'd better be," Marwan said.

The rain was coming down still harder, and the temperature

was dropping quickly. But he saw a sign for the airport. It was just ahead.

"I'd better go," he said. "I'm almost there."

"Good," Ramy said. "Stay safe, and call me in three days."

"Three days," Marwan confirmed, then said, "Ramy?"

"Yes, Marwan?"

"Thanks."

"What are little brothers for?"

14

MARWAN PULLED INTO the airport parking lot. It was exactly 8:00. He found a deserted little section near the back and turned off the engine. Then he wiped the rental car clean of all fingerprints, grabbed the garment bag out of the backseat, and dumped the keys, the pistol, and the cell phone into various trash cans as he ran to make his flight.

By 8:12, he was inside the main terminal. Walking as quickly as he could without drawing attention, he found his rented locker. He unlocked it and he fished out a small stack of fake passports and a dozen credit cards, two per alias. He also grabbed a change of clothes, a pair of contact lenses that made his eyes look green rather than brown, a small backpack, and several stacks of euros in small denominations. He slammed the door shut and tossed the photo of Claudette

Ramsey in a trash can before ducking into a nearby men's room.

At 8:21, he stepped up to the Royal Air Maroc counter and paid for his ticket.

"You'd better hurry, Monsieur Cardell," the blonde behind the counter said as she handed him his boarding card. "They are already boarding."

Marwan bolted for security and passport control. There were still a few passengers ahead of him. But police and plainclothes agents were everywhere. It seemed the place was crawling with them. Marwan entered the queue and tried to act casual, but his heart was racing. He needed to get his mind off the prospect of imminent arrest and interrogation. He needed to find a way to calm down and become the alias he had just assumed.

He surreptitiously tried some breathing techniques, but to little avail. How would the APB list him—as a witness or as a man wanted for multiple homicides? Had every airport, seaport, train station, and hotel in France and Italy been alerted, or just those within a hundred kilometers or so of Monte Carlo? More to the point, had he slipped the noose, or was it being tightened around his neck even now?

He snuck a glance at himself in a window as he passed. The snakeskin boots added a good two inches to his height. Then, of course, there were the ripped blue jeans, the black T-shirt, the faded jean jacket with a huge Grateful Dead logo stitched on the back. These and the dark sunglasses and the backpack and the iPod blaring the Dead's greatest hits made him look more like some American college kid hitchhiking through Europe than a bodyguard to former presidents and prime ministers. He barely recognized himself. And that, of course, was the point.

No fewer than eight French policemen were checking passports and faces and luggage and running the metal detectors. It felt as if every eye were on him. It had been a long time since he had bluffed his way through European security. Did he still know how? He vowed then and there that if he somehow made it through all this, he would spend a lot more time out of his office and in the field.

It was finally his turn. He tossed his backpack and the garment bag—the one he had stolen from the honeymooners in Monte Carlo—on the conveyor belt to be x-rayed. Then he handed over his fake American passport, his airline ticket, and his boarding pass.

The lead gendarme was a short bulldog of a man with a close haircut, a tight-fitting French border police uniform, and a severe look upon his face. He examined the documents closely. Too closely.

Marwan's pulse quickened.

The man asked something in French.

"Huh?" Marwan asked, peeling off his iPod and looking thoroughly confused.

The man switched to English.

"Monsieur Cardell, where are you traveling tonight?"

"Heading to Casa, dude," Marwan said in a nearly flawless Southern Californian accent. "Actually, Rabat, if I can find me some wheels."

He was just glad he was not hooked up to a polygraph.

"Alone?" the man asked.

Marwan looked around himself, then faced the gendarme with a shrug and a smile. "Unfortunately."

"Business or pleasure?"

"Pure pleasure, bro—at least I hope," Marwan laughed, hoping to elicit a bit of warmth, something—anything—he could work with to get this guy to lighten up a bit and wave him through.

He got nothing. Instead, the man's eyes bored more deeply into his.

"Are you carrying any weapons?"

"No," he said, though he almost wished he were.

"Drugs?"

That one was easy. He had never used them in his life. But he had to stay in character.

"Not today," he quipped with a wink.

The gendarme did not look amused.

"Are you traveling with more than ten thousand euros?"

Marwan did a quick calculation. As best he remembered, he had a little less than two thousand. He laughed again. "Dude, you're kidding, right?"

He saw the man's eyebrows rise.

"I had to sell my Harley to get over here," Marwan continued. "Blew most of it already! Who knew France was so expensive?"

"Where are you staying in Rabat?"

Marwan paused for a moment. He didn't recall ever being asked such questions upon *leaving* France. Were they onto him? Why not just grab him? His mouth went dry.

"Hostel Rabat," he said at last. "If I can get myself there. If not, it's going to be a cold night."

The pain from his shoulder was beginning to cloud his mind. *Please, just get this over with!*

"So no drugs?" the gendarme asked again.

"Yeah, I got some right in my pocket. You want a hit?" Quickly realizing that sarcasm was probably not the best tack to take, he resorted to pleading. "Come on, bro, my plane's leaving any minute."

"May I look in your bag?" the man asked, obviously unconvinced.

Marwan said yes, but no sooner had the words come out of his mouth than he realized that in his haste he had never checked to see what was in the garment bag he'd taken from the honeymoon suite in Monte Carlo. He had no earthly idea if it was the bride's or the groom's. And he was about to find out in the sight of eight well-armed men.

The gendarme began with Marwan's backpack.

More blue jeans. A couple of old T-shirts, desperately in need of some laundry soap. A few pairs of dirty underwear—a few clean pairs as well. A charger cable for the iPod. A dog-eared paperback of John Grisham's novel *The Firm*. A half-eaten bag of M&M's. A small shaving kit. An old toothbrush. A half-empty tube of Crest. Some deodorant. And a small velvet box with a small gold ring.

"Getting engaged?" the gendarme asked.

For the first time, Marwan saw a glimmer of humanity in the man's eyes. A flicker of sadness, rapidly turning back to steel.

Use that, he told himself. "Dude, that's why I'm here. I put three years into her, and she turned me down flat. Said I had no ambition. Said I couldn't support her lifestyle. Can you believe that?"

The gendarme cracked an ever-so-faint smile and shook his head. Then he repacked the backpack and opened the garment bag. Marwan's heart almost stopped.

To his horror, the bag was filled with women's clothes and cosmetics. Dresses. Halter tops. Tight jeans. High heels and flats. And lingerie that left little to the imagination. They were all new—some articles still had store price tags dangling from them. They were all expensive. And they all begged for an explanation that Marwan Accad—aka Jack Cardell—did not have.

Marwan wondered if he looked as surprised as he felt.

"Perhaps I should call you *Jacqueline* Cardell, instead of Jacques, *non*?" the gendarme asked.

The man began to laugh, as did his colleagues, most of whom seemed to have become intrigued by this California beach bum.

Marwan forced himself to laugh too. "Nah, stuff she left in our apartment. I've had this vision of building me a bonfire out of this stuff one night on the beach, then surfing her out of my system until sunrise."

The gendarme stared hard at Marwan for a moment, but his face softened. "*Amour.* It is not always an easy thing."

To Marwan's surprise and relief, he zipped up the bag and waved him through.

15

The Skeleton had arrived.

That's what Goddard and DuVall had dubbed Lemieux. He was all bones and no heart, they said, and he would be joining them any moment.

Goddard watched from the balcony of Ramsey's flat as Lemieux's jet helicopter landed at the public heliport below, and the rather tall and lanky fellow disembarked, got into the unmarked sedan Goddard had sent for him, and made the short drive to the front door. The heliport was less than a hundred meters from Sovereign Plaza, the luxury apartment complex that the Ramsey family (as well as one of the princesses of Monaco) occasionally called home.

The Ramseys owned four other homes besides this one, Goddard had learned since arriving. One was in Alexandria, on the southern shores of the Mediterranean, where Rafeeq had been raised. Another was a sumptuous urban town house in Maadi, an exclusive suburb of Cairo, not far from the corporate offices of Blue Nile Holdings. Yet another was a pricey ski chalet in Davos, Switzerland, which Rafeeq often lent out to clients, since he had long passed the age he could safely ski. And of course, there was their opulent forty-acre estate just outside of Paris—the city of Claudette's birth—where they had spent most of their time recently.

Buying the flat in Monte Carlo had been Claudette's idea, Goddard had gathered from their private cook, who had been in his guest quarters when the shooting began. Claudette was the ultimate socialite, he said, and desperately wanted a place where she could wine and dine her rich friends, a place she could see and be seen by the glitterati that came each summer to play.

The phone rang. Goddard answered it immediately, then hung up and announced, "He's coming. Everyone out."

Goddard's team didn't need to be told twice. No one wanted to be around when the Skeleton arrived. They had all worked with him before. So the crime scene photographers, the detectives dusting for fingerprints, the officers taking measurements, and those finding and marking shell casings all finished their work, packed up their equipment, and exited the flat as quickly and quietly as they could. They were essentially finished anyway. The bodies had been removed. They were just wrapping up loose ends. If they were needed again, they would return. For now, they were more than happy to leave, Colette DuVall included.

A few minutes after they had all departed, the elevator door opened, and Lemieux stepped off.

"Inspector, welcome," Goddard said.

Lemieux didn't nod. He didn't speak. He didn't smile. He did not even take Goddard's outstretched hand. Rather, he immediately began moving through the living room—slowly and methodically—stopping occasionally to bend down and examine certain numbered evidence markers and bloodstains. He seemed particularly interested in studying the angles from which the shots had been fired.

"When you're ready, I can show you the apartment across the way, the one the assassin—or assassins—used," Goddard offered. "My men have recovered the rifle and a scope."

But Lemieux remained silent. He was counting shell casings. Then he began counting bullet holes. He moved from one to another, noting the rounds embedded in the walls and the bookshelves and those riddled in the desk and chairs and sofas, continually looking back at the building from which they apparently had been fired.

"No fingerprints on the shells from the other apartment, I'm afraid," Goddard continued.

But Lemieux again said nothing. The silence was deafening.

Goddard studied the man as he slowly circulated the living room. He was almost six feet five inches tall and frightfully thin, and he wore a long black London Fog raincoat that hung on his bony shoulders like some kind of burial shroud. His face was drawn and somewhat gaunt, and though at 62 he was younger than Goddard's father, he was just as bald, with a small tuft of gray hair poking up over each ear and a narrow, graying mustache under a proud and pointed nose. The one glaring difference between Lemieux and Goddard's father was that Goddard was pretty sure his father still had a heartbeat.

But despite the man's cold demeanor, it was Lemieux's eyes that bothered Goddard the most. They were small and dark brown, and while they effectively communicated the man's powerful intellect and his legendary photographic memory, they projected not a hint of warmth or compassion—not even for the murdered victims or their families, much less for any of the men trying their hardest to find the killer or killers and bring them to justice.

How could such a cold man have such a sterling reputation throughout the whole of Europe? Goddard wondered. Yes, the cases he had solved were still studied by criminologists the world over. But what of the other cases under his authority, the ones that had died slow and painful deaths of starvation and neglect? Didn't anyone take these into consideration when the great Marcel Lemieux came to mind?

"I cannot tell you how much I love the look and the feel and the smell of a fresh murder scene," Lemieux said at last as he worked his way around the room. "It is like a beautiful painting, one by a master like Monet or Manet. It is pointillism, Monsieur Goddard. Up close, no single clue—no single dot or speck of color—seems to make much sense by itself. But when you step back, when you close your eyes and breathe it all in, when you stop to see the bigger picture, then the clues begin to tell you a story, a vivid and violent and fascinating story. That's what all the great detectives have done. They have closed their eyes and quieted their souls and let the narrative guide them."

Goddard said nothing. Everything about this man repulsed him. Now he could add delusions of grandeur and a wont for pontification to the list.

The Skeleton was examining one of the tiny video surveillance cameras that Rafeeq Ramsey's Paris-based security company had installed throughout the house and in the outer hallways six months earlier.

"We have all the surveillance recordings cued up and ready to go," Goddard said before he was asked. "They're all digital. They're all time-stamped. And they captured everything. Ramsey and Marwan Accad talking at some length. Then Ramsey being shot. The death of the bodyguards. Accad taking their weapons. It's all there. In fact, I just got the ballistics report back. The two bodies we found at the Méridien were killed with one of these weapons, undoubtedly by Accad."

Lemieux stopped what he was doing and looked up.

Surprised by his interest, Goddard added, "The only problem is that while the surveillance tapes show us *what* happened, they don't tell us *why*. There is no audio. No one but Marwan Accad knows what Monsieur Ramsey said in the final minutes of his life. But as I said on the phone, I'm hoping—as are you, I'm sure—that he can shed some light on this horrible crime."

"So have you found him yet, Monsieur Goddard?" Lemieux asked.

"No, not yet," Goddard conceded. "But we have a new lead."

"Oh?"

"A taxi company just reported one of its cabs missing," Goddard said. "The driver last reported in right outside the Méridien. Now no one can find him, and he's not answering his radio. The manager of the Méridien claims to have seen him pull away, heading west, out of the city."

"Toward France?" Lemieux asked.

"Apparently," Goddard said. "I'm having my men check traffic cameras to see if we can identify the car and see where it went."

One of the benefits of living in a high-tech age and in a city-state wealthy enough to afford state-of-the-art law enforcement technology was that surveillance cameras were positioned everywhere throughout Monte Carlo. A person could barely make a move without being photographed. The authorities couldn't always stop a crime, but they could often reconstruct it and follow those responsible.

"How long ago did the Méridien manager see the taxi leave?" Lemieux asked.

"Over two hours ago," Goddard said.

"And there's been no sighting of Accad in the city?"

"No."

"And no one's spotted him at the airport in Nice?"

"No."

"Cannes?"

"No."

"Hyères?"

"No."

Lemieux paced the room and then stopped suddenly and whipped around.

"He has to be heading for Marseille," he said. "Get me the head of airport security—now!"

16

Royal Air Maroc flight 256 hurtled down the runway into the rainy blackness with 140 drowsy passengers on board, and Marwan Accad—aka Jack Cardell—was one of them.

As the jet banked south and began flying across the Mediterranean at twenty-five thousand feet and almost five hundred miles per hour, the flight attendants served some refreshments. When the pilot turned off the interior lights, most of those on board began to drift off to sleep. But try as he might, Marwan could not. The wound in his shoulder was almost unbearable. He was perspiring and felt feverish and nauseated. He asked one of the flight attendants for some pain relievers and washed them down with a Coke. Then he headed to the lavatory to wash his hands and face.

Once inside, he locked the door and stared at himself in

the mirror. He looked as terrible as he felt. His face was pale. His eyes were red and watery. And as he peeled off his jean jacket, he found the shoulder of his T-shirt soaked in blood. It had soaked right through the paper towels he'd packed around the wound in the restroom at the Marseille airport when he changed clothes.

Marwan hung his jacket over the hook on the door, washed his hands with soap and warm water, and then carefully dabbed water on the paper towels on his shoulder until he could peel them off. It was a painful process and took longer than he had expected, and soon a flight attendant was knocking on the door.

"Sir," she said, "is everything okay in there?"

"Yes, thank you," Marwan replied.

"Are you sure?" she pressed.

"Yes, I'm fine. I'll be out in a moment."

"Please, sir, we will be landing soon. You need to return to your seat and fasten your seat belt."

"Yes, yes," he said. "I will be right there."

The last thing Marwan wanted to do was cause a scene or attract attention to himself. As horrible as he felt, he hurried to wash the wound—wincing as he did—and redress it with new, moist paper towels. He splashed some water on his face, dried himself off, along with the sink and small counter, and stuffed all of his used paper towels into the trash. Marwan put his jacket back on, checked himself again to make sure there were no signs of blood on him, and then stepped out of the lavatory.

"Are you sure you're okay?" the flight attendant asked as he reemerged.

"A bit of airsickness, I'm afraid," he said, hoping that would seem normal enough for her to leave him alone.

"You really don't look too good," she said. "Would you like me to have a doctor waiting for you on the ground when we arrive?"

"That won't be necessary," he said as he began to perspire again. "My girlfriend will take care of me when I get there. But that's very kind. Thank you."

She let him go for now. But as Marwan returned to his seat and closed his eyes on the approach into Casablanca, his fears began to rise again. Yes, he was out of Marseille, out of Europe. But he was drawing far too much attention to himself. This woman would remember his face, his eyes, his demeanor. How soon until she was questioned?

He had the Monaco police hunting him, and very possibly the French and Italian police by now as well, not to mention Claudette Ramsey and her thugs. How close were they to catching him? He had left too many clues in the airport, he knew. Once those were found, they would know he had headed for Morocco. He'd be lucky to live another two days.

The plane finally landed. After making it through passport control without incident, Marwan rented a car and made his way into Casablanca. A cold November rain was coming down hard, and he could not get the heat or windshield wipers to work properly, making it difficult to read street signs in a city he had been to only a handful of times.

To make matters worse, his fever was rising. He felt weak and disoriented. Twice he realized he was about to fall asleep at the wheel and had to swerve to keep from hitting oncoming traffic. He knew what was happening to him, and there was nothing he could do but press on. He had lost too much blood. His wound was becoming infected. He hadn't slept. He hadn't eaten. And his body was in danger of slipping into shock.

It was almost midnight when he reached the address he had scratched out on a small slip of paper he kept in his wallet. The two-story, whitewashed villa was surrounded by a stone wall with two openings, one for cars and one for people—both protected by heavy iron bars.

As he pulled himself out of his rental car, Marwan began questioning his decision to not let Kadeen know he was coming. Would his friend even come out and open the gate at this time of night?

But there was nothing to do about it now. What was done was done. All that mattered was getting through that gate.

Without bothering to close the car door, he stumbled around the rear of the vehicle but lost his balance and fell to the ground at the base of the wall. Delirious with pain, he shut his eyes tightly and tried in vain to remain conscious.

He wasn't sure how long he had been lying there when he opened his eyes again. He could feel small, sharp rocks pressing themselves into his cheek, and there was grit on his tongue. Gathering up all his energy, he tried calling out, but his voice just came out a whisper. *"Kadeen . . . Kadeen . . ."*

Tilting his head back, he could see a button embedded in the wall above his head. He reached his hand up, but the button was too high.

Gripping the cool iron of the gate with his one good hand, he strained to pull himself up. Slowly he began to rise, using the strength of his left hand and the leverage of his damaged right shoulder. The pain was beyond anything he had ever felt before.

He vomited, and the movement caused him to lose precious inches. *Pull! Just keep pulling!* Finally he was barely within reach of the button. Putting his full weight on his shoulder, he pressed his finger to the white plastic.

He heard nothing.

I'm going to die right here. Out in the road like a dog.

Suddenly the door to the house opened, and Marwan heard a buzzing from inside. He realized he had never taken his finger off of the button.

"What do you want? Don't you know it's midnight?"

Marwan recognized the voice of his childhood friend. Again he tried calling out his name, but this time nothing came.

A flashlight clicked on, and through his closed eyes, Marwan could see the glow of it playing across his face.

"I said, what do you want? If you don't leave immediately, I'll call . . . Marwan?"

Marwan could hear the scuff of slippers against stone and the rattle of a key in the gate. "Marwan, is that you?"

Marwan tried to speak, but no words came. Then his feet refused to support his awkward posture any longer. He slumped to the ground, and everything went black.

[illegible]

[illegible]

[illegible] finger to the white plastic.

[illegible]

[illegible]

PART TWO

17

Claudette Ramsey lounged by the pool in her bikini at a large villa in the mountains, sipping piña coladas and soaking in the rays of the sizzling São Paulo sun.

But even as she acted the part of a woman enjoying her newfound freedom, with a cabana boy rubbing coconut oil on her shoulders and back, her stomach churned while she awaited word of the latest operation. No longer would she have to live with that insufferable tyrant—the Pharaoh, as she liked to call her husband behind his back. By now he was dead. But what of the private investigator? Was he dead too? And even if he was, who else knew what he must know? Who else had he told?

Her satellite phone rang. She sat up and shooed the cabana boy away. Then, when she was absolutely sure she was alone, she flipped open the phone and asked, "Are you on a secure line?"

"Of course," said the voice at the other end. "You think I am a fool?"

"I cannot afford to take any chances. You know how much is at stake."

"You are not the only one taking risks."

"Then is it done?"

"Not quite."

"What does that mean?" she demanded.

"They got your husband. But Marwan Accad got away."

"How is that possible? I paid for *three* teams."

"He is very good."

"I thought you were better."

"We will find him," the voice assured her. "And we will kill him. But it will take more time and more money."

"Absolutely not," she growled through clenched teeth. "I'm not paying you one cent more. You said you would get them both. That's what I paid for. The rest is your problem."

"You're forgetting one thing, Mrs. Ramsey."

"Don't call me that," she insisted. "You know I hate that name."

"Nevertheless," the voice said, "I know where you are, and I know what you've done, and I have all the evidence I need to have you locked up for the rest of your life."

"Any evidence that implicates me implicates you as well," she shot back.

"Really? Well, we will just see about that, won't we?"

Claudette was now up and pacing about the pool, her face flushed with anger. "How dare you threaten me? I'm the one who—"

"Silence! Do not think you are the first 'client' who has ever tried to back out of her obligations in the middle of an operation. We have ways of handling such people, ways I guarantee you never want to experience for yourself."

"I'm not trying to back out," she said. "I just don't want to pay more than we agreed."

"You will pay what it costs, or you will pay with your life. Is that understood?"

Claudette stopped cold in her tracks. She knew he was serious, and she knew he was capable. She did not want to die. She simply wanted to be free, and rich, like she had always deserved. The collateral-damage death of her stepdaughter, Brigitte, had been unfortunate, but luxury and alcohol were helping to soften that pain. Now she feared she could suffer the same fate.

"Very well," she sighed. "How much more will you need to finish the job?"

18

THE SURREALNESS of seeing his childhood best friend—a friend he hadn't laid eyes on in almost ten years—collapsed against his front gate quickly gave way to action. Kadeen al-Wadhi reached back into his house and pressed a button on the wall next to the door. A buzzer sounded, and the gate's lock clicked.

Because the gate swung outward, Kadeen had to push hard to shift Marwan's weight in order to give himself enough of an opening to squeeze through. Once outside the gate, he placed a large rock into the gap—a rock he kept there just for that purpose, having locked himself out of his property one too many times. Then he took hold of his friend.

"Marwan! Marwan, speak to me!"

Marwan's head lolled back. There was no response. It was

obvious by the numerous small scabs on his friend's face that he had recently seen some trouble. But obviously, those tiny cuts were not enough to cause unconsciousness. There had to be something more.

A dog barking down the street reminded Kadeen of his location. He had to get Marwan off the street and inside.

"Kadeen, what's going on?"

Kadeen turned and saw his wife, Rania, in her yellow robe, standing in the doorway.

"Quickly—come hold the gate open," Kadeen said in a strong whisper.

When he saw her hesitate, he added firmly, "Rania, now!"

She rushed to the gate and pushed the rock away with her foot. As Kadeen slid Marwan's arm around his shoulder and hefted up his weight, Rania asked, "Who is it?"

"It's Marwan Accad," he answered as he grunted his way around her. The toes of Marwan's shoes formed two serpentine tracks in the dirt as Kadeen struggled toward the front door.

He heard the gate clank closed behind him and felt his burden lighten as Rania placed herself under Marwan's other shoulder. They worked themselves sideways, then edged their way through the narrow door and into a small living room.

They dragged Marwan across the floor, knocking a vase off an end table as they passed, and dropped his body onto a couch. Both were panting when they straightened up, but Kadeen's breath suddenly caught in his throat. The left shoulder of Rania's robe was stained dark with blood.

"*Habibti*, are you . . . ?" Then he realized the source of the blood. "Help me get his coat off."

Together, they slid Marwan's arms out of his jean jacket.

Kadeen could see that although Marwan had padded his right shoulder, blood had soaked through and covered the upper quarter of his shirt. He looked up to ask his wife what to do next, but after seeing the blood on herself and on Marwan, her nursing training had already kicked in.

"Get me some scissors—the ones from the block in the kitchen," she ordered.

Kadeen jumped into action, thankful that Rania had taken charge. He felt very comfortable in a lot of areas, but this was not one of them.

As he ran through the house, he wondered what Marwan could be doing there. Was he running from something? Was he hiding? Had one of his dubious-background, high-powered clients turned on him? Were the police after him?

Whatever the situation, two things were certain: Marwan was in trouble, and Kadeen was the one he had come to for help.

He scanned the kitchen, looking for the butcher's block. *I really need to spend more time in this room,* he thought, getting frustrated. *There it is!*

Once he had the scissors, he turned to run back to the living room and almost stumbled over his eight-year-old daughter.

Glancing over her shoulder to make sure that the four-year-old wasn't up too, he said, "Laila, what are you doing—"

"Who's the man in the living room, *Abi*?"

Kadeen squatted to look her in the eye. "He's a friend of mine, my little *simsimah*. He's hurt, and he's come to us for help."

"Is he going to die?"

Lord, please, no, he thought. "I don't know. I don't think so."

"Can I help you?"

A feeling of pride swept over Kadeen. Laila hated to see anybody or anything hurting—a wonderful quality in a little girl when directed at people, a little more difficult to deal with when she brought home the occasional mangy street dog.

"You certainly can. Go to Maryam's room and quietly get into bed with her. Sleep with her tonight. She's too little to see this, so please make sure she doesn't come out."

"Should I pray while I'm in bed?"

Kadeen cupped Laila's cheek in his hand. "Of course, *simsimah*, pray. Now scoot."

Moments later, Kadeen was back in the living room. While he was gone, Rania had managed to tear open Marwan's shirt. Kadeen dropped the scissors into the pocket of the jeans he had slipped into before he had answered the door and looked over Rania.

Marwan's shoulder was a nightmare.

"Sorry I took so long," he said. "Laila was in the kitchen."

"I know. She heard the vase. I sent her there after you. This is not good, Kadeen."

"That much seems obvious."

"He needs to get to a hospital. This is too much for me to handle."

"He can't go to a hospital."

She stood and faced Kadeen. "What do you mean he can't go? Either we get him to a hospital, or he is going to die tonight on our couch!"

Gently taking her by the shoulders, Kadeen said, "Listen, *habibti*, there is a reason he came here instead of going to the hospital. He is obviously in some sort of major trouble."

"He's in trouble if he stays here! Dying on our couch is pretty serious trouble!"

Kadeen released his wife and turned away. "I know, I know. Just give me a minute to think."

Brushing past him, Rania left the room. Moments later, he heard pots rattling and water running.

Turning around, he stared at his friend. It was hard to know for sure, but it appeared that the years had aged him well. *After all this time, this is how you step back into my life. That is so like you—always a flair for the dramatic.*

Rania came back around him. In her hands she carried a pot of water with several rags floating in it.

As she knelt and began cleaning the wound, Kadeen asked, "You don't think this is something you can handle?"

Without turning, she replied, "It's a gunshot wound. The bullet has to be taken out. Then all the fibers from his clothing have to be removed. Finally, it's already infected, so we need to get him on heavy doses of antibiotics—greater amounts than I have access to."

Kadeen nodded. *Please, Lord, guide me.*

19

An airport security officer identified the stolen rental car just as the sun was coming up over Marseille. Fifteen minutes later, the area was surrounded by police, and by seven thirty, Inspector Jean-Claude Goddard's cell phone was ringing in Monte Carlo.

"Yes, yes, what is it?" he asked, startled out of a catnap in his office, where he had been all night. "You're kidding. . . . Where? . . . Has the area been secured? . . . No, no, we'll grab a chopper. . . . Have everything ready by the time we arrive. . . . Good work."

He called Colette DuVall to make the necessary arrangements, then called Lemieux and delivered the news. They had a lead.

Goddard splashed hot water on his face, brushed his teeth

and hair, and changed into a clean shirt from one of his desk drawers. He stopped in front of the mirror and realized that he still looked as bad as he felt. Then he gathered up his badge, sidearm, wallet, and keys and met DuVall out front. She drove him to the heliport to meet Lemieux.

"You look horrible," DuVall said as she sped through nearly empty streets.

"I feel worse," Goddard said.

"Didn't you go home last night?"

"How could I?" he said, sifting through his notes. "Have you found any more on the four men who engaged in the shoot-out with Accad in Saint Michel?"

"No. No identification, no fingerprint matches. There wasn't even any registration for the vehicles. Just like the two from the Méridien; it was like they were ghosts that just appeared from the great beyond."

"That's odd. Smells like professional security on a level that's even beyond what Accad was doing. Probably Ramsey's people. It's almost too coincidental that they could be from another case he was dealing with. But we can't rule it out either. What about the taxi driver?"

"It seems that Accad killed him, then stuffed his body in the backseat. He was an immigrant from Algeria."

"No previous connection to Accad?"

"Doesn't appear so, sir."

Goddard drummed his fingers on the dashboard as he thought. Out of the corner of his eye, he saw DuVall give him a would-you-please-stop-it look. He ignored her and kept up the percussion solo. It helped him think.

"So work this through with me. Accad kills Rafeeq Ramsey. Goes to the Méridien. Kills two mystery gunmen—"

"Remember, one was a woman."

"Whatever," Goddard said, dismissing her interruption with a wave of his hand. "I don't care if one was a chimpanzee. They were armed and shooting. He goes back outside, kills his taxi driver. Steals the taxi. Is ambushed by four *gunmen*," he continued, daring her to say anything, "whom he promptly dispatches. He goes to La Turbie, steals a rental car at the Trophy of Augustus, then drives to the Marseille airport, where he promptly disappears. That sound about right?"

"Yes, sir," DuVall answered matter-of-factly, apparently still stinging a little bit from Goddard's sarcasm.

"Pretty full day for one man." Goddard began his dashboard drumming again. "Did you find any more background on him?"

"The e-mail I sent you at four was all I've found so far," DuVall said. "But I've got a conference call with Beirut and Paris at ten. I'll call you as soon as I get more."

DuVall pulled into the parking area. The chopper was already warmed up and ready for takeoff. Goddard got out and grabbed his briefcase.

"Sure you don't want to take my place?" he yelled over the roar of the rotors.

"A whole day with the Skeleton?" she yelled back. "Tempting, but I'll pass."

"Very funny," Goddard shot back. "Just get more on Accad—fast."

"Will do."

A few minutes later, Inspector Lemieux arrived, and they were soon in the air.

"All right, Monsieur Goddard," Lemieux said after they had been airborne for a few minutes. "What do you have on our suspect?"

It was showtime.

"His full name is Marwan Adeeb Musa Accad," Goddard began as they flew over the French countryside. "He was born in Sidon, Lebanon, on February 14, 1978. His father, Adib, was a banker. His mother, Sarah, was a schoolteacher. The family moved to Beirut in '83. Beyond that, it's a bit sketchy. We know that Accad's only brother, Ramy, was born in '82. We know that Accad joined the army in '96, and that he did well, got noticed, got promoted, and served in several elite units. He was then assigned to the secret services, serving as a bodyguard for the defense minister in '98 and then on the prime minister's protective detail from 1999 to 2001."

Goddard scanned through the printout of DuVall's e-mail.

"From there," he continued, "Accad left the government in 2003. He set up Accad & Associates, an executive security company. That was right about the time that Ramy got out of the army and joined his brother's business. As far as we can tell, most of their work is protecting Western oil executives and their staffs currently working in Iraq and helping track down victims of kidnappings. More recently, they've begun protecting Western oil company executives working in Libya. And apparently they're developing quite a brisk business working with other Fortune 500 clients in and around the gulf. There's no bio on his company Web site, just a client list and contact information for their main office in Beirut. My colleague,

Colette DuVall, put a call into the office last night. It was closed, but she will try again in about an hour."

"That's it?" Lemieux asked.

"So far, yes," Goddard said, taken off guard by Lemieux's intensity.

"You think I don't know all that already?" The Skeleton's voice dripped with disgust. "I got all that with a single phone call to my office. It took me all of five minutes. My secretary knows more about Marwan Accad than you do, Monsieur Goddard. Is this the best Monaco has to offer? Heaven forbid!"

Goddard was determined to keep his composure. *What I wouldn't give for five minutes alone with Lemieux, no badges, no rank,* he mused. But he knew he could not afford to lose his cool. Nor did he want to give Lemieux the satisfaction of knowing he was getting under his skin.

"You asked me to pull together what I could," Goddard replied. "We should have more in a few hours."

"In a few hours, Marwan Accad could be in either Japan or Alaska," Lemieux said. "We don't have the luxury of time. We have a killer on the loose, and at this point he has a twelve-hour head start."

Goddard felt his neck and face turning red and his ears growing hot. Everyone in the chopper had just heard him get chewed out, and he wanted to strike back. But now was neither the time nor the place.

"I'm curious, Monsieur Goddard," Lemieux went on as they continued toward Marseille. "Why did you say nothing about how Marwan Accad and his brother survived the 1982 invasion of Lebanon—hiding in the bathtub and in the hallways of their apartment building, huddled in the arms of their mother, trying to avoid getting hit by glass and shrapnel?"

"I'm afraid I didn't—"

"Why did you say nothing about the day Accad saw his two uncles and two aunts and their children killed by a mortar round during Ramy's first birthday party?" Lemieux continued. "Did you know that Accad and his brother watched their own parents die in a car bombing on the streets of Beirut a few years later?"

Goddard looked out the window at the barren trees and the muddy farms after a night of drenching rains.

"Well, did you?" Lemieux demanded. "January 3, 1993? Does it ring a bell?"

"No," Goddard said. He felt humiliated. And what made it worse was that Lemieux was right. He should have had more. He should never have brought Lemieux bread crumbs instead of a full meal. Goddard knew how this guy operated, and he had only himself to blame.

Unfortunately, Lemieux still was not done.

"Accad was just shy of his fifteenth birthday," the Skeleton said without a trace of emotion. "Ramy was not quite eleven. It was a day that would haunt them for the rest of their lives, a day of which they never speak. Not to each other. Not even to themselves. You want to solve this case? Then you had better come to understand the real Marwan Accad. You want to know how a man can be driven to blackmail? to murder? to terrorizing an entire community of innocents? Then you had better start by understanding the events that shaped him and the demons that drive him.

"The narrative begins with the day his parents were

murdered. Everything changed on that day, did it not? Accad at once ceased to be a brother. He was now a father. There was no one else left to raise Ramy. Their uncles were dead. Their aunts were dead. The rest of their relatives had fled Lebanon for Europe and the United States. All of a sudden, Accad had to raise his little brother all by himself. Feed him. Clothe him. Protect him from harm. Even in the army, Accad had to clear the way for Ramy. He got Ramy accepted into an elite unit. He got Ramy choice assignments, even a coveted spot on the deputy prime minister's protective detail, just one step removed from the inner circle of power.

"But why? What were they after? Was their real objective so noble, to protect the leaders of their country from harm and the children of leaders from having to suffer as they had suffered? Come now, Monsieur Goddard, tell me you are not so naive."

Goddard said nothing. He had had just about enough of this.

"Marwan Accad is not driven by a love of country," Lemieux said. "He is driven by pure greed. Believe me. I have spent a lifetime pursuing such men. I know them by sight. Accad wants what he believes is rightfully his. He wants what was ripped from his hands—riches, the indescribable sense of invincibility that goes with real wealth, fabulous wealth. And to satisfy his nearly insatiable hunger, he preys upon the rich and the powerful, lulling them into a false sense of security before bleeding them dry. Mark my words, monsieur, Marwan Accad is a son of the devil. He comes only to rob, kill, and destroy. Which is why we must find him before he strikes again."

20

By the time Goddard and Lemieux landed in Marseille, the local authorities had gathered significant new evidence. The inspectors proceeded to the office of the director of airport security and began by reviewing surveillance tapes.

The first showed Marwan Accad's stolen rental car entering the airport grounds. Another showed Accad himself entering the airport a few minutes later. Other camera angles showed him emptying his locker, entering the men's room, picking up his ticket and boarding pass, and going through security as Jack Cardell.

"What's that he just tossed in the trash?" Goddard asked.

"Who knows?" Lemieux said. "It could be anything."

Goddard turned to the director. "Someone needs to go through all the trash collected last night and find what that was."

"But, monsieur, the inspector is right," the director said. "It could be anything."

"Or it could be something," Goddard insisted. "Find it."

Next, Lemieux called in the gendarme who had cleared Accad through security. He interrogated him so intensely that Goddard thought the man was going to have a nervous breakdown. The man was promptly suspended without pay.

A review of computer logs, meanwhile, showed that someone using a Lebanese Internet provider had purchased the Royal Air Maroc ticket for Marwan online.

"It has to be Accad's brother," Lemieux said.

"We don't know that for sure," Goddard cautioned.

"Who else could it be?" Lemieux asked.

"I'm just saying, we are trying to build a case," Goddard said, "one built not on conjecture but on solid facts, provable in court. If Accad is really guilty—and he may very well be—we need a lot more evidence than what we have. Right now, it's all circumstantial."

"I have won many cases with less," Lemieux boasted.

And how many have you let die with more? Goddard wondered, but he said nothing.

"Suit yourself," Lemieux said. "But I am getting on the next flight to Casablanca to find our killer. I want you to go to Beirut. Find out who purchased that ticket. But watch your back, Monsieur Goddard. Marwan and Ramy Accad are dangerous men. The closer you get, the more dangerous they'll become."

21

Marwan ducked behind a plaster half wall. Bullets flew all around him, sending grit and white dust puffing up, stinging his eyes. Peeking around the side of the wall, he saw blood splash from the neck of one of his assailants. The man crumpled to the ground.

Looking to his left, he saw another man firing at the enemies, but because of the angle, Marwan couldn't see his face. *At least I'm not alone,* he thought as he began returning fire.

He couldn't miss. It was almost as if he had an angel on his shoulder directing each bullet. As quickly as an attacker came through the door or around a corner or up from behind a piece of furniture, Marwan took him out. But for each man he killed, it seemed like two more took his place. Soon, his arm began to ache and the smell of powder burned his nostrils.

At long last, the last man fell. Then there was silence.

My partner, he thought, realizing he hadn't heard any shots from him for a while. With his gun trained toward the front door, he slowly sidestepped the length of the room. At the end, sitting with his back to the wall and his face turned away was the man who had had his back throughout this shoot-out.

Marwan could hear his ragged breath—shallow and intermittent. He dropped next to him and took hold of his chin. Everything seemed to move in slow motion as he turned the man's head.

"No!" Marwan screamed.

Kadeen al-Wadhi's face was covered with blood from a wound to the top of his head. On his chest, Marwan could see three more bloody holes. His friend's lips were moving, but no sound was coming out.

"Kadeen! Hang on, my friend. I'll get you help."

Marwan began backing up so he could get to the door, but a barely perceptible shake of Kadeen's head froze him in his tracks.

"What? I need to get you help!"

Still his friend's lips kept moving.

He's trying to tell me something! "What are you trying to say?"

Taking two strides forward, Marwan squatted in front of Kadeen. His friend's eyes showed no recognition of him. As he listened to his breathing, it became obvious that he was beyond help. Marwan had seen plenty of people die before; he knew the signs.

Slowly, he leaned in. With each inch he moved forward, the soft whisper began gaining definition.

". . . . . here? . . . . . dead. . . . . . . burn . . . . . . Why . . . . here? . . . . all dead. . . . . you burn . . . . Why did . . . here? . . . all dead. I . . . you burn in . . . Why did you come here? . . . They're all dead. . . . I hope you burn in hell. . . . Why did you come here? . . . They're all dead. . . . I hope you burn in hell. . . . Why did you come here? . . ."

Marwan stumbled back from Kadeen, lost his balance, and fell to the floor. His head rapped the tile, and he was momentarily stunned. As he lay there, he tried to process his friend's words.

It's my fault! If I hadn't come here, Kadeen would still be alive! Wait. . . . He said, "They're all dead." A knot formed in his stomach. *Oh, please, it can't be! Tell me it's not true! Maybe if I don't look, it won't be true; this all won't be real!*

But even as these thoughts raced through his mind, he knew he had to look. Keeping his eyes squeezed tight, he turned his head toward the back of the room. *Come on, you have to look! You need to know! Open your eyes on three. One . . . two . . . three!*

Marwan snapped his eyes open. Sitting on the ground, leaning against a doorway were Kadeen's wife and two little girls. Oddly, they were arranged exactly how they were in the one picture that Kadeen had e-mailed of them with the older daughter next to her mom and the younger one in her mother's lap. The only difference from the picture was the 6mm hole in the center of each forehead.

"No!" Marwan tried to get up, tried to go to them, but something held him down. He kicked and thrashed, but still he couldn't seem to move. "No! Please, no!"

"Marwan! Marwan, stop! Wake up! Marwan!"

Marwan's eyes popped open. Kadeen was leaning over him, holding him down with one arm on his left shoulder and the other across his chest. There was blood dripping from Kadeen's nose.

"Marwan, wake up! It's okay. You're safe."

"I've got to get out of here," Marwan said, still trying to sit up. "I've put you all in danger!"

A slight smile crossed Kadeen's face, but he didn't let up his hold. "You're not going anywhere, my friend. Now stop moving around before it's more than just my nose that's bleeding."

Marwan couldn't understand why his friend was having such a hard time comprehending the danger he and his family were in. "You're not hearing me, Kadeen! I'm in real trouble, and I've brought it here with me!"

"It's obvious you're in trouble. But like I said, you're not going anywhere—at least not yet. The doctor said you need to rest to get your strength—"

"Doctor!" Marwan yelled, renewing his attempts to get up. "Did you bring a doctor here?"

"Relax! Dr. Ajjedou is a friend. He and I work together on a kind of . . . underground operation. I trust him completely. He knows how to be discreet, and he knows when to ask no questions. Now, please, would you stop moving around? You're scaring my daughters," Kadeen said with a nod behind Marwan's head.

Immediately Marwan stopped struggling. Tilting his head back, he saw two little girls holding tightly to their mother. The younger one had tears streaming down her cheeks.

"I . . . I'm sorry," Marwan said, embarrassed and ashamed. Looking at the girls, he added, "I was just having a nightmare. But it's over."

"That's right; it was just a nightmare," Kadeen echoed. "Mr. Accad is awake; right, Mr. Accad?"

And for the first time since his eyes had opened, Marwan was fully awake. The terror of the dream had left him, and he could finally assess his surroundings.

It was obvious by the furniture that he was in a living room—nicely decorated but not ostentatious. As for himself, he was lying on a couch, shirtless, with his right shoulder heavily bandaged. He knew that he must be on some serious pain meds because, although it seemed that his body really wanted to tell him how messed up his shoulder was, his brain just didn't seem to want to hear it.

Marwan forced a smile onto his face. "Rania, it's good to see you again. I'm so sorry to cause such a fuss."

"You are welcome in our home," Rania said with a slight bow of her head. She continued to hold on tightly to her daughters.

"You must be Laila," Marwan continued. "And that means you're little Maryam. It's so good to see you in person. Your daddy's told me so much about you."

"Welcome Mr. Accad to our home, girls."

Laila said a quiet "Welcome to our home." But Maryam just burst into tears again.

"*Habibti*, would you take the girls into the other room so that Mr. Accad and I could have a talk? Thank you."

Marwan watched as Rania led the two girls through an arched entryway to another part of the house. When he turned around, Kadeen had a smile on his face but was shaking his head.

"You certainly know how to make an entrance," Kadeen said. "You ready to tell me what's going on?"

"Any chance I could get you off of me first?"

"You're not going anywhere?"

"Seems I don't have a choice but to stay."

"That's all I needed to hear," Kadeen said, lifting his arms from Marwan's upper body. He snatched a couple tissues, then lowered himself into an out-of-place chair that looked like it had been pulled over for whoever was on Marwan duty.

Kadeen held the tissues to his nose to stop the blood and said, "Well, I always knew you were hardheaded."

Marwan chuckled quietly. "I'm sorry. I wasn't quite myself. Although . . ."

"Although what?"

"Although you probably deserved what you got—trying to hold me down like that!"

Kadeen laughed. "There wasn't any 'trying' about it. You were locked up tighter than a widow's purse."

Marwan joined his friend's laughter. "Believe me, if I hadn't lost all that blood, there's no way you could have kept me down."

"Probably not . . . probably not." Kadeen pulled the tissue from his nose, looked at it, then put it back in place. "Now please, Marwan, tell me what's going on."

The details were still a bit sketchy in Marwan's brain. But as he told his friend the story, the memories became much clearer to him, as did the plan for what he had to do next.

22

"BUT THAT'S ALL the more reason for you to stay here," Kadeen protested as Marwan finished his story.

"No, it's all the more reason for me to go. I don't know who I'm going up against. I don't know how many there are. I don't even know exactly what it is they want, other than me dead." Marwan was getting more exasperated as he spoke, the helpless ambiguity of his situation causing his gut to tighten. "If I had been fully in my right mind, I never would have come here to begin with."

"But you are here. And whatever the situation, I am glad you came. And you must promise me that you will at least consider staying here for a few days to recover."

"We'll see," Marwan said simply.

"We'll eat in twenty minutes," Rania called from the kitchen.

Ever since Kadeen's family's departure from the living room, Marwan had seen little of them. Rania had brought in cold drinks and a plate of *M'hanncha*, but though the almond pastry looked and smelled delicious, Marwan bypassed it; he didn't think his stomach was quite ready for something that sweet.

No, I think I'll save my appetite for what's still in the kitchen. For the past twenty minutes, the smells coming from that room had been drawing Marwan's attention to the point of distraction. *I hope I can keep the food down. If I can, I'll leave right after we eat.*

"If I can't convince you to stay, where will you go?" Kadeen asked, revisiting a line of conversation that Marwan had twice deflected already.

He was about to deny his friend again when he saw Laila and Maryam in the doorway to the kitchen. They were staring at him, and Laila held a sheet of paper in her hand. Thankful for the distraction, Marwan waved them over. He grimaced at the pain the movement caused but tried to cover it with an oversize smile.

Slowly, cautiously, the girls walked toward him. Laila held out the paper. It was decorated with hearts and crosses and the words *We hope you feel better. Love, Laila and Maryam.*

"I made the crosses," Maryam said.

"They're wonderful. Thank you, girls."

They continued to stare at him, and Marwan, who never really knew what to say around children, continued to stare back.

Just as it reached the point of awkwardness, Kadeen leaned forward and whispered something in the girls' ears. Their faces lit up. Laila picked up the leftover *M'hanncha*, and the two girls ran from the room.

Despite the pain he was feeling, Marwan had to smile.

"They're beautiful, Kadeen."

"On that we agree, my friend."

"I look at them. I look at your wife. You know what I wonder?"

"Whose family they really are?"

Marwan chuckled. "No, I wonder what you're doing here in Morocco. With your education and your intelligence, you could be living the high life anywhere—Paris, New York, Dubai. Instead, you're here in Casablanca—not exactly the hotbed of cultured civilization."

"My company transferred me here. Simple as that."

Marwan rolled his eyes. "'Simple as that,' my foot. From what you told me before you came here, you could have had your company send you anywhere. So come on. Spill it."

"You really want to know?"

Marwan's silent stare gave his answer.

Reaching to a small table, Kadeen picked up a leather-bound Bible and flopped it down on the coffee table in front of Marwan. "There you go."

Partly wishing he had never brought it up, yet partly curious, Marwan asked, "So God told you to come? What, did you come across a burning bush or something?"

Kadeen laughed. "Or something. No, this book is not just the reason I came to Morocco, but it is also my true work here."

Instead of taking time to sort through his friend's riddle, Marwan leaned back farther into the couch and nodded for Kadeen to continue.

"I'm here working for my company. That is my daytime

job. As long as my work gets done, my employer doesn't care what I do with the rest of my time."

Marwan looked up sharply, then grit his teeth at the screaming of his shoulder with the sudden movement. More slowly, he reached for his bottle of water. "And just what do you do with the rest of your time?"

"Smuggle Bibles."

Marwan almost spit the water out of his mouth. "You do what?"

"Well, actually, we don't really call it smuggling anymore. We prefer 'Bible couriers.' But be that as it may, Rania and I felt the Lord leading us to get the truth of God's Word into as many hands as is possible. We chose Morocco because it is the perfect launching point to reach Mauritania, Algeria, Tunisia, even as far as Libya."

"But that's crazy! Why would you risk your job, your freedom—possibly even your life—all for this book?" Marwan said, picking the Bible up from the coffee table and letting it drop with a thud.

"You ask why. Let me put it this way. Suppose you had the cure for cancer. What kind of person would you be if you kept it to yourself? Think about it. Even if the government was against you, even if everyone laughed and called you a fool, even if it meant a risk to yourself or your family, wouldn't it still be worth getting that cure out to the world?"

"Okay, I get your point. But the fact is, this isn't a cure for cancer."

"You're right. It's not a cure for cancer. It's more important." Kadeen leaned forward in his chair. "I'm not doing this to save people's lives. I'm doing it to save people's souls."

Marwan dismissed the claim with a wave of his hand. "Now you're being melodramatic. Come on, Kadeen, when it comes down to it, the Bible is just a book. No offense—I mean, it's got a lot of good stuff in it, but . . ."

"No offense taken. And I hope you will take no offense when I tell you that you've got the Bible all wrong. It's not just a book with 'a lot of good stuff in it.' It is the very Word of God."

This had rapidly turned into a religious discussion, something Marwan had promised himself long ago he would never get into with Kadeen. He knew about his friend's conversion to Christianity in college. He had also witnessed the change in his life from hard partyer to what Marwan considered to be a much more boring version of the original. On the flip side, if he was forced to admit it, he had also seen peace and purpose enter Kadeen's life for the first time in as long as he had known him.

The truth was, Marwan was happy for Kadeen—even proud of the changes that had taken place in his life. But he also knew religion wasn't for him. He was doing just fine without God in his life. He had made that very clear early on after Kadeen's transformation, and his wish to not be preached at had always been respected. Until now, apparently.

Still, if he had to admit it, he was a bit intrigued. Picking up the Bible again, Marwan said, "Okay, if this is really the Word of God, what about all the contradictions?"

"Like . . . ?"

Marwan was momentarily flustered. He began flipping through the pages, not knowing what he was looking for, much the way someone who doesn't know a thing about automobiles still looks under the hood when their car stalls along the side of the road. Finally he put the Bible down with a grunt of pain and a laugh. "You know that's not fair, Kadeen. I'm not a Bible scholar."

"Then how do you know there are contradictions?"

"Well, everyone knows," Marwan answered weakly.

"Listen, if there was one provable contradiction, don't you think that those who are against Christianity would have published it in every single newspaper and shouted it on every street corner of the world?"

Marwan shrugged his acceptance of the point.

Kadeen opened the Bible to the table of contents and passed it to Marwan. "The fact is that the Bible was written by around forty different authors over a period of fifteen hundred years, and yet it is still entirely consistent throughout. Think about that! How utterly unlikely, if not impossible, is that? Friend, you can trust the truth of that book."

"Okay, then, what about the changes that have taken place over the years?" Marwan countered, passing the Bible back to his friend.

"Again, give me an example," Kadeen said with a smile, offering the Bible back. Marwan waved his hands, refusing the book, so Kadeen continued, "Did you know we have more ancient manuscripts of the New Testament than any other written work in history?"

"It's a popular book. So what?"

"So what? Think about it. Archaeologists have found some twenty-four thousand ancient New Testament manuscripts and manuscript fragments—some from as far back as AD 130—more than any other ancient work, and all are essentially identical."

Shaking his head, Marwan said, "Again, so what?"

"The 'so what' is that it proves that the New Testament that we have today has been accurately copied and transmitted through the ages. Do you know we only have 643 ancient manuscripts of *The Iliad* by Homer, putting it in a very distant second place? Yet does anyone doubt the historical authenticity of what we read back in university?

"And take Caesar. He wrote his history of the Gallic Wars somewhere around 50 BC. There are only nine or ten known copies in existence in the entire world, and all of them date to almost a thousand years after his death. Aristotle wrote his poems around 343 BC, but the earliest copy we have is dated AD 1100. That's nearly a fourteen-hundred-year gap. Yet nobody doubts the veracity of either of these works.

"But the Bible—that's a different story. Never mind the Old Testament with its ridiculously detailed ancient copying processes. Forget those twenty-four thousand New Testament copies I mentioned. It still can't be trusted. Sense a bit of a double standard?"

"Fair enough," Marwan said in order to buy himself time. His mind was racing, trying to come up with a hole in Kadeen's argument. Then he halted in midthought. *Why? Why am I trying so hard to prove him wrong?* "Okay, what if I concede the point that the Bible is all true? Still, I ask, so what? How about I get you an accurate history of ancient Greece. Are you going to risk your life to get that into people's hands?"

Kadeen smiled. "Good question. The answer is obviously no. But you're missing a critical point. The Bible is not just a true book; it is also a book of truth. It doesn't just tell you what happened in the past; it tells you how to live now. And most importantly, it tells you how to prepare yourself for when this life is over."

"Meaning what?"

"Meaning it tells you how you can have eternal life in heaven. The Bible contains the good news about Jesus Christ, who said, 'Greater love has no man than to lay down his life for his friend.' That's exactly what Jesus did—he laid down his life so that anyone who believes in him and accepts the sacrifice he made can enjoy eternity with God. He died for you, Marwan."

Marwan fidgeted, feeling increasingly uncomfortable with the conversation. Talking about the authenticity of the Bible was one thing, but all this talk about Jesus and dying and eternal life . . . this was something very different. "All that's in the Bible, huh?" he finally asked.

"Exactly. And that's not all—"

"The food's on the table. Are you two ready to . . ." Rania, who had just come walking into the room, stopped short. Marwan could see the frustrated look that Kadeen gave her.

"Could we have just five more minutes?" Kadeen asked.

"Of course. I'm sorry," she sputtered. "I didn't mean to—"

"Not at all," Marwan said, taking the opportunity to extricate himself from the conversation. It had been interesting, but it felt like Kadeen was about to take it to a deeper level than he was ready for. "If you could convince your husband to help me off this extremely comfortable couch, I think I might actually be ready to eat something."

Rania gave an apologetic look to her husband, who smiled his forgiveness.

Reaching for Marwan's extended left hand, Kadeen said, "Old friend, you are about to experience the reason I married this woman."

"The only reason?" Rania said playfully.

"Well, I can think of a few others," Kadeen answered with a wink. "But this is probably not the time to get into those."

23

It was almost nine when Marwan Accad drove away from the al-Wadhi home and into the night. Where was he supposed to go? He didn't know anyone else in the country. He didn't dare stay at a hotel. And he had to assume that those hunting him would track him to Morocco soon, if they weren't already here.

It had been a bittersweet parting. Kadeen was clearly unhappy with Marwan's decision to leave, calling it foolish and unnecessary. *While* foolish *may be accurate, I have to believe it was necessary.* Marwan just wished it were possible to erase any trail that someone could follow to Kadeen and his family.

He glanced at the passenger seat, at the Bible that Kadeen had given him as he was walking out the door.

"This is my personal Bible," Kadeen had said. "Believe it

or not, it's the only one I have currently in the house. Hope you don't mind, but I've been studying with it for years and it's marked up quite a bit."

"Thank you," Marwan said, embracing his friend. "I will cherish it deeply." *Although the chances of my actually opening it are slim.*

Now, as he drove, he ran his thumb along the book's cracked and peeling binding. *It would be nice to have the kind of peace and clear direction that Kadeen and Rania have. Maybe someday. But there is definitely no chance for peace today.*

He was still managing a fever, though it was down to 101. Every joint in his body ached, and the throbbing in his shoulder was intense. And as he drove, he continued to beat himself up. Going to Kadeen's had been a stupid mistake. How could he have been so foolish?

He was the center of this whole problem. He was the lightning rod. If it weren't for him, no one would be in any danger. Darkness began to creep into his thinking—thoughts of taking his own life, thoughts of ending all his pain and escaping into the abyss.

But then, too, came thoughts of his brother, who was working so hard to help him get to safety. He could never abandon Ramy. His parents would never have forgiven him, and no matter what happened, he couldn't dishonor their memory.

But what exactly was he supposed to do? He had nowhere to stay, no one to turn to, and the clock was ticking. Someone was coming after him, and one wrong move could be fatal. All the planning he had done while at Kadeen's now either seemed ludicrous or had dissipated into a pain-soaked fog.

Marwan was able to think clearly enough to know that the

rental car was one more link to his whereabouts. So he drove it several kilometers away from Kadeen's neighborhood and abandoned it on a quiet side street, leaving the keys in the trunk. Then he flagged down a taxicab and took it back to Mohammed V International Airport, where he called his brother from a pay phone using a credit card linked to one of his aliases.

"Ramy, it's me, Marwan. Sorry to call you at home."

"What are you doing?" Ramy asked. "I told you to call from a satellite phone."

Marwan shook his head. He didn't want to start the conversation with an argument. "I know, but I didn't have time."

"And you were supposed to wait three days. It's barely been one."

"I need to come home."

"Why? What's wrong?"

"It's a long story," Marwan said.

"How long could it be?" Ramy asked. "You haven't even been there twenty-four hours."

"Look, I can't talk about it, not on an unsecure line," Marwan insisted. "Just book me a ticket."

"No," Ramy said. "Beirut is not a good idea. Not yet."

"Why?"

"It's not safe. Not right now."

Marwan pounded the wall above the phone, sending shards of pain shooting through his arm, shoulder, and neck. "Well, I can't stay here. I can't go back to Europe. How about São Paulo?"

"Very funny," Ramy said, sounding exhausted.

"Why not?" Marwan asked. "I can help track down Claudette."

"I've got people doing that, but not you."

"The U.S. is out?"

"You'd never get a visa."

"How about Cairo?"

"Why Cairo?"

"Why not?" Marwan said, spotting several Moroccan police officers gathering by one of the exits. "There are 7 million people there. I can disappear."

"I still don't understand," Ramy said. "Why can't you just stay in Casa?"

"I just can't," Marwan said, knowing that his visit to Kadeen al-Wadhi would be the one thing that would set his brother's blood to boiling. "I'll tell you later."

"Fine, I'll book you to Cairo. When do you want to leave?"

"Now."

"What do you mean, now? Where are you?"

"I'm at the airport."

"Already? Wait, hold on a moment."

"What's the matter?"

"There's a breaking news story on French television."

"What?" Marwan watched the police as he waited for Ramy. They seemed to be just talking, but . . .

"They've found the car you left in Marseille, not to mention the body of the taxi driver in Saint Michel," Ramy said.

"What else are they saying?" Marwan asked, the sweat coming now from more than just his fever. "Have they said anything about me or about Morocco?"

"No, not yet," Ramy said. "They're saying police are still gathering information, no leads yet."

"They're lying," Marwan said. "They're onto me. I've got to get out of here now."

"Okay. What name should I use for your departure?"

Marwan quickly ran through his aliases in his mind. "Book the flight under the name of Tariq Jameel."

"Got it," Ramy said. "What else?"

"I need a place to stay when I get there."

"Hotel?"

"No, too risky, too easy to track me down."

"Then what?" Ramy asked.

"Get me a flat."

"A flat? How long are you planning to stay?"

"I have no idea, but it could be a while."

"How long is 'a while'?" Ramy asked incredulously.

"I don't know," Marwan said. "But you said it yourself, Ramy. I can't come home. I can't go after Claudette. Where else am I going to go?"

Ramy said nothing.

"Just find me a place quickly—I don't care how much it costs." Marwan's head was starting to spin. He knew he needed to finish the call quickly. "FedEx me a satellite phone, some cash, and some business cards."

"Business cards?"

"Something to make me seem legitimate."

"Like what?" Ramy asked.

"I don't know," Marwan said. "Make me a computer salesman—no, a consultant. Make up some company name and logo. And put up a fake Web site for it right away."

"You're kidding, right?"

"Hey," Marwan said, managing a small grin, "what are little brothers for?"

24

By 11:30 p.m., Marwan was boarding EgyptAir flight 848, which departed at five minutes past twelve. By 7:05 a.m., he had landed in Cairo, though for the life of him he did not know how he had made it.

No one had stopped him. No one had questioned him. No one appeared to be following him. Why? Was it a trap? maybe some kind of gift from heaven? It didn't feel like a trap. But why would God suddenly be merciful to him now?

It didn't make sense, but he would take whatever sliver of good fortune he could find. The more important question was not how he had gotten here but what he was going to do.

To begin with, he had to remember that he was now Tariq Jameel. That's what his passport said. That's what his tickets said. That was the name on the lease for the flat. He had to start getting used to it. He had to start thinking of himself as Tariq Jameel. And he needed a convincing cover story to go with it.

He worked his way through the airport crowds, paid for his visa, and caught a cab to Sheraton Royal Gardens on Helmiat Al Ahram Street, just a few kilometers from the airport. He wasn't going to check in. He just needed a base camp for a few hours from which he could contact his brother, have something to eat, and plan his next moves.

He went to the business center and found a clerk.

"Good morning," the clerk said upon seeing him. "May I help you?"

"I'd like to rent a computer."

"Of course, sir. Are you a guest here at the hotel?"

"No, I'm meeting a colleague, but I forgot my laptop and I need to check my e-mail."

"No problem, sir," the clerk said. "How long will you need it?"

"Just an hour or so."

"My pleasure, sir. I just need you to fill out this form. May I have your name?"

"Tariq Jameel," he replied without hesitation.

"Very good, Mr. Jameel. You will also need to buy a wireless access card."

"How much?"

"One hour is forty-five pounds, sir."

"Fine. Do you take Visa?"

A few minutes later, Marwan/Tariq was sitting in a dark corner of the lobby, sipping some orange juice. He logged on to the Internet and opened up an instant messaging system.

Ramy, you there? . . . It's me, Tariq. . . . I've made it.

He waited a few moments, and then a reply popped up on his screen.

You're okay?

Fine . . . clear sailing. Any luck with a flat?

Sort of.

Meaning?

I found a place, but it hasn't been lived in for a while. The owner says it needs a little work, but he also said you could move in today if you don't mind.

The pain in Tariq's shoulder had dissipated some with time and a load of painkillers that Kadeen had supplied him with. However, he still found himself having to type one-handed.

How much work?

A little cleaning, some painting, a few repairs—who knows? Obviously I haven't seen it.

Where is it?

Heliopolis—near the airport.

That's perfect. I'm at the Sheraton Royal Gardens right now.

The owner can meet you there whenever you'd like. . . . I think he's just happy to get rid of the place.

Will he rent by the month?

No. He wants a minimum six-month guarantee.

Tariq shook his head. Six months was way too long, but there was probably a way around the owner's demands.

No way. Tell him we'll pay the first month in cash, but we won't sign anything until he's made all the repairs . . . then we'll consider six months.

Will do.

Good—what else?

I found out who's working on your case back in Monte Carlo.

Who?

There's two of them, actually. One guy's name is Jean-Claude Goddard. Born in Nice, grew up in Monaco. 46 years old . . . chief of detectives . . . smart guy, good reputation, highly respected, married with one daughter. The other guy is Marcel Lemieux. 62 years old. Born in Grenoble, grew up in Normandy, now the chief homicide detective in Paris . . . widely considered the best cop in the country. Arguably one of the best inspectors in Europe. He's cracked some of the EU's biggest cases. Twice divorced . . . no kids.

Marwan scribbled the information onto a pad. Then a thought struck him.

Which one is headed to Morocco?

How did you know?

Instinct.

Lemieux—he could be landing any minute.

What about Goddard?

He's coming here to interrogate me.

You're joking.

Wish I were.

Get out of the country. You can't let them find you—not yet.

I can't just disappear. I've got the business to run.

Run it from the road—you've done it before.

And where am I supposed to go?

Don't we have a team in Baghdad right now with those execs from Exxon Mobil?

This time Tariq had to wait a full minute before the reply came back.

Have you completely lost your mind? You want me to fly all the way to Iraq to avoid talking to some cop from Monte Carlo?

Tariq answered immediately.

Absolutely. You can't stay there. . . . If Goddard finds you and you don't give him what he wants, he'll have you arrested and extradited on obstruction of justice charges and hindering the prosecution. God only knows what might happen to you then. You absolutely can't let that happen.

What if Goddard follows me to Baghdad?

He won't. He'd rather stay alive.

25

For two days, Tariq Jameel did not emerge from the flat.

He still had a fever, but with no thermometer, he had no idea how high. It was obvious that Kadeen and Rania had saved his life. However, he was still a long way from well. He had no energy to go out and find a doctor. He had no appetite, so he simply sipped cans of soda and bottled water that he'd brought from the Sheraton Royal Gardens, trying desperately to rehydrate his body. He took the antibiotics that the al-Wadhis' doctor friend had given him, but he tried to leave the painkillers in his backpack as much as possible.

Ramy was not kidding about the flat. It was large—much larger than he needed—with three bedrooms and three baths and an enormous living room. But to say that it needed "a little work" was putting it mildly. It had no doubt been a grand and lovely place back in the 1950s and '60s, but Tariq wondered if it had been cleaned since.

Dust covered everything, floor to ceiling, and the kitchen table and counters were overlaid with a film of grease. Two of the three showers didn't work. Two of the three toilets leaked. The kitchen sink didn't work. The oven didn't work. Only one of four burners on the stove worked. And at night it got quite cold, and Tariq couldn't get any of the heaters to work.

The artwork left much to be desired as well. There was an array of paintings on the walls, including a miniature Mona Lisa and a life-size portrait Tariq dubbed, *Spanish Lady with an Attitude*. In the dining room hung two identical paintings of a young boy smoking, while in one of the hallways there was a three-dimensional picture of four kittens, one of which had its face punched in. The living room had three large brass statues of Asian dragon-men of some sort and an enormous painting of zoo animals hanging out at a bar. And they were all covered in dust.

Not that the decor mattered much. Most of the lightbulbs in the place had blown out so that even in the daytime Tariq couldn't see that well anyway.

The landlord had promised to have everything cleaned and fixed immediately, but Tariq needed a few days to rest. Having workmen scrubbing and pounding and making all kinds of racket would certainly not be conducive to his recuperation. So he had asked the man not to send the cleaners until Monday. Until then, all he wanted was a thick blanket and a clean pillow and a couch on which to lay his head. Unable to find the first two, he had settled for the couch in the living room, where he had collapsed and slept almost around the clock.

On the third day, he was suddenly awakened by a knock on the door.

Instinctively Tariq reached for his gun, then remembered he no longer had one. He checked his watch. It was almost noon, though with the drapes closed and most of the lights not working, the flat was quite dark.

The knocking began again, louder this time. Tariq's pulse quickened. No one knew he was in Cairo, much less Heliopolis, and it was only Thursday—no workmen should be there yet. But the knocking continued.

Tariq got up, grabbed a small lamp, and moved quietly to the door. Had they found him? If so, why were they knocking? His hand tensed around the midsection of the lamp. It would be little protection if someone was here to take him by force. But he refused to go down without a fight. He reached the door, looked out the peephole, and breathed again. It was a FedEx deliveryman with a stack of large boxes in his hands. He opened the door and saw the man's startled expression.

"Are you Tariq Jameel?" the man asked.

"I am," he said, realizing how awful he must look—unshaven, unshowered, and in the same clothes he'd had on since he left Casablanca.

"Sign here."

Tariq did, then tipped the man and took the packages. Sure enough, they were all from Beirut. He ripped the first one open like a little kid on his birthday.

Inside was a brand-new satellite phone with batteries, a charger, and an instruction booklet. Also inside was an envelope containing ten thousand Egyptian pounds—plenty to get him started—and a stack of business cards that read, *Tariq Jameel, Managing Director, ICT Consulting, Brussels, Belgium*, complete with a Web site, an e-mail address, a post office box number, and a Brussels-area phone number.

Tariq powered up the sat phone and called the number.

"Thank you for calling ICT Consulting," a woman's voice said in French on the recording. "No one can take your call right now, but please leave your name, number, and a brief message, and someone will get back to you as soon as possible." The message repeated in English and then again in German. Ramy had thought of everything.

Tariq ripped open the next box and found a large leather briefcase inside. He pulled it out, unzipped it, and found himself staring at a high-end notebook computer complete with fingerprint security access and a USB satellite hub. Digging further, he found several pairs of blue jeans, khaki trousers, several new shirts, socks, underwear, a couple of sweaters, a shaving kit, and toiletries—toothbrush, toothpaste, mouthwash, soap, a nail clipper, and so forth.

But it was the third box that surprised Tariq the most. On the top layer was a brand-new handheld digital TV and radio receiver, still in its box. He assumed that was Ramy's way of helping him keep up with the news, particularly of the intensifying hunt for him. Below that were maps of the city, a list of computer consulting companies based in Cairo, and a stack of newspaper stories—printed off the Internet—on the state of the computer industry in Egypt, all designed to help him build and maintain his new cover.

Finally, underneath everything else, there was a small,

locked, lead-lined strongbox with a key taped to the top. He inserted the key, turned it, and opened the lid, revealing a .45-caliber pistol and ammunition.

26

Tariq Jameel was beginning to feel guilty for sending his little brother to Baghdad. Ramy obviously knew what he was doing. He would never have given him up to Jean-Claude Goddard or anyone else. He felt an ache in his stomach. If Ramy died in Iraq, he could never forgive himself. He had to find a way out of this nightmare, and quickly.

He booted up the computer, activated the sat hub, and logged on to the Internet. Then he ran a quick search for recent stories about the Ramsey family. As he had expected, the European and Egyptian media were awash with reports about Rafeeq's and Brigitte's deaths and the kidnapping of Claudette. And pictures of Marwan Accad, now wanted for murder, were everywhere. Perhaps coming to Cairo had been a mistake, but he still believed he'd had no choice.

The latest news was right at the top of the *Le Monde* home page. It boasted "exclusive" details of the events leading up to the assassination in Monte Carlo, including the fact that a ransom note had arrived at the Ramseys' estate in Paris via a DHL package from Berlin the day after Claudette's disappearance. The note had provided a Swiss bank account number and demanded one million euros be wired to the account within twenty-four hours "if Mr. Ramsey ever wanted to see his wife alive again." Ramsey, the story reported, had promptly paid.

"Several days later," *Le Monde* went on to say, "a second DHL package, this one from Brussels, arrived at the Ramsey home. It contained a video of Mrs. Ramsey, bound and gagged but still alive, and a note demanding 10 million euros or Mrs. Ramsey would be executed live on the Internet. The package directed Mr. Ramsey to wire the money within seventy-two hours and then come to Brussels and await further instructions."

The story noted that "an anonymous package" was left at the front desk of Mr. Ramsey's hotel, containing "a grainy new photo of his wife," a note demanding 25 million euros, and details of where Mrs. Ramsey could be found in Madrid "in precisely one week, assuming the money is paid in full."

It was all true. It was why Accad & Associates had been brought in by Rafeeq Ramsey in the first place. But what worried Tariq most was the next paragraph: "Police now believe Marwan Accad, the CEO of a Lebanon-based executive security company, may be the mastermind behind this shocking crime. Sources close to the investigation say they have hard evidence of Mr. Accad's involvement and note that he fled the scene of the crime and has been missing ever since. Repeated phone calls yesterday by *Le Monde* to Accad & Associates in Beirut went unreturned, but an extensive manhunt for Mr. Accad is under way."

Suddenly there was another knock at the door—a slight tap at first and then a hard pounding.

Tariq froze. It couldn't be the FedEx man again. But who?

He quickly loaded the .45 and moved carefully to the door. But when he looked through the peephole, he was again stunned by what he saw. Outside his door stood three beautiful young women, each probably in her twenties. The one in the middle was holding a basket of fruit and sweets.

Baffled, he put the gun in his back pocket and covered it with his T-shirt. Then he opened the door a crack and said, "Good morning."

The one on the right smiled. The one on the left giggled shyly. The one in the center did the talking.

"Good morning. My name is Dalia—Dalia Nour. These are my friends, Dina and Mervat. We live right above you, and we heard you were new."

Tariq wasn't sure what to say.

"Well, it's nice to meet you, Dalia, ladies. May I help you somehow?"

"We just wanted to welcome you to the building," Dalia said, "and to give you this little present from the social committee."

She offered him the basket of fruit, which Tariq gratefully accepted. As he did, he found himself captivated by Dalia. She had the most gentle face and gorgeous brown eyes that twinkled when she smiled, as she was doing now. She was dressed like a European girl, not a local, and she obviously didn't mind spending money on clothes. Her sweater was a soft pink cashmere. Her black jeans and designer shoes were more likely from London or Paris than Cairo or Alexandria. While the others wore all kinds of rings and bracelets and necklaces, the only jewelry Dalia wore were two small diamond earrings in gold settings and a gold watch that looked like a Cartier around her wrist.

"Well, this is very kind," Tariq said, his eyes locked on Dalia's. "Thank you."

"Our pleasure," Dalia said, her expression changing ever so slightly.

Was she as attracted to him as he was to her? Or was it the fever deceiving him? He sensed they were about to leave and remembered how horrible he looked.

"I would invite you ladies in for a cup of tea and to share these treats," he said, trying to think of a way to keep the conversation going for a few more minutes, "but I'm afraid my place looks worse than I do at the moment."

That elicted a laugh from Dalia and Dina and another giggle from Mervat.

"That's okay," Dalia said. "I'm afraid we can't stay anyway, but we would like to invite you to a small party on the roof tonight. It starts at nine, and you don't need to bring anything but yourself—and perhaps a clean shirt."

Tariq wanted to accept. There was something about this woman that fascinated him. But he was supposed to be keeping his head down, maintaining a low profile, not partying with the neighbor girls.

Still, how could he turn them down? Refusing to go would only get the whole building talking about this rude new stranger, and the last thing he needed was people gossiping about him.

"I'd be delighted," he said at last. "And for you, I'll even scare up a clean shirt."

27

Inspector Goddard was getting nowhere. He had arrived in Beirut the night before only to find Accad & Associates all but deserted. A lone receptionist informed him that no, Marwan Accad had not checked in; no, she did not know where he was; and sorry, but Ramy was out of the country until further notice. Everyone else in the company was scattered around the Middle East on assignment. Goddard left a number where he could be reached and went back to his hotel to check in with the Skeleton.

He called Lemieux at the Hyatt Regency in Casablanca and found—to his relief—that Lemieux was faring little better. Airport surveillance videos showed a Jack Cardell arriving on the Royal Air Maroc flight and promptly renting a car. But so far the APB that Casablanca police had put out on the car had turned up nothing.

Moroccan intelligence, meanwhile, said Accad had been there only twice before, each time with the Lebanese prime minister, and they had no known contacts in the country for him. They did not even have a file on Jack Cardell and had no record of such a person—alias or otherwise—ever being in the country. For the moment, Lemieux was at a dead end.

"Accad had to be headed to Morocco for a reason," Lemieux said, thinking aloud. "He knew we'd pick up his trail. He knew he couldn't use the Cardell alias for long. He had to be meeting someone."

"Didn't he tell the gendarme in Marseille that he was headed for the Hostel Rabat?" Goddard asked after a moment of pondering the impasse.

"That was just part of his cover," Lemieux said.

"Maybe," Goddard said. "But what if he really meant it?"

"I told you," Lemieux replied, "there's no evidence Accad has been here in years, much less to any specific hostel."

"Well, he must have stayed somewhere," Goddard pressed. "Have you checked all his known business associates?"

"Don't be a fool! Of course I have."

Trying to let Lemieux's insults slide off his back, Goddard continued, "Have you gone farther back? College roommates? High school chums? Childhood friends?"

"Hmmm. With his parents' dying when he was so young, it's possible he forged some very strong friendships. What do we know of his childhood relationships?" Lemieux asked, curious now.

"Very little, I'm afraid," Goddard admitted.

"Am I the only one with a functioning brain? Ask the brother," Lemieux ordered.

Goddard explained why that wasn't possible.

"You're telling me Ramy Accad left the country just as you were heading there to interview him?" an incredulous Lemieux asked. "Where did he go?"

"The receptionist wouldn't give me that information," Goddard answered, "but I tracked his flight through airport manifests—he flew under his own name—and discovered him on a plane to Baghdad. On the surface, it does seem odd. But the receptionist said he typically travels three weeks out of four anyway."

"How long ago was the trip planned?"

"She said it just came up."

"I bet," Lemieux said. "Go back to her. See what she knows about Marwan Accad's childhood. Then contact me as soon as possible."

28

Tariq couldn't remember the last time he had been to a party—at least one when he was not carrying a gun and protecting a dignitary. His life in recent years had been so consumed with work—often dangerous work, at that—he didn't even take vacations, much less mix and mingle with people he had never met before. But now he found himself actually looking forward to the evening.

Showering was no easy process, his shoulder wound was still raw. But the antibiotics were clearly working. He was feeling a bit better. He sensed his appetite was starting to come back, and he had already finished the big, juicy oranges in the fruit basket Dalia and her friends had given him earlier.

Dalia Nour.

Her face came to mind as he stared in the mirror and

shaved. Who was she? What was her story? He saw no engagement ring on her finger. Was it possible a girl that attractive was still single?

Grateful for Ramy's care package, Tariq finished dressing and slipped the gun into his waistband at the small of his back, then took the elevator to the rooftop terrace. There he found about two dozen people, all under thirty, laughing and dancing and chatting away. The latest Amr Diab album was playing loudly over a large sound system. Several tables were covered with hors d'oeuvres, baklava, and other various pastries, and there was a cash bar set up in the corner serving liquor of all kinds.

The sight and smell of the liquor actually reassured him. These were not religious people, and that was good. After the conversations with Kadeen, he had no interest in talking about God, whether the Christian one or the Muslim one. Using his own experience and his own ingenuity, he had made it to safety with no help from any God, thank you very much.

He walked over and bought a beer. He had tried to sleep away his pain the last few days. Maybe it was time to drink it away for the next few hours.

And then he felt a tap on his right shoulder. He tried not to let his grimace show.

"Nice shirt," a soft voice behind him said.

He turned and found Dalia smiling up at him.

"You clean up nice," she said, obviously flirting with him, but just as obviously high on pot. She took another drag on her joint and offered him one of his own. For a moment he wondered what his mother would say, but he quickly shook that off. Tonight was not about feeling sad or guilty, he decided. It was about forgetting his predicament and having some much-needed downtime.

"Thanks," he said, taking the marijuana cigarette from her small, delicate hands and lighting it up. "What's the occasion?"

"It's a Thursday," Dalia said with a wink.

"And?"

"And it's time to relax and enjoy a day off."

"You guys do this every Thursday night?"

"Some people do."

"What about you?"

She shrugged. "Sometimes I prefer to go dancing or to the movies."

"And tonight?"

"I was curious to see if you'd show up."

"You didn't think I would?" Tariq asked.

"Honestly? No."

"Why not?"

Dalia took another hit from her joint. "I don't know. You just strike me as a loner."

Tariq held up his hands in mock surrender. "Guilty as charged."

"Really?" she laughed as she playfully put a hand on his chest and leaned into him. "And what else are you guilty of?"

The question cut deeper into his heart than she had intended or noticed.

"Name it," Tariq said quietly.

She gazed into his eyes as if she were trying to read his thoughts. Tariq was captivated and couldn't turn away.

Finally she broke into a wide smile. "Come here," she said. "I want to show you something."

She took him by the hand and led him through the crowd and around the corner to a quiet, private garden where they could look out over the twinkling lights of Heliopolis and the planes taking off and landing in the distance.

"It's stunning," he said.

"Isn't it?" They stood there for a few minutes, just the two of them, savoring the view.

"So what's your name, bad boy?" Dalia said at last.

"Tariq."

"Tariq what?"

"Tariq Jameel."

"And what's your story, Tariq Jameel? Who are you, and what are you doing here?"

He could only imagine the look in her gorgeous eyes if he told her the truth.

"I'm a consultant," he said, stomping out his cigarette, then taking a sip of beer.

"What kind of consultant?" she pressed.

"Computers."

"It sounds boring."

"It is."

"So where are you from?"

"All over," he said. "I've lived in Europe for most of the last five years."

"Really?" she said, and her eyes lit up in anticipation. "Like where?"

"Madrid, Paris, Berlin, you name it. But my company's based in Brussels."

"Mmm, I love Paris, especially in the spring," she said, ignoring any talk of business, for which he was grateful. "The air is so fresh and sweet, and the flowers are in bloom, and the streets are filled with couples in love."

"Did you grow up there?" Tariq asked between sips.

"No; Jordan. But I'm a flight attendant for British Airways, and I sometimes get to fill in on flights to Paris."

"Sounds like a fun job."

"It can be," she said a bit wistfully.

"But . . . ?"

"But it's hard to have a life of your own."

"What do you mean?"

"I mean when they hire you, they make you these dazzling promises—not just the Brits, but all the airlines—free travel, see the world whenever you want, you know. But the truth is you work all the time, at crazy hours. You're always living out of a suitcase. You barely know where you are when you wake up. You're not sure where to call home. It's hard to make friends, except with other employees. And unless you fall in love with a pilot—and they're all married—or a flight attendant—and they're all gay—then . . . well, whatever. At least it pays the bills."

She took another drag on her cigarette.

"What about your roommates?" Tariq asked. "You're all friends, aren't you?"

"Not exactly," she said.

"What does that mean?"

"No, no, don't get me wrong," Dalia said. "They're sweet girls. I'd do anything for them and vice versa. But we haven't really known each other all that long. We're just sharing an apartment because none of us could afford the rent on our own. And besides, they both work for Air France, so I hardly ever see them. And they just got transferred to New York. Now I'll never get to see them."

"That's too bad."

"That's life," Dalia sighed. "No rest for the wicked."

"Why don't you do something different?" Tariq asked.

"Like what?" she said. "Computer consulting?"

"It pays the bills."

"You like it?" Dalia asked.

"It's okay," he said. "But like you said, I'm a loner. It's not so bad for me. But someone like you, well, I don't know. You may need something more."

"What's that supposed to mean?"

Tariq noticed the quick defensiveness that often accompanies pot smoking. *Gotta take it easy with her. It's been a while since you've had someone this good-looking and this young interested in you.*

"I just mean you're so nice, beautiful, outgoing, vivacious—you need something better."

She turned from the city and looked into his eyes, her head tilting to one side.

"You think I'm beautiful?"

"Why else would I be at this party?"

Tariq leaned down and kissed her gently. She responded instantly and with an intensity he had not expected. The two made out as a 747 roared overhead on approach to Cairo International. And before long, Dalia made him an offer he couldn't refuse.

"Dina and Mervat are leaving straight from the party to the airport," she said softly as she kissed his ear. "I have the apartment all to myself until tomorrow afternoon."

Tariq felt his temperature rising again.

"Care to join me?" she whispered in as seductive a voice as he had ever heard.

He wanted nothing more, but two hesitations rushed to the fore—Dalia's safety and the festering wound in his shoulder. He pushed away both thoughts.

Nobody could possibly trace him to this flat. Ramy was too good to let that happen. The second issue was tougher. He'd need to come up with an excuse, an accident of some kind. But why let that stop him from a night with this gorgeous, willing young woman?

"Love to," he whispered back.

"Good," she said. "Apartment 901. Mingle a bit. Then meet there in ten minutes. My room is in the back, the third on the left. I'll leave the front door unlocked."

Tariq watched her as she swaggered away. Just before reaching the door, she accidentally bumped into a large standing vase. It teetered, but she caught it. Dalia turned and gave him a bit of an embarrassed smile, then blew him a kiss.

"The girl's wasted," Tariq said to himself, a little disappointment starting to cloud his mood. *How's she going to feel in the morning waking up with me next to her? If she was sober right now, would she have given me that invitation?*

A battle ensued in his conscience. Here was this gorgeous woman just waiting for him to spend the night with her. Yet her judgment was impaired and he hardly knew her. *But what do I care? I'm not her father. She's a grown woman who's made a grown-up decision. On the other hand, she didn't make it with a fully functional, grown-up mind. Besides, there's something special about her. I'd hate to waste my shot at getting to know her with a meaningless one-night stand.*

In the end, he went back to his flat, sat in his kitchen, popped open the first of four bottles of Stella, and spent the next two hours second-guessing himself. When he could no longer keep his eyes open, he laid his head on the table and fell asleep.

29

Tariq woke with a jolt, sending two empty beer bottles crashing down from the table.

"Just great," he said, trying to spot a path away from the table that would protect his bare feet from the broken glass. Carefully choosing his steps, he tiptoed out of the kitchen. After slipping on his shoes, he took a broom and dustpan back in to clean up the mess.

It was the dream again. Kadeen, Rania, the girls—all shot, all dead. *If you hook up with Dalia, will she end up joining that dream? Is it really safe or fair for you to bring her into your crazy life right now?*

Tariq brooded over that question as he swept up the glass. He didn't think anyone could know where he was staying; Ramy was too careful to allow that. And even if someone did know he was in Cairo, the chances of connecting him to Dalia were slim at best.

In the end, his desire for some companionship won out. He got dressed and left his flat to begin exploring the neighborhood a bit. After a while, he found what he wanted.

Walking into the small shop, he scanned the merchandise. *Ah, those will do.*

He waved the shop owner over and pointed to the arrangement of a dozen lilies, each one displaying a wide array of pinks. Tariq watched the man's smile widen when he realized he was about to be over six hundred pounds richer.

After making preparations for the delivery of the flowers, Tariq wrote a note to be attached.

Dalia,

Forgive me for last night. I was not in the condition an exquisite beauty like you deserves from a man like me. Please allow me to make it up to you this evening. I will be at your door at 8:00 p.m. If you answer the door, be prepared for a night on the town. If you don't, I will understand.

Tariq

He paid for the flowers, leaving a sizable tip to ensure the delivery would be handled properly, then wandered the streets for a few more hours. Eventually, he could feel his body starting to wear down. Tariq could tell he was still not 100 percent. He made his way home, took a short nap, and spent the afternoon gathering whatever information he could off the Internet on the investigation into the whereabouts of Marwan Accad.

At 7:55 p.m., he closed and locked his door. Two minutes later he arrived at Dalia's flat. *What are the chances she opens the door?* he asked himself, looking down at the time ticking away on his watch. He knew he wasn't a bad-looking guy, but he also knew he wasn't anywhere near Dalia's league. And after standing her up last night . . .

From inside, he heard female laughter. *She and her girlfriends are probably in there laughing right now about the fool who's going to be standing at the door knocking until his knuckles bleed, desperate to get some time with a woman far above his class.*

He had just about talked himself out of knocking on the door at all, when he saw the second hand on his watch sweep past the twelve. *Why not?*

As he raised his hand, the door flew open, and Dalia wrapped her arms around his neck. She kissed him hard enough to cut off his air supply for a moment.

She finally stood back. "I've been watching you through the peephole. We were wondering when you were going to knock."

Tariq looked over Dalia's shoulder and saw her two roommates, whose names he had already forgotten.

"Hi, girls," he said sheepishly.

"Hi, Tariq," they said in unison.

"Nice flowers," the darker of the two said.

"Oh yeah," Dalia said, kissing him once again. "Do you know how long it's been since someone sent me flowers?"

"Really? I would think a beauty like you would be receiving flowers on a daily basis," Tariq said, seeing an opening and taking advantage of it.

"Ooooo," one of the roommates said.

"He's smooth," the other said.

"Ta ta, girls," Dalia said, slipping her arm through Tariq's. "Don't wait up for me."

They took the taxi Tariq had waiting and traveled through town until they crossed the bridge to Zamalek, a large island in the middle of the Nile. Once there, they pulled in front of La Trattoria, a trendy Italian eatery located in the heart of the restaurant and coffee shop district. Earlier in the day, acquiring the reservation had taken a promise of some significant cash, which Tariq slipped to the maître d'.

When they were situated at their cozy corner table, Tariq said, "You know, only in today's world could a Lebanese man and a Jordanian woman enjoy a romantic Italian dinner in Egypt."

Dalia laughed. "Welcome to the world of a flight attendant. Half my life I spend wondering what country I'm in, trying to find foods that remind me of home."

"What foods are those?"

"Oh, there's *kanafeh*, *mansaf*, but my favorite has to be *mrouzia*. My mother spent some time in northwestern Africa and came back with an amazing *mrouzia* recipe."

Tariq sensed a cloud sweeping across Dalia. "Is everything okay?"

"Yes, of course," she answered, forcing back her mood. "I just don't really want to talk about home."

"Fine with me," Tariq said, reaching across the table to take Dalia's hand. "Instead, why don't we talk about you and me and us?"

"The very things I had in mind," Dalia said playfully.

The dinner progressed nicely. The food was wonderful and

the company was better. As they ate, Tariq watched the people entering and exiting the restaurant—a habit he had picked up early in his career.

As they waited for their dessert of caramelized pears in red wine sauce, two men entered the restaurant. It was past the time when reservations mattered, so they were shown to a table across the room from Tariq and Dalia. They were obviously European by their appearance. Tariq watched as they took their seats; then he stiffened. Both were sporting the subtle, telltale bulge of a shoulder holster.

"Tariq? Tariq, are you with me?" Dalia followed his gaze to the other table just as the two men looked their way. The larger of the two nodded; then they turned back.

"Do you know them?" Dalia asked.

"No. Do you?"

"I don't think so," Dalia said. "So, I was telling you about Prague. We had a three-day layover, and each day we walked up to the castle to take a tour. And each time we arrived, they were just closing it down for one reason or another. The first day, they had to . . ."

Tariq watched Dalia as she continued to talk, but his mind was far gone from the conversation. He didn't have his gun because he'd thought they would be totally safe. *Be honest. You didn't bring it because you didn't want to have to explain it to Dalia later tonight if things go how you hope they'll go.* He didn't even have his SOG pocketknife with him—an absolutely inexcusable mistake.

Dalia was now talking about walking Wenceslas Square and eating Stroganoff in the downstairs restaurant at the National Museum. Tariq hoped he was giving the requisite *wow*s and *huh*s at the right times. Twice he had again caught the two men looking at their table.

He still had the steak knife from his veal dish, and now as he pretended to listen to Dalia, he carefully palmed it and slid it into his lap.

"Am I boring you?" Dalia asked.

"Boring me? You? Never," Tariq protested. "It's just that sometimes I get lost in the deep, rich brown of your eyes."

"Oh, you're good," Dalia laughed. "You're really good. So, my girlfriend and I are on the Charles Bridge . . ."

Tariq's body tensed. Both men were standing up. They started on their way toward Tariq and Dalia's table. Tariq gripped the steak knife. He watched the men's hands. The moment one of them reached into his jacket, Tariq would have a split second to react.

The table's going to have to go into Dalia. Then drive the first one into the second and go wild with the knife until you get one of their guns.

The men were getting near. Adrenaline was surging through Tariq's veins.

"Tariq? Earth to Tariq?"

"Excuse me," the first man said.

Tariq had one hand on the knife and one hand on the table.

Seeing that Tariq wasn't going to answer, Dalia said, "Yes?"

"I'm so sorry to disturb you, but maybe you can settle a bet for my friend and myself."

"I can try," Dalia said, totally unaware of the potential danger.

"Do you fly for British Air?"

A smile spread across Dalia's face. "Yes, I do."

The second man's hand went into his jacket.

Do it! Do it! Tariq shouted to himself. But something didn't feel right. He held still a moment longer.

The man's hand came out with his wallet. He pulled out a twenty-euro note and passed it to his friend, who accepted it with a laugh and an "I told you so."

"Were you on one of my flights?" Dalia asked.

The second man said, "We've each been on a couple. We're air marshals for British Air."

"I thought I recognized you," Dalia said, laughing. "I'm Dalia, and this is my friend Tariq."

Tariq let go of the knife and reached his hand out. As he shook their hands, the men introduced themselves.

"Nervous?" the first man said, wiping his hand on his jacket.

"First date," Tariq admitted.

"Well, congratulations. I know a few guys who have been after her for a while—to no avail."

After a little more small talk, the men returned to their table.

"Are you really that nervous?" Dalia asked.

"I am not used to being in the presence of such loveliness," Tariq answered very formally.

"Oh, you're so full of it."

They finished their dessert, and while Tariq had a couple other activities planned, Dalia said she was ready to head home. Her roommates had another late-night flight.

The night ended as Tariq had hoped it would, and the next morning when he woke up, it was in the nicely decorated bedroom of Dalia's flat.

30

Accad & Associates was located in a small office building near the American University of Beirut. *In many ways it's suggestive of its founder,* thought Goddard, now back for his second visit. Discreet, unassuming, and a bit mysterious, just like Marwan Accad.

The sign on the door gave the company's name but offered no logo, no Web address, no hint of what its employees did. The furniture in the waiting room was tasteful, even on the expensive side, but there were no brochures, no pictures on the wall, nothing to suggest the millions of dollars that poured into its coffers every month from clients worth billions. Only the thick, bulletproof street-side windows and the surveillance cameras positioned over the main entrance, in the hallways, and in the company's lobby provided any clue as to the security-conscious mind-set of its owners.

But for all Marwan and Ramy Accad's precautions, there was one weak link—Jasmine Zeitoun.

"Good morning, Mademoiselle Jasmine." Goddard smiled as he sidled up to the reception desk. "So good to see you again."

Jasmine, an attractive young graduate student, smiled back and batted her eyes at Goddard, as if he were the first good-looking man who had walked through these doors in months, if not years.

"Welcome back, Inspector Goddard. What can I do for you today?"

"I'm heading home, but I just wanted to check again to see if either Monsieur Accad—or any of their associates—has checked in today."

"No, I'm sorry," she said, seeming to be genuinely disappointed she could not help him. "It's been very quiet."

"Very well," he said. "You can't blame a guy for trying."

"Not at all," she said. "It is my pleasure."

"And you still have my number?"

"I do," she said, finding his card on her desk and showing it to him. "I will have one of the Accad brothers call you as soon as I hear from them."

"You're most kind," he replied, preparing to leave. "Oh yes, one more thing."

"What is that?" she asked.

"Marwan's old friend in Morocco," he said. "I need to talk to him—part of the routine investigation, you know—but I seem to have misplaced his number. Do you have a number where I can reach him?"

"You must mean Kadeen al-Wadhi," she said innocently, typing a name into her computer. "He's the only friend of Marwan's that I know of there. It's a shame that he and Ramy don't get along. He always seems so nice on the phone."

"I thought so too. Ramy and Kadeen didn't get along? I wonder why," Goddard said, mining Mademoiselle Zeitoun for all she had.

"Well, the story is, monsieur," she confirmed in a whisper, though no one but the two of them were in the office, "it all goes back to when they were kids and Mr. al-Wadhi was always mean to Ramy. Ramy just never forgave him and never forgot."

"What a shame."

"Oh, it is. Whenever a letter or something comes from Mr. al-Wadhi for Marwan, I always have to hide it so that Ramy won't know about it. Such silly games for grown men. From how Marwan describes Mr. al-Wadhi and his family, they seem like wonderful people." Jasmine handed a Post-it note to Goddard with a number neatly printed across it.

"They certainly do. Thank you so much, my dear. You have been most helpful."

Ten minutes later Goddard was in his car, racing for the airport and speed-dialing the Skeleton.

"The friend's name is Kadeen al-Wadhi," Goddard said breathlessly when he had gotten Lemieux on the line. "They've known each other since they were kids. He lives in Casablanca with a wife and two daughters."

"What does he do there?" Lemieux asked.

"I'm not sure yet," Goddard said. "I've got DuVall working on that right now. I'll know soon."

"Good work, Goddard," Lemieux said, sounding genuinely happy for the first time in days. "You might just end up making a fine detective after all."

31

"My poor Tariq. Was the other driver hurt badly as well?"

Tariq heard the question but had no interest in answering it. He pretended he was still sleeping, but Dalia asked him again.

After a few moments, he rolled over and slowly opened his eyes to the golden morning sunshine pouring through the curtains. Dalia snuggled her warm body close to his, waiting for an answer. He was used to lying. It didn't usually bother him. But for some reason lying to this girl on this day made him feel ashamed, though he couldn't imagine why or how to get around it.

"I'm afraid he was," he said at last. "The police said he had been drinking a lot. He'd just come from a party, wasn't paying attention, and then—*wham!*—I never even saw him."

Dalia winced. "You could have been killed."

Tariq hesitated again. "I don't like to think about that." He scooped his shirt off the floor and put it on.

"Dying or the accident?" she asked.

"Both," he said, then slipped out of bed and pulled on his khakis.

"Is that what you were having a nightmare about last night?"

"Nightmare?" he asked.

She nodded. "You don't remember?"

"No, I don't," he lied again. What had he said? How much had she heard?

"It was around three," she recalled. "You were grinding your teeth, tossing and turning, and then you started mumbling something."

"Like what?"

Dalia pulled the sheet up to cover herself. "It was something like 'No, stop, it wasn't my fault! I didn't know!' But I couldn't get it all. I was still half-asleep myself."

Thank God, he thought. But what he said was "And then what?"

"And then it was over. You rolled over and went back to sleep. You don't remember any of that?"

The truth was he did. It was a nightly occurrence, only this was the first time he had actually seen the bullets being shot into the little girls' heads.

It was a terrible dream, and he was still a bit shaken over it. But there was no way he was going to tell her. His only chance of survival at this point was living a double life. He couldn't afford any more mistakes. More mistakes meant a higher chance of people getting killed. And while he wasn't squeamish about killing when it needed to be done, neither did he relish pulling the trigger.

"Sorry, I don't." He leaned down and kissed her. "Now I've got a question for you."

"Okay."

"When's your next flight?"

"Not until Monday night," she said. "Why?"

"So you've got the whole weekend free?"

"I was going to go to Alex to visit a friend."

"A guy?"

"No." She smiled. "A girlfriend."

"Cancel," Tariq said.

"Why?"

"Let's do something together this weekend."

"Like what?"

"I have no idea," he said. "But let me take you to breakfast and we'll come up with something, anything you want."

"Anything?" she asked, looking a bit suspicious.

"Anything," he said, desperately hoping she'd say yes. He knew the risks of starting a relationship now of all times, but he was sure he could manage them, and he couldn't bear the thought of going back to his dingy, filthy flat all by himself. Dalia was beautiful and fun and full of life, and the way he figured it, every minute he spent with her was time he wasn't thinking about Ramsey and Goddard and Lemieux.

"You're on, Tariq Jameel," Dalia said at last. "Let's play tourists."

Despite having lived in the Cairo area for almost a year, Dalia had never taken the time to see the city. Tariq was new in town. (He had been to Cairo several times with the Lebanese prime minister, but he'd never had any time for himself.) So after quick showers and a buffet breakfast at the Sheraton Royal Gardens, the two took a taxi to the Khan Al-Khalili bazaar, where they spent the morning like a newlywed couple on their honeymoon. They strolled the aromatic alleyways, browsed in shops filled with jewelry and antiques and various Oriental curiosities, and sipped Turkish coffee at the Naguib Mahfouz Café.

"Have you ever read any of Naguib Mahfouz's novels?" Dalia asked as they nestled together in a private little booth whose walls were covered in sheets of bright red cloth, making it feel as though they were hiding in a tent.

"Only one," Tariq answered, munching on a small pastry. "*The Day the Leader Was Killed.*"

"That one was sad," Dalia said.

"Aren't they all sad?"

"Not all," she said. "But regardless, I read them for the love stories. 'My sweetheart pulls the hook out of the water; it is empty but the hook pierces my thumb which leaves an indelible mark, one that has remained to this very day. On the banks of the River Nile in front of our home, I told her that she was no good at fishing but that she had hooked me all the same, and I have bled.'"

"I'm impressed," Tariq said.

"My father got me 'hooked' on Mr. Mahfouz, pardon the pun. When I was a little girl, he used to read his novels to me every night before I went to bed, at least a chapter but sometimes more if I could beg persuasively enough. And when I got old enough, I began reading them myself."

"Have you read them all?"

"Not all his plays, but all of his novels and most of his short stories. They're magical, like escaping my life and entering another world. For a long time, I thought I wanted to be a writer when I grew up, until the day Mr. Mahfouz was attacked by that maniac with the knife. I remember exactly where I was when I heard the news."

"Really? That was a long time ago—'95 or '96, wasn't it?"

"October 14, 1994," Dalia said.

"Wow, you really do remember."

Dalia stared into her coffee. "It was my thirteenth birthday. I had just gotten home from school and my mother told me. I didn't believe it at first, so I called my father on the phone and he said yes, it was true. I ran to my room and locked my door and started crying, and I didn't come out until the next morning. No one I had cared about had ever died before. It was like losing my own grandpa, even my own father. I can't even explain why. But then I heard that he would live, and I felt so happy, so relieved, like a big burden had been lifted off of me, and I began to cry again. My friends thought I was crazy, but I didn't care. I was just glad Mr. Mahfouz was still alive and I prayed that he would one day be able to write again, and he did. Have you ever felt like that, Tariq? Have you ever lost someone close to you? or thought you did?"

Tariq's instincts told him to lie again, to keep his distance, to give her nothing that could ever let her get close enough to him that she might discover his real identity. But his heart said just the opposite. True, they barely knew each other. They had met less than forty-eight hours earlier. But he heard himself say, "My parents. They died when I was fifteen. It was a car bomb. My brother and I both saw it happen. A few meters closer, and we would have been killed as well."

"Oh," Dalia gasped. "I didn't mean . . . I didn't know . . ."

"It's okay," he said gently. "It was a long time ago."

"I'm so sorry."

There was a moment of awkward silence.

"You've seen a lot of death, haven't you, Tariq?"

He didn't nod. He didn't speak. He wanted to, but for the moment, he couldn't.

Dalia reached out and touched his hand. He felt the urge to pull away. He didn't want to be pitied. He had never wanted that. But neither did he want to offend this girl. And besides, her skin felt warm and soft and reassuring, and he couldn't remember the last time someone had even cared what he thought or felt, much less asked.

"Maybe we could go and do something else," he said after a while.

"Sure," Dalia said. "I'd like that."

32

An hour later they were strolling hand in hand through the cavernous Egyptian Museum, trying to absorb four thousand years of history in about four hours, while Dalia read snippets from a guidebook she had bought in the gift shop.

"Guess how many artifacts are housed here," she said as they admired the limestone statues of Prince Rahotep and his wife, Nofret, then turned to wind their way through the treasures of Amenhotep III and Queen Tiy.

"I have absolutely no idea," Tariq replied, never a big fan of museums but trying to enjoy it because Dalia obviously was.

"Come on, just guess."

"Fine, a million."

"Be serious. How many?"

"Okay, half a million."

"Very funny. It's 120,000 on display—and they say there's another 150,000 in the basement."

"That's it?" Tariq quipped. "And they call this a museum? What a sham!"

"You're hilarious," she said, playfully elbowing him in the ribs. "You should have been a comedian."

"That's right," he said. "The world's first computer consultant comedian. Now why didn't I think of that?"

"Come on," she said, ignoring his sarcasm, "let's see the treasures of King Tut."

They took the stairs to the second floor and entered the Tutankhamen Galleries. They began by studying the two life-size black and gold statues that once guarded the entrance to his tomb in the Valley of the Kings near Luxor. Soon they were peering into the massive glass cases containing the gold-painted wooden burial vessels found by the famed British archaeologist Howard Carter back in the 1920s and still intact after so many centuries.

"Isn't it amazing?" Dalia said. "Look. Inside this big gold chamber fit this smaller one, and inside that one fit this even smaller one, and so on."

A few minutes later they entered a special, darkened, climate-controlled gallery in which a small tour was being held.

"And look—inside of all that fits this solid gold sarcophagus," she continued in a whisper, "with a smaller gold and wood sarcophagus inside that, and an even smaller one inside that and so forth until Tutankhamen himself was sealed inside, behind this gold mask."

They stopped in front of a glass case, lit from within, surrounded by museum guards, containing the most remarkable artifact Tariq had ever seen.

"Is this it?" he whispered back. "Is this the real thing?"

"Absolutely," she replied. "Look at the colors and the craftsmanship. It's extraordinary."

She was right. The life-size burial mask was made of solid, burnished gold and painted with brilliant blues and yellows and reds in a stunning likeness of the face of the boy king who once ruled the Nile and all who lived within its care and keeping. What was more, in glass cases all around them were other priceless gold and silver objects and precious gems and jewels that had been found buried with Tutankhamen as well.

"Can you imagine having so much wealth?" Dalia asked as she gazed around the room at what had to be hundreds of billions of pounds' worth of treasures, if they could even be priced at all.

"Can you imagine having it all buried with you, thinking that you could take it with you and use it in the afterlife?" Tariq asked.

"You're right. That is kind of sad."

"But all the ancient Egyptian kings believed it," Tariq added. "Look at the pyramids. That's why they were built—to store up riches for heaven, riches that were ultimately looted by bandits and grave robbers."

A guard asked the two of them to please be quiet, and they decided to continue working their way through the museum. But soon they were walking through room after room of additional treasures that Tutankhamen had insisted be buried with him—his spears and his bows, game pieces he liked to play with, gold fans he must have used to cool himself in the sweltering summers, even the actual golden throne from which he once ruled his mighty empire.

Thirty minutes later they paid a small fee and entered the Mummy Room. The first mummy they saw was King Ramses II, and Tariq couldn't help but think of Rafeeq Ramsey, whose body no doubt still lay cold in a morgue back in Monte Carlo. They leaned in and stared at the gaunt face and the bony fingers and the dark brown wrappings that still covered most of the ancient king's body.

"Dalia?" Tariq whispered, glancing around to see if the guards were close enough to hear him.

"What?" she whispered back.

"Do you believe in heaven?"

She turned and looked at him with a quizzical expression. "Of course. Don't you?"

"I guess."

"You guess?"

"No, I do—I . . . I don't know. . . . Never mind."

She suddenly straightened up. Her expression changed and she whispered in his ear. "I'm sorry," she said. "I shouldn't have brought you here. I wasn't thinking. All this celebration of death."

"No, no, it's not that," he said. "I'm fine. I just . . ."

"Just what?"

"I don't know. Lately I've been thinking a lot about what happens after we die. All these pharaohs thought they could take their wealth with them, but here it still is. I've always thought that if I was a really good person—you know, the good stuff I've done outweighs the bad stuff—I'd make it to heaven. But what if I'm wrong?"

Dalia was silent for a moment, then said, "You know, if you were to ask my dad, he would tell you that no one could be good enough to get into heaven."

Tariq shook his head, not liking that answer. "So what you're saying is that we're all out of luck. What good is heaven if no one can get there?"

"I didn't say that no one could get there. I said you can't work your way there. According to my father, only through believing in Jesus can someone get to heaven. It's a gift, not a payment for what you've done."

"You say that's what your father believes. What do you believe?"

Tariq could sense Dalia's discomfort with the conversation and was about to change the subject when she said, "I don't know anymore. I grew up believing what my parents did. But then I moved away from home, and their beliefs seemed so provincial, so antiquated when compared with the modern new world I was living in. Now, honestly, I just try not to think about it."

Tariq took her hands. "I'm sorry. I shouldn't have brought it up. Let's keep looking around. By my guess, we've got eight more hours of things to see and less than two hours to do it in."

But as they continued their tour, Tariq couldn't keep his mind off their conversation. Despite what he had said to her, he knew that he wasn't a good man. He had shed too much blood and caused too much pain to too many people to feel that he had any possible shot at making it into heaven.

Yet she had given him a possible alternative. *"It's a gift, not a payment." I've got to process that. But not now. I'm in a room full of priceless antiquities with a beautiful woman on my arm who thinks I'm a pretty special guy.* There would be plenty of time to think about those things later.

33

THE CELL PHONE buzzed, and Inspector Goddard grabbed it.

"Colette, please tell me you've got a lead on Kadeen al-Wadhi," he said as he stood in line at the ticket counter in the Beirut airport, trying to get a ticket that could get him to Morocco by the end of the day. "Anything I can go on."

"Actually, I do," DuVall said.

"Yes!" Goddard nearly shouted. "He's in Casa?"

"That he is. And I've got a home address for him."

"Really? Give it to me."

Goddard scribbled down the address in his notebook.

"Do you have a photo yet?"

"Just got it."

"E-mail it to my phone immediately."

"Will do."

"Excellent work, Colette. Really sharp. You didn't contact the Moroccan police yet, did you?"

"No, I figured you'd want the information first."

"Brilliant. How did you find him?"

"The phone company," DuVall said, the pride in her voice evident. "The hard part was simply finding the right manager who could authorize a search of their records and, of course, convincing them that I was who I said I was. After that, it went quite quickly."

"Well done," Goddard said again, not believing his sudden good fortune. "All right, I want you to learn everything you can about Kadeen al-Wadhi. Track down every person he's called in the last few days, who his neighbors are, what kind of car he drives—everything. And let's try to keep the Moroccan police out of this as long as we can. I don't want any jurisdictional skirmishes slowing us down. In the meantime, I'll call the Skeleton."

* * *

Inspector Lemieux hung up with Goddard and checked the text message that had just arrived on his cell phone. Goddard and his little blonde deputy had come through after all. Imagine that.

It could hardly be more perfect, Lemieux thought. Either Accad was at al-Wadhi's house, hiding out—a high probability—or else this al-Wadhi knew where he was and could lead them to him. Either way, he had to get to him fast. He stormed out of the Hyatt Regency and jumped in his car.

The sun was just starting to set when Lemieux pulled up

outside the gate of the al-Wadhi villa. He inspected the fence and saw what could have been the remnants of blood by the front gate. If it was blood, it wasn't fresh.

Next he went to the gates in front of the carport. There was one car parked there, and he could see oil stains on the cement next to it. *Interesting. Looks like either Mama or Papa isn't at home. That could prove beneficial.*

Walking back to the front gate, he looked for movement in the house. Not seeing any, he pulled his weapon, chambered a round, then tucked it back in its shoulder holster with the safety off. *You just never know what kind of people you're going to run into,* he thought with a smile as his hand reached for the buzzer.

34

Kadeen was sitting at the desk in his office. His eyes were getting tired from staring at the computer screen. His time spent caring for Marwan had put him behind in his work, and he still wasn't completely caught up. He needed to get these reports in by tomorrow. Unfortunately, the numbers were just not adding up.

His frustration level had been slowly rising all day, and having Laila and Maryam running in and out of his office hadn't helped his mood much. Finally he had pleaded with Rania to take the girls out for ice cream or shopping or anywhere as long as it was out of the house.

Rania had smiled, kissed him on the forehead, then collected the girls. The resulting silence had been helpful, but the work was still a long ways from done.

When the front gate buzzer rang, he ignored it. But when it rang a second time, he remembered about Rania's gate opener. After the first gate opener had accidentally been crushed under the tires of his car, he had gotten her a new one. Unfortunately, that cheap replacement worked only about 50 percent of the time. In those times when it didn't work, she would either have to use her key to open it or send one of the girls to buzz him so that he could open it for her.

As he got up from his desk, he looked at his watch. *They've only been gone forty-five minutes.* The frustration he had been feeling began to surface again. *Couldn't she have kept them away a little longer?*

Keep a smile on your face. Don't let the girls think they've always got a grumpy daddy, he thought as he swung open the front door.

Instead of seeing one of his smiling girls at the gate, he saw a tall, gaunt man in an overcoat.

"Can I help you?" Kadeen asked, trying to control his nerves. This man had *police* written all over him. Already Kadeen was running through the contingency plans he had laid out in case the Bible-smuggling operation was ever found out.

"Mr. Kadeen al-Wadhi?" the man asked.

"Yes, I am. May I ask who you are?"

The man reached into his coat and pulled out an ID wallet. He opened it and held it up, saying, "I'm Inspector Lemieux with Paris homicide."

"Paris? Aren't you a long ways from home, Inspector?" Relief flooded Kadeen as he realized that this wasn't about the Bibles, but just as quickly it faded away when he put two and two together and came up with Marwan.

The inspector gave a humorless smile and said, "Yes, I am. I'd like to explain to you what I'm doing down here. Would you mind if I came in?"

"Of course. Please pardon my manners," Kadeen said, his mind going a mile a minute. He had rehearsed many times how he would answer the authorities if they came regarding the Bibles. *Now you just have to apply that to Marwan's situation.* He pressed the buzzer unlocking the gate.

As the inspector approached, Kadeen watched him glancing up and down the street, almost as if he didn't want to be seen entering. *Watch out for this one.*

The inspector held out his hand, and Kadeen took it.

"I'm sorry to barge in on you like this. Is your family at home with you?"

The inspector's icy grip sent chills down Kadeen's spine. He quickly released the man's hand. "No, they're out for a while trying to give me some quiet so that I can finish a project for work."

"Well, I promise I won't keep you long," Lemieux said, brushing past Kadeen into the house.

Closing the door behind him, Kadeen turned and said, "Welcome to my home. I will try to be of whatever assistance I—"

Suddenly Lemieux swung out with a small leather sap. The metal ball in the end caught Kadeen on the temple, causing his vision to blur momentarily. Then Lemieux was on him. He hauled Kadeen up by the collar and threw him onto the coffee table, which collapsed beneath him.

The air shot from Kadeen's lungs as the inspector straddled his chest. His large hand grasped Kadeen's windpipe and began squeezing. Kadeen tried to call out, but he couldn't. Stunned, he watched as Lemieux pulled a silenced gun from a shoulder holster and pressed it against Kadeen's forehead.

"Accad," the inspector called out. "Accad, I know you're in here! Come out now, or I swear I'll put a hole in your friend's head!"

Kadeen tried to shake his head to indicate that Marwan wasn't there, but he could barely move. Already, blackness was starting to creep in from his peripheral vision.

"Accad! I'll give you until three to come out! One! Two! Say good-bye to your friend! Three!"

Kadeen squeezed his eyes shut, ready to meet his Maker. Instead, the grip around his throat was released, and air came rushing back into his lungs. He coughed and gasped for breath, rolling onto his side when Lemieux stood.

"I guess that means Accad is not still here," Lemieux said, sitting back on a chair and lighting a cigarette. Kadeen noticed that he kept the gun in his lap.

"I don't know what you're talking about," Kadeen answered, his voice more gravelly than usual.

"Come now, let's not play games. Your family will be home shortly, and I'm guessing that you would rather have me gone when they arrive, would you not?" Lemieux slapped the leather sap several times into his hand as he talked, the cigarette dangling from the corner of his mouth.

Lord, please get me out of this, but more importantly protect my family. Give me wisdom for their safety and Marwan's.

"What makes you think Marwan was here?"

"Quit stalling," Lemieux said, his lips spreading into that serpent's grin again. "Time is something that is working against you right now. So please start by admitting to me what I already know—Marwan Accad was here."

"Yes, Inspector, he was here. But he's gone."

"I can see that he's gone. Please tell me where he has gone to."

Finally a question that Kadeen had no qualms about answering honestly. "I don't know."

Lemieux leaned forward in his chair. He tapped ash onto the floor. "Come now, Mr. al-Wadhi. You don't really expect me to believe that."

"It's the truth! I promise you. He stayed here less than a day. I tried to convince him to stay longer so that he could heal. . . ." Kadeen stopped himself, realizing he had said too much.

"Ah, so our Mr. Accad is injured, is he? Please relate to me the nature of his injury. And let me again remind you that every minute you waste is one minute closer to the return of your lovely family."

"He was shot . . . in the shoulder. We patched him up as best we could. He left the next night."

Standing to his full height, Lemieux towered above Kadeen, who had only managed to prop himself up on one elbow. The inspector dropped his cigarette to the floor and ground it out with the toe of his boot, then picked up the butt and slipped it into a pocket. "I return to my previous question—where did Marwan Accad go?"

"I told you, I don't know."

With speed belying his age, Lemieux was on him. Kick after kick landed on Kadeen's head and stomach. Then, as quickly as it started, it stopped.

Kadeen gasped for air. He could feel the blood pouring down his face, and the pain when he moved told him he had multiple broken ribs.

When he opened his eyes, he saw Lemieux's face inches from his own. The inspector was holding Kadeen's head by the hair. In a menacing whisper that reeked of coffee and tobacco, he said, "Tell me where he's gone, or I will do the same—and worse—to your wife and children."

"I told you I don't know where he's gone," Kadeen said, watching Lemieux's face darken even more. "But . . ."

"Yes?"

"But he left me a number."

"He left you a number?" Lemieux said, letting Kadeen's head drop to the ground with a thunk. "Well, why didn't you say so?"

Grabbing Kadeen's hair again, Lemieux lifted him off the ground. "Let's make a call," the inspector said with another vicious smile.

35

"My cell phone is in my office. That's the number he'll recognize," Kadeen slurred through his swollen mouth. The rest of his face felt just as bad. Blood dripped to the floor as he stumbled down the narrow hallway. The silencer-extended barrel of Lemieux's gun felt cold on the back of his neck.

Lord, help me to do the right thing, he prayed. *Please watch over my family. Do what you will with me, but please protect Rania and the girls.*

Upon reaching his office, he stumbled through the door. One of his eyes was almost completely closed, but through the other he saw his phone. *Is this the only way? Can I think of no alternative?*

He stopped in the middle of the room and turned toward Lemieux. "I can't believe you're a police officer and you're doing this. Can't we even discuss this?"

"Tick, tock, Mr. al-Wadhi," Lemieux answered, raising the gun so that it was between Kadeen's eyes.

Kadeen reached for the phone, and the inspector lowered himself onto a wooden chair in the corner of the room.

"Before you call, let's make it clear what you are to say. You will tell Accad that your family is in great danger and he must return. You must not mention my name! Are we clear on that?"

Kadeen nodded, but in doing so the room started spinning. He leaned against the edge of his desk.

"If you mention my name, your family will die. If you try any tricks, your family will die. And you'll want to be sure to be persuasive, because if Accad refuses you, your family will most certainly die."

The thought of his little girls in the hands of this monster was all the motivation Kadeen needed. Cradling the phone in his hands, he tried to focus his vision on the small numbers. When they began to clear, he started pressing buttons.

Lifting the phone to his ear, he waited.

"Marwan? This is Kadeen. . . . Yes, I know my voice is strange. You've got to help me. Remember how you said there might be people coming? You were right. . . . It's really bad, Marwan. You must come back. . . . Please, my friend, you must. . . . But Rania and the girls—he'll kill them if you don't. . . ."

Kadeen watched as Lemieux leaned forward in the chair. He knew time was short before the inspector blew again.

"But, Marwan, you must come back. After all we did for you . . . I don't know what to say. I thought—"

Suddenly Lemieux was off the chair. He snatched the phone from Kadeen's hand.

"Listen, Accad, you better get back here, or I swear I will make those little girls die slow deaths! And what I'll do to the woman, you don't even want to know! Do you hear me, Accad? Accad?"

Lemieux held the phone away from his face and saw that the screen was black. He redialed the last number, and a moment later the house phone began ringing.

A painful smile spread across Kadeen's battered lips as he watched the inspector try to figure out what was going on.

"What have you done? What did you do? What were all those numbers you were dialing?" Then a thought must have occurred to Lemieux, because he quickly began pressing buttons.

"What is this text you sent?" he said, grabbing Kadeen by the back of the neck and holding the phone in front of his face.

Relief washed through Kadeen's damaged body as he saw the confirmation that his message did indeed go through. Written on the screen were the words:

To: Rania's Cell
Acts 9:24-25
Kadeen

Slapping Kadeen's face with the side of the gun, Lemieux again shouted, "What does this text mean?"

With a bloody grin, Kadeen said, "It means you will never see my family, Monsieur Inspector."

A number of years ago, when Kadeen and Rania first got involved in couriering Bibles, they had worked out a code in case either of them was ever arrested. Both were well aware of the dangers involved in their work and found special meaning in the story of the apostle Paul's escape from Damascus in the book of Acts. Rania would see the reference and immediately use the escape routes and safe houses established for them and other Bible couriers. Once they disappeared, they could stay underground for days, weeks, or months.

"Looks like your leverage is gone. What now?" Kadeen asked, no longer afraid of the answer.

A look came over the inspector that resembled that of the devil himself. Lemieux brought the handle of the gun down on Kadeen's head once, twice, three times. But when Kadeen began to crumple to the ground, Lemieux held him up.

Kadeen was very near blacking out when he felt the inspector slapping him on the face and heard his voice as if it were coming from a great distance. "Wake up! Wake up! I'm not done with you yet!"

Kadeen's mind was on autopilot as he teetered just this side of consciousness. "How may I help you, Inspector?"

The barrel of the gun pressed up against the bridge of Kadeen's nose. He heard Lemieux growl, "I will give you one last chance to tell me where Accad is before I put a bullet in your brain!"

"But don't you know, Monsieur Inspector? Greater love has no man than to lay down his life for his friend." The peace Kadeen felt in his heart overwhelmed the pain in his body. *Lord, I am yours. . . .*

"Well, if that's true," Lemieux said through clenched teeth, "you're about to show a whole lot of love." Then he pulled the trigger.

PART THREE

36

GODDARD FINALLY ARRIVED in front of Kadeen al-Wadhi's house.

"What took you so long?" Lemieux sniffed when Goddard got out of his cab.

"It's a long way from Beirut," Goddard replied, refusing to take the bait. "Any sign of Accad?"

"No, it's been quiet."

"What about the family?"

"I said it has been quiet."

"But you're certain they are in there?" Goddard pressed.

"I am not certain of anything at this point," Lemieux said. "From the look of the carport, one vehicle might be gone. But we must not waste any more time. We need to go in now. I've circled the house, and cut glass tops the entire wall. If anyone is in there, the only way out is through one of these two gates."

Goddard walked around one corner of the wall. In the shadows of the setting sun, he could see that the cut glass did surround the villa as Lemieux said. However, it seemed to him that a heavy rug or rubber mat of some sort, if it were thrown on top of the glass, could easily provide safe passage over. Looking at the impatience on Lemieux's face, though, caused him to decide to keep that thought to himself. Instead he mentally prepared himself for a possible foot chase.

As he approached Lemieux, the inspector sneered, "I trust my analysis of the situation has met with your approval?"

Rather than answer to the negative, Goddard replied, "How do you want to work this?"

"If Accad is half the man we give him credit for, then he already knows we are here. So you ring the buzzer while I cover the carport gate."

Grateful to get a little distance from this man, Goddard quickly agreed.

"Remember—he is a very dangerous man," Lemieux said as he trudged along the wall.

Goddard stared at the light behind the front window for a minute, trying to detect any shadows or movement. Seeing none, he pressed the button. He faintly heard the buzzer inside. After waiting half a minute, he pressed it again.

Still there was no answer. He looked at Lemieux, who signaled for him to go in. Goddard sighed as he pulled out a small leather packet with tools for picking locks. *A European policeman gains entry without permission into a house on Moroccan soil. Is this technically breaking and entering? I suppose that's the one nice thing about having Lemieux along; I can't imagine anyone trying to put cuffs on him.*

With a click, the gate opened. After a couple knocks on the front door, he used the same tools to enter the house.

As soon as the door opened, he saw the damage. Pulling his gun, he dropped to a squat. A fight had occurred in the front room. Furniture was broken, and there was blood on the floor. The blood began in a small pool in the middle of the room by a broken table, then trailed down the hall.

After getting his bearings, Goddard stood and cautiously made his way through the house, sweeping each room as he passed it. The blood droplets he was following led to a closed door at the end of the hall.

He leaned with his back against the wall to prepare himself, then pushed hard through the door. Leading with his gun, he rapidly surveyed the small room. It was clear of threats, but not clear of people. Lying back across the desk with his legs still hanging over the side was a man with a bullet hole between his eyes. He had obviously been beaten, and he was now just as obviously dead.

Goddard fought revulsion at the sight. It didn't matter how many dead bodies he saw, he still had a visceral reaction each time. Walking back to the front door—partly to alert Lemieux and partly to avoid the smell—he called the inspector in.

"What's happened here?" Lemieux asked when he saw the damage in the front room.

Goddard pulled out his phone to check the photo DuVall had sent. Although his face had been disfigured, there was still enough resemblance that Goddard could be confident that this was the man in the back room. "Follow me," he said.

"Marwan Accad's killed him," Lemieux said immediately upon entering the study. "We're too late."

Goddard was still stunned by the murder scene. "But why would Accad do it? Our information is that they were close friends."

"That's not the issue," Lemieux insisted. "The only issue is hunting down Accad before he kills again. Get this place dusted for prints and searched for physical evidence immediately. But first, get Accad's picture to every police station, bus station, train station, TV station, airport, and seaport in Morocco. He's very likely still in this country. We cannot let him escape."

37

At eight Monday morning, Tariq's satellite phone rang, but he didn't care. He was serving Dalia breakfast in bed and didn't bother to answer it. An hour later, it rang again, but this time Tariq was in the shower and did not hear it. An hour later, it rang yet again, but this time he had left it in her apartment. He and Dalia were spending yet another day together, so all of Ramy's urgent calls went unanswered.

Winter was almost upon them, but the romance of Tariq Jameel and Dalia Nour was blooming like the Nile Delta in spring. After breakfast that chilly morning, they headed to the Cairo Tower, 185 meters high, and held hands as they gazed out across the teeming city below and competed to see who knew more landmarks than the other. They quickly spotted the Egyptian Museum and the Citadel and the Rafeeq Ali

Mosque and the Mosque of Ibn Tulun, but after these the skyline began to blur into a never-ending sea of hotels and apartments and office buildings, all shrouded in a brown, dusty, polluted haze.

"Have you ever been to the pyramids?" Dalia asked.

"I'm ashamed to say it," he said, "but no, I actually never have."

"Me neither," she exclaimed. "Let's go! I want to see them up close and race camels in the desert!"

"You mean *ride* camels in the desert?" Tariq asked.

"No way—I mean *race* them!" she replied with a mischievous twinkle in her eye.

Tariq was amazed by her energy and her passion for life. It was refreshing—and addicting—so he shrugged his shoulders. "Let the race begin!"

They took a taxi to Giza, where they climbed the shaft inside the Great Pyramid and peered into the great empty sarcophagus, imagining all the treasures this ancient wonder once held. Then they hired a guide and two camels and trotted deep into the desert.

Nothing more was said about Naguib Mahfouz's brush with death or about Tariq's parents or about the car accident he said he had been in or the injuries he had supposedly sustained in the wreck. There was no need to speak of Goddard or Lemieux or Monte Carlo or Rafeeq Ramsey. With her, he wasn't on trial or under investigation or having to watch his back. They could just play like young lovers, and for Tariq, it was a cup of cool, refreshing water for a dry and thirsty heart.

"Hey, Tariq, bet I can beat you to the Sphinx!" Dalia shouted. "Loser pays for dinner!"

No sooner were the words out of her mouth than she gave her camel a good, hard slap on its backside and took off down the dunes.

Tariq's competitive juices started flowing immediately, and he quickly gave pursuit, leaving their bewildered and not-too-happy guide behind, shouting curses into the fall breeze. Dalia was good, as if she had been raised riding animals. By now, she was forty or fifty meters ahead of him, her beautiful dark hair blowing wildly behind her. But he wasn't about to go down without a fight. He crouched, kicked harder, and began to pick up speed.

Up the first dune they went and down the other side. Then again and again, and as they approached the crest of the last dune, Dalia briefly vanished from sight. But only for a moment, as Tariq was closing fast.

Dalia was shouting back at him, taunting him, teasing him, making him all the more determined to win. He kicked harder and harder still, trying to extract every last bit of energy from the three-year-old camel beneath him, but in the end it was not enough. Dalia reached a startled group of tourists near the base of the Sphinx about half a length ahead of him and then veered back toward the desert to slow down and catch her breath.

She was laughing so hard she was practically crying, as was he, and he was suddenly stirred with a passion he never imagined he could feel for anyone.

"Buy me something!" she said as they embraced.

"*Buy* you something?" he asked, startled by the request. "Like what?"

"I don't know," she laughed, drawing him close to her and

kissing him again on the neck and the ears. "Something special, something different, something I can remember you by when you vanish into the night and I never see you again."

"What are you talking about?" he asked, not sure if she was joking or not. "Why would you say that?"

"Isn't that what men do? Take what they want and then cut you loose when you least expect it?"

She still had a playful look in her eyes, but her words—however innocently and laughingly spoken—had their intended effect. Tariq knew now that he was playing with fire. Someone had hurt this girl badly, and not that long ago, and here he was, stoking the still-hot embers. She was his for the asking, but she did not want to be toyed with or taken for granted, and within his heart it forced an issue he'd had neither the time nor the interest to confront thus far.

Whatever he felt for her, he wasn't really going to stick around for long, was he? How could he? In a few days or a few weeks or perhaps a month or two, Ramy would call, warning they were onto him, and he would have to disappear. He would have to "cut her loose" when she "least expected it," wouldn't he?

It would be easier on him, of course, if all he wanted was a one-night stand or a weekend fling. But to Tariq's surprise, he found her feelings mattered to him. There was something about this girl he really liked, and he didn't want to hurt her.

"Some men, maybe," Tariq said as he pulled her close to him and kissed her gently. "But not me."

38

Hoping to change the subject, Tariq led Dalia arm in arm down a street lined with shops and crowded with tourists, then finally into one of Cairo's famed papyrus institutes.

"All right," he whispered as they first walked in. "I'll tell you what. I'll buy you anything in the store."

Dalia's eyes lit up. "Anything?" she asked with delight.

"Anything," he said. "Just say the word."

She squeezed his arm and looked around the large shop whose walls were covered with the most beautiful paintings in the most vivid colors, all done on large sheets of papyrus.

"May I help you?" a clerk asked, apparently able to see the "big sale" look in Dalia's eyes. "I can give you a very good price today."

"Perhaps you could show us around," Tariq said, and Dalia quickly nodded.

"It would be my pleasure, sir," said the young man, no more than twenty.

He guided the couple to the back, where he began by giving them a brief demonstration of how stalks of papyrus are cut into long, thin strips; soaked in water to remove most of their natural sugars; pressed together in a crisscross pattern; and finally dried over many days to make the remarkably strong sheets upon which skilled artisans painted their dazzling scenes, many of them from legends of ancient Egypt.

"Tell me about this one," Dalia said when he was finished, pointing to one of the larger scenes of people and animals and hieroglyphics, painted in brilliant blues and reds and gold, all set in a hand-crafted wood frame and hanging on the wall beside them.

"Ah yes," the clerk said, "*The Final Judgment*. This one is very famous. Copies of this painting used to hang in homes and tombs and temples all over Egypt."

"Why?" Tariq asked. "What does it mean?"

"Well," the clerk explained, "ancient Egyptians believed that when people died, they would face a final judgment, a final reckoning for what they had done in their lives. You see the man up there in the top left corner, kneeling before all those figures across the top of the painting?"

"Yes."

"That is man in the afterlife. He is kneeling before fourteen judges, swearing that he is not guilty, offering sacrifices to them, and pleading with them to let him go to paradise."

"What about the man down there?" Tariq asked. "Is he the same man?"

"The one in the lower left?" the clerk asked.

"Yeah."

"Yes, he's the same man," the clerk said. "He's being led into the palace of justice, where it will be determined whether he is good or bad, guilty or not. You see those giant scales before him?"

"Yes."

"The heart of the deceased is placed on the left side of the scales," the clerk explained, using his finger to identify the various parts of the picture, "and a feather of justice is put on the right side. If his heart is heavier than the feather, it means the man's heart is full of sin. It means that he is not good enough for heaven and will be sent straight to hell. But if his heart is lighter than the feather, then he is a good man—a pure man—and he will go to paradise. This man in the painting? He was pure, so he is being led into the throne room of heaven by that figure holding the key to eternal life. Do you like it?"

"No, I don't," Dalia said, visibly uncomfortable. "Show me something else. Something not having to do with hell and judgment."

She turned her attention to another painting, one with two doves perched in a large tree. But Tariq remained fixated on *The Final Judgment*, studying it with great intensity.

"How can you know for sure?" Tariq thought out loud.

"Know what for sure?" the clerk replied.

Startled by the clerk's response to his thoughts, he said, "Oh. Well, I was just wondering, how can you know for sure if your heart is pure enough, if you're headed for heaven instead of hell?"

But the clerk just stood there blankly. It was obvious he had never been asked that question during one of his tours.

Tariq felt a wave of fear wash over him. The question echoed through his soul again and again. *How can I know? Any moment now, I could have a bullet take my life away. Is my heart too heavy in the scales or not? What did Dalia tell me her father says—heaven is a gift and not a payment? Is it possible heaven is something God just offers us, not something I can earn? And what about Kadeen's claim that the Bible contains the truth about life and death?* He had to find the answer before his own fate was sealed.

He bought Dalia a painting—a different one, of course, an exquisite and expensive one of two lovers sailing a felucca down the Nile—but Tariq could not shake the anxiety *The Final Judgment* had stirred within him. It was as if he could hear his mother's voice in his head, weeping over all the foolish, selfish choices he had made in his life, begging him to change course and make a fresh start while he still could.

But where would he start? To whom should he turn? He was ready to make a change. His life was coming undone. But "changing course" was easier said than done. *When all this calms down, I think I'm going to have to spend an extended time with Kadeen, asking questions.*

On returning to Dalia's flat, they showered and changed, and he took her to the Mövenpick Hotel. There the two of them had a candlelit dinner before Dalia worked the evening flight to London. She could not have been more happy. He could not have been more miserable.

"Dina and Mervat sent me an e-mail last night," Dalia said. "I forgot to tell you."

"Really," he said without looking up from his plate of barely eaten dinner.

"They're still in New York. They just found a flat. Dina says they're coming home next weekend to pack up their things and ship them back there." She paused for a moment. "I can't believe they're really leaving. I guess I've got to find new roommates. I'll never be able to afford that flat on my own."

"Right," he said, picking at his beef fillet.

"Tariq, are you all right?" she asked.

"Yeah, I'm fine," he said, pouring himself a third glass of wine.

"You seem . . . distracted, far away. Not like this morning. Not like all weekend."

"No, no," he said, "I'm just . . ." His voice trailed off.

"Just what?"

He didn't want to lie to her. He didn't want his heart to be any heavier than it already was. The very thought bothered him now as it never had before. But then again, wasn't his whole life a lie at this point? He wasn't Tariq Jameel. He wasn't a computer consultant from Brussels. He wasn't setting up a branch office in Cairo or looking for a girlfriend or a wife. He wasn't any of the things he had told her.

"I'm just going to miss you," he said, looking at her at last. "I've really enjoyed the past few days together."

"So have I," she said, taking his hands.

"You're a very special girl."

Dalia was still smiling at him, but she seemed a bit skeptical as well. "Special as in 'I want to spend more time with you'? Or special as in 'That was fun; you'll never see me again'?"

"Special as in 'I want to spend *a lot* more time with you,'" he insisted, squeezing her hands. "What time do you get back tomorrow?"

"I should be here by lunchtime—noonish, I think."

"Perfect. I'll be waiting."

"You promise?"

He smiled. "I promise."

39

Inspector Lemieux paced the floor of the hotel suite. The longer this dragged on, the more irrelevant became his people's slight lead on the investigation. Goddard was good, and that woman, DuVall, might be even better. If they found Accad before he did, this whole thing just might lead to his own downfall. However, if he could ensure Marwan Accad's permanent silence, then it was likely he could end up pulling this off after all.

From the beginning, things had fallen apart. The death of Ramsey's daughter was not supposed to happen, and if there was one thing that Lemieux regretted in this whole affair, that would be it. But what was done was done. It was too late to go back. Besides, why should he mourn Brigitte Ramsey when her own stepmother seemed to have gotten over her?

Claudette Ramsey—she truly was a piece of work. Rarely had he met anyone so greedy, heartless, and self-focused. He knew he was ruthless—one had to be in his line of work—but he at least had some scruples, one or two lines he refused to cross. Yet she seemed to be completely without conscience.

In one sense, that made her easy to work with. In the past, most women he had dealt with had cringed a time or two at the methods he had been forced to employ in order to get the job done. No such problem with Claudette.

The downside was that her lack of any moral compass could make her careless. A temper tantrum could easily lead to violence, and violence, if not carefully controlled, could lead to discovery. Already he had been forced to commit two of his teams just to babysit her. If she didn't hold the purse strings to such a large fortune, she would have become expendable long ago.

Lemieux stopped at a long table situated under a window that looked out into the Casablanca night. The table was made of a rich, beautifully burled thuya wood, and its surface was bare except for a cell phone. He stared at the phone, as if just by the sheer strength of his will he could make it ring.

He turned and began the slow walk to the other side of the elegantly decorated room.

The worst of the mistakes already made had been allowing Marwan Accad to live. How could the snipers have missed him? And then somehow Accad had found a way to kill two of Lemieux's best assassins in that hotel. The woman, Alix Pelletier, had been a special prize. No man could resist her seductive skills, including Lemieux himself a time or two.

Accad had cost him resources and aggravation. It was time for him to die.

Back at the phone, he again stared at it. As he was preparing to return to his pacing, he was startled when it actually rang. Smiling to himself, he picked it up.

"Hello?"

"We have found him."

"Well, are you going to make me guess? Where is he?"

"We spotted him on an airport security tape. He's very good. He knows just where not to look to avoid the cameras, but finally we caught him as he boarded an EgyptAir flight from Casablanca to Cairo."

"Good work, Edgard. Where is he now?"

"We don't know for sure," Edgard replied.

"Well then, you haven't really found him, have you?" Lemieux shouted, his legendary short temper instantly in full bloom. "Cairo is a city of 7 million people, and the whole country of Egypt has, what, another 70 or 80 million on top of that! And you call to tell me that you have found him, you imbecile?"

"My apologies, sir. I should have said that we know where he went from Morocco."

"You're right, you should have! Words mean things, Edgard! Tell me what you are doing to find him!"

"Again, we are looking for friends, girlfriends, relatives. We're checking hotels and hostels. We're also looking at flats and houses that may have recently been rented by an expatriate individual or a corporation."

"Don't forget the possibility of a preexisting safe house," Lemieux reminded his man. "Also, I want you to create a false rental car trail leading south to Asyût. Make it complex but discoverable. And do it quickly! If you found this lead, then

Goddard's people will be just behind you. We need to throw him off the scent."

"Yes, sir."

"Then I want you to send five of our two-man teams to Cairo. I do not want Accad getting away again."

There was a brief pause. Lemieux could hear Edgard sucking in his breath. "Sir, we only have four teams available. They are there in Morocco as we speak. The rest are either with Claudette Ramsey or searching for Ramy Accad," Edgard said matter-of-factly. But Lemieux could hear the anxiety in his voice, which was exactly how he wanted it. *When subordinates fear you, that is when they will follow you without question.*

"Take one of the two teams from the other Accad brother, then! Must I make every decision? I want you to listen to me closely, Edgard. You will find Marwan Accad, and when you do, you will make sure he is dead. I can't go to Cairo without Goddard and his little minions following me, so I am counting on you. I don't have to tell you what the consequences are for failure!"

"Don't worry, sir. We'll find him."

When Lemieux heard the click on the other end of the line, a smile spread across his bony face. *You may have won when you knew we were there, Accad. But wait and see what happens when you don't see us coming!*

40

Tariq spent the night alone at Dalia's flat. The cleaners and repairmen hired by his landlord had been working in his flat for most of the day, but one could barely tell. There was so much work still to be done. Besides, while Dalia's flat was considerably smaller, it was far warmer (partly because her heaters worked and his didn't), far better decorated, and actually felt like a home.

She had curtains on the windows and fresh flowers in colorful vases on the kitchen table. She had clean linens on the beds with big, thick comforters and soft, fluffy pillows, and knickknacks of all kinds, collected from the many countries where she had traveled. What's more, her dishes were washed, there was good food in the refrigerator and pantry, and her stove worked, which would have settled the issue had there been any doubt in his mind about staying there in the first place.

Tariq made a hot cup of coffee and helped himself to some cookies he found in the pantry. Then he began poking through Dalia's things, trying to get a sense of who she was.

Beside her entertainment center, he found racks of hit CDs and DVDs of the latest Egyptian, European, and American films, all neatly arranged in alphabetical order. He found closets lined with new clothes and shoes, velvet boxes filled with jewelry, stacks of *Vogue* and *Cosmo* and other fashion magazines. He also found scuba and snorkeling gear and bookshelves lined with travel guides to resorts throughout the Mediterranean and the Caribbean, not to mention a complete collection of Naguib Mahfouz novels. And eventually he found her stash of marijuana as well, to which he helped himself.

What struck him as curious, though, was that he could find no diaries, no personal journals, not even a family photo album. There was nothing that could give him the kind of clues he was looking for. Who was Dalia Nour, really? Where did she come from? Where was she headed? He was intoxicated with her, but it suddenly dawned on him how little he really knew about her.

He knew she had grown up somewhere in Jordan but didn't know where. He knew she had left home at eighteen, but he didn't know why. He knew she had graduated from a little college in France but didn't know which one or what she had studied. He knew she had joined British Airways to see the world and travel for free. He also knew that she had already been to twenty-three countries and hoped to go to

Australia later that year for her third vacation in as many years because, she said, the snorkeling was amazing there. But besides that, there wasn't much more to go on. She was as much an enigma to him, apparently, as he was to her.

In search of answers, Tariq opened a drawer in the small nightstand beside her bed, and there he found a stack of brochures for two- and three-day vacation packages to various resorts in Sharm el-Sheikh. She really was a traveler, wasn't she? He couldn't even remember the last time he had taken a vacation. But Dalia seemed obsessive about seeing the world and drinking her fill from the cup of life. It was as though she couldn't sit still for more than a few days at a time. Whenever she had a few days off, she was jet-setting to another exotic locale. But why? What exactly was she running from?

Tariq flipped through the stack. One was for the Hilton. Another was for the Ritz-Carlton. Yet others were for the Four Seasons, the Marriott, the Jolie Ville, and several more as well. At the bottom of the stack was a small notepad embossed with the British Airways logo. It was marked up with all kinds of notes, all of them in Dalia's handwriting, with pricing options for three people staying in a single suite, possible dates for travel, and pros and cons for each of the various resorts.

He was about to put it all back in the drawer and continue his quest to learn more about this mystery girl when he noticed that the dates Dalia had circled as the best time to go—and then had crossed out—were coming up soon, between Christmas and New Year's. Just then he realized why Dalia wasn't going. Dina and Mervat had been transferred. Dalia was barely going to be able to pay the rent on this flat, much less spend a fun-filled weekend in Sharm. And that got Tariq thinking. *What if . . .*

By the time Dalia returned home, the plans were set, their tickets were bought, their suitcases were packed, everything—including Dalia's snorkeling gear—was loaded into a waiting taxi, and Tariq was on the front steps of the apartment building with a big bouquet of flowers.

She couldn't believe it. Dalia's eyes said it all: They were both going to Sharm? Really? Right then? All expenses paid? How had he known? How had he made all the arrangements so quickly? How could she be so lucky to be falling for a guy like this?

Tariq answered all of her questions—except the last—as they boarded the one-hour flight to the Sinai Peninsula. He laughed at Dalia's joyful, playful, amazed reaction. Tariq had never been so spontaneous in his life, but it felt right, and he suddenly hoped this was just the beginning. Getting out of Cairo would be good for so many reasons. He needed the sun and the sand and the surf to get his mind off all his troubles. And he needed as much time with Dalia as he could possibly get.

"This is incredibly generous," Dalia said at last. "I still don't understand why you did it."

"I missed you," he told her as their plane was coming in on final approach.

She squeezed his arm and nestled close to him. "Really?" She smiled.

"Really. You've got a great little place in Cairo, but it's not the same without you. I was getting lonely in there, and then I found your calendar and noticed you had the next couple of days off. I couldn't resist. I hope I wasn't being too forward to plan this whole thing on the spur of the moment."

"You absolutely were," she replied. "And I couldn't be happier."

41

They checked in at the Ritz-Carlton, and for the next two days they played like newlyweds. They slept in late and had breakfast in bed. They sunbathed by the pool. They spent their afternoons snorkeling in the Red Sea, just off Tiran Island, not far from the coast of Saudi Arabia, and then went to fancy restaurants before retiring to their suite for nights of unrestrained passion.

The temperatures during the day hovered in the mideighties, with a slight breeze coming in from the north. At night, it never dipped below sixty. *No clouds. No rain. No smog. No pollution. No phone calls. No e-mails. No guns. Nobody trying to kill me. It couldn't be more perfect. Does this really ever have to end?*

On the third day, he got up early and went jogging in the

cool morning air. His body was recovering nicely from the wounds he had sustained in Monte Carlo. He was steadily regaining his strength, and in many ways, he had never felt better. He was laughing. He was singing in the shower. He was flat-out drunk with love. It was the only explanation he could come up with.

Tariq had never experienced anything like this with any other girl. Sure, there had been relationships in the past—even one brush with an engagement. But for some reason, it was different with Dalia. She wanted him. She needed him. And she made him feel special. He was falling for this girl, and it was all going so fast.

After a four-mile run along the beach, Tariq got back to the Ritz and slipped into their room as quietly as he could. Dalia was still sleeping. She looked like an angel—so beautiful, so peaceful, it had to be a dream.

He took a shower and then got dressed. Perhaps they could do a little sightseeing or a little shopping. Maybe they'd rent bikes or go parasailing. It didn't really matter to him. Whatever she wanted, so long as they were together.

"Hey, good morning," Dalia said softly as he came out of the bathroom.

"Good morning to you." He kissed her gently. "How are you feeling?"

"Great," she replied with a smile. "Hungry."

"Me too. Why don't you take a quick shower and then we'll go down to breakfast and make a plan for the day?"

"Sounds good," she said, insisting on another kiss before slipping into the bathroom and closing the door behind her.

While he waited for her, Tariq straightened up the room.

He gathered some of Dalia's clothes that had been drying on their balcony. He folded them neatly and tucked them into her suitcase. He also found her keys and her cell phone under the bed. But when he went to put them back into her purse, several pieces of paper tumbled out—mostly an assortment of old receipts and a few presumably unpaid bills. At the bottom of the stack, though, was an envelope that caught Tariq's eye.

It was a letter, not a bill, and it was postmarked from Jordan, just the week before. Unlike the others, this one was already opened. Curious, he slid the letter out. As he opened it, a little handmade lace cross slipped out and dropped to the bed. Tariq placed it on the nightstand, then sat on the bed and began reading.

My dearest Dalia,

Thank you so much for your recent letter.

I can't tell you how glad your mother and I are to hear that you are no longer dating Kalim. You know we didn't care for his way of life—the drugs, the alcohol, all the late-night parties. He was not the kind of young man we raised you to marry. He was not a Christian or even a very kind or serious man. We are proud of you for breaking up with him and moving on with your life.

Are you ready for us to find a good and godly man who will love you and care for you all the days of your life? What about Youssef? Did you know I hired him as my assistant pastor last month? He is doing wonderful work at the church, especially with the children—teaching Bible studies and Sunday school classes and running the youth group. I believe he still cares for you very much. Could we give him your number and ask him to call you? It would make your mother and me so happy.

When are you coming home? We would love to see you. You could see Youssef. And all your cousins would love to see you again. So would I. Please write again soon.

Love, Father

The letter was carefully typed on the letterhead of something called "Petra Bible Church" with a post office box address in the town of Ma'an in southern Jordan.

Tariq was surprised. *Is Dalia's father some kind of priest? She said she had been raised in a Christian home, but not* this *Christian!*

So how is this going to weigh in the scales—corrupting the daughter of a man of God? I'm drinking with her. I'm doing drugs with her. I'm sleeping with her. That feather is getting lighter and lighter, and my heart is getting heavier and heavier. And who is Kalim? Who is Youssef? What in the world is going on, and what else is she hiding?

Determined to get some answers, Tariq approached the bathroom door. Then he stopped. *You complain about her secrets? What about your own? Maybe it's best just to let us each hold a bit of our lives back until we're both ready to come completely clean.*

After putting the letter back, he waited for her to get herself ready. Then they went down to breakfast; Tariq held tightly to her hand the whole way.

42

Dalia excused herself so that she could freshen up before they began the day's activities.

Tariq, who had been hoping for such an opportunity, took the satellite phone out of his pocket, powered it up, and dialed his brother.

"Marwan, where have you been?" his brother shouted when he answered the phone. "I've been calling you for the last several days. I was terrified. I thought you were dead."

"No, no, I'm fine," Tariq said calmly. "I've just been . . . uh . . . I've been busy. Why? What's happening?"

"Busy?" Ramy asked. "Doing what?"

"None of your business."

"Are you insane, Marwan? I'm risking my life to help you stay alive and out of jail, and you just disappear for a couple of days and then have the nerve to say it's none of my business?"

"You're right," Tariq said, trying not to sound too defensive.

"You better believe I'm right," Ramy shot back, obviously furious but trying to control his emotions. "Look, a lot has been happening since you dropped off the face of the earth. I'm leaving Baghdad on the next flight and heading back to Beirut. The prosecutor in Monte Carlo has issued a subpoena for me to be interviewed by Inspector Goddard."

"I guess that's to be expected," Tariq said.

There was a long pause, and Tariq knew something else was wrong.

Finally Ramy came right out and asked, "Why didn't you tell me Kadeen had moved to Casablanca?"

Tariq was stunned. How could he have known? Quickly, he got up and walked out of the restaurant. He found a deserted corner of the lobby and tucked himself into it. "I'm not sure what you're—"

"Forget it, Marwan. It won't work. I know you were there. What I want to know is why? You said you were going to lie low, no friends, nothing familiar. You promised."

"I didn't know where else to go," he admitted. "I needed his help."

"Why?" Ramy demanded.

"Because I'd been shot, Ramy. There. You happy? I got hit by one of the assassins in Monte Carlo, but I couldn't go to a hospital there or in France. I didn't know who was after me. I didn't know whom to trust. All I could think of was Kadeen. So I went to him. He took care of me, and I got out of there as quickly as I could."

"It was a stupid mistake, Marwan," Ramy said.

"You're probably right," he conceded. "But it worked out, didn't it?"

"No, it didn't."

"What do you mean?"

"Kadeen is dead."

Tariq felt as though the wind had been knocked out of him. All the terror of the nightmares he had been experiencing since being there came on him full force. "What are you . . . ? How did you . . . ?" Tariq couldn't think. He couldn't breathe.

"The police found his body in his house in Casablanca," Ramy explained. "He had been beaten, then shot at point-blank range."

"What about Rania and the girls? Please tell me . . ." He couldn't finish the sentence. The picture of them with bullet holes in their heads caused his breakfast to rise to his throat.

"They're in hiding. They're safe."

"What? How do you know they're safe?"

"Because she called me. Apparently Kadeen had given her our office number a long time ago in case she was ever in trouble."

The relief caused Tariq's knees to buckle. He leaned against the wood paneled wall. Then guilt washed in and wiped the relief away.

"Where is she? We need to do something. We have to help them." Tariq felt frantic and helpless. "We need to get her to safety. We need to get her some money. We need to make sure she's taken care of. We need—"

"Marwan, stop! Stop!"

Tariq stopped. But his mind was racing.

"She said that she couldn't say where she was, only that she and the girls were safe. She said that she would get in touch with you when the time was right. And she told me to tell you one other thing."

Tariq waited silently. Whatever words she had for him, he deserved. Whatever blame she was going to throw onto him, he was already putting on himself tenfold.

Ramy took a deep breath, and when he spoke, Tariq could hear the emotion in his voice. "She told me to tell you that she forgives you."

Tariq was stunned. Tears began to pour down his face, and he tucked himself even deeper into the corner.

"I . . . can't . . . I don't . . ."

"Listen to me, Marwan. You can grieve later. Right now I need you here with me. Are you listening?"

But he was far from with his brother. Images of his childhood with Kadeen were racing through his mind, interspersed with bits of their last conversation as well as the faces of Laila and little Maryam as they gave him their get-well card. *What will become of them? How will they survive without Kadeen?*

"Ramy, I want you to—"

"Shut up! Just shut up and listen. I will make sure Rania and the girls are taken care of, even if you do end up finding a way to get yourself killed. I need you to focus on what I'm saying to you so that we can keep that from happening. Are you with me?"

Tariq took a deep breath and wiped his face with his sleeve. *Ramy's got it under control. I just need to trust Ramy. You can't help Rania if you're dead, so get focused.*

"I'm with you, Ramy," he said.

"Good. Now, Inspector Goddard left a message on my voice mail back at the office," Ramy said. "That's how I found out about Kadeen. He said they found your fingerprints all over the crime scene. He said they found your hair fibers on a pillow on the couch. A shopkeeper around the corner ID'd you, says he saw you walking around the neighborhood. They found your car a few kilometers away.

"Inspector Lemieux insists you did it, and based on that evidence, I can see why he came to that conclusion. They've issued a warrant for your arrest, and Goddard says if you have an explanation, you'd better turn yourself in and give it now. Otherwise, there's nothing anybody will be able to do to help you."

Tariq didn't want to hear any more. He was sick. He was seething with anger and toggling back into disbelief and about to throw the phone across the room. And then Ramy said, "I'm afraid that's not all. It gets worse."

"How?" Tariq managed to say. *How could it possibly be worse?*

"If they've traced you to Morocco, it will only be a matter of time before the police follow you to Egypt. And if the police can find you in Egypt, you know that Claudette's people will too. And they won't just be looking to arrest you. They'll be gunning for you with everything they've got. You've got to get out of there."

As much as he hated to admit it, Ramy was right. If Claudette Ramsey's team of assassins could follow him to Kadeen's home in Morocco, they could certainly find him in Egypt. He was being framed for crimes he hadn't committed, and now every police force in Europe and North Africa would be looking for him.

He certainly couldn't go back to Cairo. But he couldn't leave Dalia either. He knew he shouldn't be falling in love with her, but it was too late. He couldn't help himself. And he would never forgive himself if any harm were to come to her now.

The dream Tariq had been living in for the past few days had been completely shattered. The nightmare was returning. It was time to run again.

43

Tariq took a few more moments to compose himself, then turned to face the lobby. When he did, he saw Dalia looking for him. She was wearing a pale blue sundress and matching shoes. From behind she looked absolutely amazing.

Then she turned.

On her face was a look that he had yet to see on her. Her eyebrows were knit together, and her normally olive skin had taken on a dark reddish hue. When she spotted him, her brows arched down even more, and she stormed toward him.

"Do you want to explain this?" she demanded, holding out the lace cross that had been in her father's letter.

Still reeling from the news of Kadeen's death, he was unprepared for this sudden onslaught. Instinctively, he went to his default mode, which was to attack back.

"It's an ancient symbol of Christianity," he said sarcastically. "It seems you should recognize that better than I."

Not getting the reaction she expected, Dalia was momentarily flustered.

Tariq stepped into the silence. "Listen, I was just straightening up the room and there was the letter. I was curious, so I read it. What's the big deal?"

"What's the big deal? The big deal is that you had no right! This is a personal letter that you read without permission!"

"Oh, please! We've been as intimate as two people can be, and you're going to get uptight about a letter from your dad?"

"Still, you had no right," Dalia answered, dissolving into tears. "You had no right to snoop through my things, Tariq Jameel. You have no right to judge me. Do you hear me? You have no right."

"Judge you? What are you talking about?" he said, gaining control of his temper and stepping toward her. "I wasn't snooping, and I'm not judging you. Why would I? I was just curious. That's all. I want to find out all I can about you."

"Just go away," Dalia said, moving away from him. "You're going to do it eventually anyway. So you might as well do it now."

"Forget it," Tariq replied as firmly but as calmly as he could. He stepped toward her again and reached out for her. This time she didn't back away. "I'm not going anywhere, Dalia. I'm falling in love with you. I want to know *everything* about you. I want to know about your parents. I want to know about your faith, whatever it is. I want to know about this guy you were dating and why you broke up. Everything."

Dalia stood there staring at the ground. Tariq took one more step and wrapped her in his arms. Her arms stayed at her side, but she laid her head on his chest.

"Dalia, please forgive me. Finding the letter was an accident, I swear to you, but you're right; I shouldn't have read it. But please believe me when I tell you that I wasn't trying to hurt you. It never even occurred to me that you'd be upset. Let's not let this ruin the magical time we've been having."

He was begging, he knew—not something he was used to. But it seemed to be having its desired effect. Slowly, Dalia seemed to be calming down. She was sniffling now, rather than crying, and her breathing had slowed considerably. Eventually her arms went around him.

"Did you really mean what you just said?" she asked after a long pause.

"All of it," he replied.

"You're really falling in love with me?"

"Yes—absolutely yes—I'm head over heels in love with you. Why else would I have swept you off your feet and brought you to this paradise?"

Tariq could hardly believe the words coming out of his mouth. He barely knew this girl. She barely knew him. He was in no position to settle down, but he couldn't help it. There was something irresistible about her, something that seemed to be warning him not to let her slip away.

"I don't know," she said softly. "I'm still trying to figure that out."

"So do you forgive me?" he asked.

She hesitated. "I'm still trying to figure that out too."

He took her face in his hands. Her eyes were red. Her

mascara was smeared. But she looked more beautiful to him than ever. He kissed her until she began kissing him back. Soon she stepped away, took his hand, and led him to the elevator. When they got in, she punched the button for their floor. Then she wrapped his arms around her, and she leaned into his chest.

He still could not for the life of him understand why she had reacted the way she had. But in the grand scheme of things, did it really matter? What did matter was that the woman he was falling in love with was herself falling in love with a computer consultant named Tariq Jameel. What would she do when she found out he was really Marwan Accad, high-priced security company owner and international fugitive wanted for murder?

The doors opened, and he followed Dalia down the hall. He knew he was wasting precious time. If he was going to make a move, he was going to have to do it soon. He had to get out of Sharm before Lemieux, Goddard, and the Egyptian police tracked him down and cut off every avenue of escape.

As he reached to unlock the door to their room, she pulled him against her. And in that moment, all thoughts of dead friends, live French inspectors, and narrowing international manhunts faded into the softness of Dalia's kiss.

44

Dalia lit up a marijuana cigarette and offered one to Tariq.

"Is this your way of making up?" he asked with a grin.

She nodded and inhaled. "The second part, at least."

He accepted her little peace treaty and inhaled as well. They sat together in silence for a few minutes, the bedroom slowly filling with smoke.

"Can I ask you a question?" Tariq began, a little hesitant to reopen a seemingly resealed can of worms.

"Sure, I guess."

Tariq processed wording for a moment. "Why did you freak out on me like that?" *Well, that certainly came out wrong.*

But Dalia only shrugged and looked away. "I don't know."

"Sure you do," he said.

Dalia took another drag on her cigarette. "I guess I was embarrassed."

"About what?"

"About my dad being a pastor. About how far the apple has fallen from the tree. I mean, I think it's fine that my parents are Christians. It's just that it never really took with me. I acted the part when I was a little girl—I didn't really have a choice. But I don't think I ever really believed all that my parents believed. It's one of the reasons I finally left home."

"How long ago was that?"

"It's been a while," she said. "Since I left for college, at least."

"And you haven't been back since."

"No." Dalia turned her head down. But not before Tariq saw her eyes moisten.

"Don't you miss your folks, your friends, your town?"

Dalia thought about that for a bit. "Actually, yeah, I do. My parents are good people, and I know they love me."

"Then why don't you go back?" Tariq asked.

Dalia sighed. "Because my father is a tyrant."

"A tyrant? Wait, didn't you say . . . ?"

Dalia laughed a little to herself. "Yeah, I guess that didn't come out quite right. It's just . . . he has all these religious rules and regulations, and it's always been his way or the highway. I decided I didn't want to live by them, so I took off and never looked back."

Tariq could hear the bitterness creeping into her voice, but he pressed on anyway. "What kind of rules?"

"Does it really matter?" Dalia asked, getting up abruptly and walking to the window. Tariq waited while she stared out at the glistening water of the Red Sea. "You know, *rules*—no dating, no drinking alcohol, no using drugs, no this, no that, no, no, no. . . ."

"As opposed to the fathers who say, 'My dear daughter, please drink alcohol; please use drugs'? What do you expect him to say?" Tariq joked, getting up to join her at the window. He wrapped his arms around her and rested his chin on her shoulder. "He's a dad. That's what dads are supposed to do—protect their daughters—right?"

"Hey," Dalia said, trying to pull away, "whose side are you on?"

But Tariq held her close and gave her a kiss on her ear. "Come on, think about it. When you have a daughter one day, you're really going to tell me that you'll let her get drunk and smoke and date guys like me?"

They kissed by the window. Finally, holding her close, he asked, "Is your dad really a priest?"

Dalia laughed and pushed him away. "You're just not going to let this go, are you?" She dropped into a cushy chair.

"I'm curious," Tariq said, scooting himself up on a table next to her. "So?"

"He's not a priest. He's a pastor," she said.

"There's a difference?"

"I guess. Kind of."

"Does he run the church, tell people about Jesus, care for the poor, that kind of thing?"

She nodded. "Pretty much."

"Sounds like a priest to me."

Dalia slapped him on the leg.

"So what's Petra Bible Church?" he asked.

"Argh," Dalia groaned, rolling her eyes. "It's the church I

grew up in. My dad's been the pastor there since before I was born. It's named for the ancient city of Petra, which is near Ma'an, my hometown."

"Is it big?"

"What, the church?" Dalia shrugged. "It's actually getting bigger. There were only thirty or forty people when I was a kid—and hardly anyone my age. But now, the last I heard, there were about a hundred and fifty people there, most of them young couples and families—and lots of kids."

"And that's where you met what's-his-name? Kalim?"

She shook her head. "Hardly."

"Then where?"

"College—my sophomore year. Some girlfriends and I went to Paris for a weekend. We met at a café."

"Ooo, sounds romantic." Tariq laughed, trying to cover his creeping jealousy. "So what happened to your *petit ami de Paris*?"

"He liked me. I liked him. We started to date. It didn't work out. No big deal."

"That seems to me like describing World War II as 'These countries didn't like each other, so they fought for a while; then it ended.'" Tariq leaned his back against the warmth of the window. "I sense you might be leaving out a few details."

"Yeah, well, the detail you need to know is that my father hated him," she said, ignoring his little dig. "Actually, I don't think he *hated* Kalim. I think my father is incapable of *hating* anyone. But he certainly *disapproved* of him."

"Why?"

"Because Kalim wasn't a Christian. He wasn't anything,

really. He didn't care about religion at all. That didn't go over well with my father. Ever since I was a little girl, he has insisted that I marry a Christian, period, end of sentence, end of story."

Ouch, Tariq thought. *I don't think Daddy's going to be so happy to meet me.* "So if you knew that, why did you date Kalim?"

"Because who cares what my father says?" Dalia shot back with an air of defiance. "I'm going to date whomever I want, and I'm going to marry whomever I want, whether my father likes it or not. It's my life. Not his. It's really none of his business whom I marry or if I even get married. I certainly don't intend to let him judge me for not living by all his rules and regulations."

"You say you dated him despite how your dad would feel about him. Could it be that you dated him because you knew exactly how your dad would feel about him?" Tariq hypothesized with a barely suppressed smirk.

Dalia leaned forward in her chair and looked like she was ready to unleash on Tariq, until she saw his face. She dropped back into the cushions and chuckled. "Okay, Dr. Freud, you may be right. Now, can I make a suggestion?"

"Anythink," Tariq said in a bad German accent.

"Would the good doctor object to joining me in some outdoor activities, rather than wasting the day in here in deep analysis?"

"Ja, ja," Tariq said, sliding off the table.

But before he could get too far, Dalia caught his arm. "Oh, and, my dear, next time it's you who gets to go under the interrogation lights."

"You got it," Tariq said with a kiss to her forehead, already mentally planning the day so that their busy schedule would "unintentionally" crowd out any opportunities for getting deep again.

45

Goddard walked out the front door of the Moroccan police headquarters and stopped under a large portrait of King Mohammed VI. His cell phone was ringing, and he didn't want to take the call inside with all the eavesdropping ears around.

Lifting the phone to his ear, he said, "Tell me you've got something, Colette."

"I think I do, sir. This might be big."

"You've found Accad?" Goddard asked, anxious for some good news after days of nothing.

"No, sir, I'm afraid not."

"Then what?" Goddard pressed, hearing the disappointment in his own voice.

"Well, sir, remember the surveillance video from inside Rafeeq Ramsey's apartment?"

"Yes."

"And remember the footage of Accad showing Ramsey something that he pulled out of a manila folder?"

"Sure, I remember," Goddard said. "A photo of some kind."

"Exactly."

"What about it, Colette?"

"Well, sir, our tech guys were finally able to create a usable computer enhancement of that image. You won't believe what they came up with."

"What?" Goddard demanded, increasingly pressed for time. In a few hours, he would be on a plane to Beirut to interrogate Ramy Accad. He didn't have time to play twenty questions with Colette DuVall.

"It turns out that image is a photograph of Claudette Ramsey," DuVall explained. "It was taken by a security camera in a bank in São Paulo, Brazil."

Goddard was stunned. Almost too stunned to talk. He sat on the low, whitewashed brick wall that surrounded the police station and leaned against the wrought-iron fence.

"Claudette Ramsey?" Goddard asked, his voice much softer than it had been before. "You're sure?"

"It's her all right—a 100 percent match," DuVall said, her excitement evident in her words. "There's a time and date stamp on the bottom of the photograph, and the bank's logo is on the back wall, just over Mrs. Ramsey's left shoulder. I e-mailed you all the details."

Goddard could hardly believe it. This *was* a dramatic development, but what did it mean? He had no idea. He was still too shocked to process it, so he put the question to DuVall, since she, at least, had had a bit of a head start on considering the photo's implications.

"I don't know, sir," DuVall conceded. "I'm just as stunned as you are."

"What do you think it could mean?" Goddard asked again, unwilling to let her off that easily. "Give me your best guess."

DuVall took a moment to consider her words. "Well, sir, it strikes me as proof that Marwan Accad knows where Mrs. Ramsey is, and therefore that Mr. Accad was, in fact, directly involved in blackmailing Rafeeq Ramsey. After all, why else would Mr. Accad have such a photo?"

"Maybe," Goddard said, trying to consider the new development from every angle. "But there's something about that theory that doesn't completely ring true."

"What would that be?" DuVall asked.

What would that be? Goddard thought. *What* would *that be?* He stood and began walking—slowly moving past the various crests that hung on the metal fence. This was a good lead—an important lead.

He stopped in front of a newsstand and scanned the headlines of the daily papers. The most recent developments in the case hadn't yet been fed to the press, but they soon would be. By tomorrow morning, Marwan Accad's face would be plastered all over every newspaper and every news Web site, as would the story of the trail of blood from Monaco to Morocco and the rapidly intensifying international investigation. In twenty-four hours, most likely, Accad would have nowhere else to run.

Goddard bought himself a cup of coffee and kept walking.

"Colette," he said at last to his assistant, who was used to waiting through his long pauses, "if Accad was really involved in kidnapping Claudette Ramsey, why would he go to Rafeeq Ramsey's apartment and meet with him directly, face-to-face? Why would he risk exposing himself and his operation? And even if Accad were stupid enough to go mano a mano with one of the richest and most powerful men in the Arab world—and I don't think of Marwan Accad as a stupid man—why in the world would he have Rafeeq Ramsey assassinated while he was standing in the room? Does any of that make sense to you?"

There was a long pause, and then DuVall said, "Maybe to give Mr. Accad an alibi."

"No, that makes no sense," Goddard countered. "If he wanted an alibi, he would have found somewhere else to be, not standing in the room while the murder went down. Besides, what about the car bomb? Why was Accad almost killed with the car bomb? And who tried to kill him at the Méridien in Monte Carlo? And what about those guys in Saint Michel? We still don't know who they were, but there is little doubt that they were trying to kill Accad. None of that makes any sense if Accad is really involved in kidnapping, blackmail, and murder, does it?"

"No, sir, I guess it doesn't," DuVall admitted. "But why then would Accad have had that photo of Mrs. Ramsey? And what about that friend of his he killed in Casablanca?"

"*Allegedly* killed," Goddard reminded her.

"Sir, with all due respect, Marwan Accad's fingerprints were all over Kadeen al-Wadhi's house," DuVall said. "He was definitely there. The evidence is clear and incontrovertible. What's more, there's no evidence that anyone else was in that house until you. How do you explain that? What other conclusion can you draw except that Marwan Accad is responsible for those two murders?"

A ridiculous thought bloomed in the back of Goddard's mind. He quickly stuffed it away as being just too far out of the box to even consider. "I don't know, Collette. I just don't know." Goddard stopped at an intersection and realized he had no idea where he had wandered off to. "What I do know is that something isn't right here, and we're running out of time to figure out what it is."

46

Tariq and Dalia strolled through the narrow streets of Sharm el-Sheikh. As they passed through the various souks, it seemed every shop owner was waiting for them with a "Hey, where're you from?" or a business card held out. Occasionally they'd step into a shop if something caught their eye. But after a particularly disagreeable episode trying to disengage themselves from an overly aggressive proprietor, they decided to keep to the street.

The image of Kadeen's dead face kept asserting itself in Tariq's mind. He had seen it in his dreams night after night since he had first arrived in Casablanca. He couldn't believe that it had happened.

Then there was Rania. She had every right to hate him, every right to wish him dead. *So what does she do? She forgives me. What kind of person does that? "Greater love has no man than to lay down his life for another." Those were the same words Kadeen told me about Jesus, about him dying for me. And now Kadeen has died for me too. I'm racking up a pretty high body count.*

He felt his body tense, and he fought back the emotions that he'd hoped he had thoroughly dealt with that morning.

"Are you okay?" Dalia asked. "You've seemed a little distant today. What's going on in that mind of yours? Are you still mad about earlier?"

"No, of course not. You're the one who had the right to be angry. It's just . . ."

"Just what?"

Tariq kept walking, trying to sort out what he was feeling—about the manhunt, about Kadeen, about Ramy, about Dalia. As they passed a small jewelry shop, an idea blazed in his mind. Wrapping his arm around Dalia's waist, he pulled her into the shop.

The store owner was welcoming them and promising to show them marvelous items that they would find nowhere else in all of Egypt. But Tariq ignored him. He examined a glass-fronted case, then pointed to a simple gold band.

"But, sir, I have much better examples of Egyptian gold in the back. If you'll please let me show them to you, I'm sure—"

Tariq pulled out his cash and peeled off four large denominations, then pointed once again to the gold band, knowing he was probably offering about eight times more than the ring was worth. The proprietor quickly opened the case.

He handed the ring to Tariq, who in turn faced Dalia. Then, dropping to one knee, he said, "Dalia, I know this seems fast. All right, I guess it really is fast. You asked what's going on in my mind. There's a whole lot of stuff—crazy things, some things you know about and some things you don't. But in the midst of all that craziness and uncertainty, there's one thing that stands out firm and strong. I love you, Dalia Nour. I love you more than I've ever loved anyone in my whole life. When you know something is right, you just know, and I know this: I want to spend the rest of my life with you. I want to make you the happiest woman in the whole world. And I know that you would make me the happiest man in the world if you would agree to be my wife.

"Dalia Nour, will you marry me?"

"Tariq, I . . . I don't know what to say."

"Yes, you do. Say yes."

Dalia's face brightened, and in that moment she was the most beautiful woman Tariq had ever seen in his life.

"Yes."

Tariq stood up, and Dalia threw her arms around him. The crowd that had gathered in the front of the shop cheered. Even the owner threw in a matching necklace and earrings for the newly engaged couple, each even poorer quality than the ring.

Walking out of the store, they received congratulatory handshakes and pats on the back. Tariq kept the presence of mind to never take his hand from his front pocket, thereby blocking at least two attempts at his wallet. Once they were back out in the sun, Tariq gave Dalia another hug. Then they continued walking through the souk.

Tariq couldn't believe what he had done. He was a wanted man, people were dying all around him, and he'd just proposed. *What kind of an idiot am I?* But he knew the answer to that question immediately. He was an idiot in love. He couldn't imagine losing Dalia, and he was afraid that if he didn't get some sort of major commitment from her right away, then when she found out the truth of who he was, he'd never see her again.

When they reached the beach, they both slipped off their shoes. Tariq carried both pairs in his right hand while he kept his left arm tight around Dalia's shoulders.

"I do have one condition," Dalia said tentatively.

"A better ring? Trust me, I will get you the most exquisite—"

"No, it's not that. Although there is that, and that is important, this is not that. This is much more important than that."

"I have no idea what you just said," Tariq said with a nervous chuckle, having understood exactly what she had said. There was a hitch, a snag, a problem that could blow this whole thing apart.

Stopping in the soft sand, Dalia turned toward Tariq. "I need to get my parents' blessing."

"What? But you haven't even seen them in how many years?"

"I know, I know. But it's important to me. It'll be important to my family. This is how we do things. It has to be done."

Tariq turned from her and started walking toward the water. Then, turning back, he said, "That's great! Your dad's going to love me."

Dalia ran to Tariq. "He will! I know he will! He'll fall in love with you just like I have."

"When? After he converts me? Didn't you say that they expected you to marry a Christian? If you couldn't tell by the time we've spent together, I'm definitely not a Christian!"

Tears welled up in Dalia's eyes, then began to spill down her cheeks. "Obviously, I'm not much of one either."

Tariq pulled her against him. "I'm sorry, Dalia. I went too far. If we need to get your dad's blessing, we'll get your dad's blessing. And if I need to convert, for you I'll convert. I mean, how hard can it be? I'll say what he wants me to say, then let him sprinkle some water on my head and he'll be happy."

Dalia chuckled softly against his chest. "You make it sound so businesslike, like it was some spiritual transaction. My dad always said that becoming a Christian is about the heart; the head and hands come later."

"Meaning . . . ?"

"It's not what you do; it's what you believe."

That idea sounded familiar. "Is that what you meant before, in the museum? When you said heaven is a gift, not a payment?"

"That's exactly it," Dalia said as she looked up at him.

This conversation was reminding Tariq of the one he had had with Kadeen. Abruptly Dalia reached up and wiped away a tear Tariq hadn't even realized was sliding down his cheek. "Tariq, what's wrong?"

"I recently found out that a friend was killed."

"I'm so sorry, sweetheart," Dalia said, replacing the tear with a kiss.

"I just wish I knew whether, when he got to the other side, he was disappointed or whether it was exactly what he had expected it to be."

"I wish I knew too," Dalia said quietly. They stood there holding each other for a long time. The warm sea breeze blew through their hair, and the gulls cried out over the water. Neither wanted to move. Neither wanted to face the questions that remained in their minds about life, about the future, about death.

Eventually, with a long sigh, Tariq said, "Shall we head back to the hotel? I think we have to make some travel plans to Jordan."

"What? Now?"

Tariq chuckled. "Of course now. We're halfway there. There's no use going back."

"But I have to give them warning."

"Let's make it a surprise."

"I don't have enough clean clothes for the trip."

"I saw this cute little shop on the way," Tariq said with a smile.

"What about my job? I have a flight tomorrow."

"Call in sick. Better yet, tell them an unexpected family issue has come up."

Tariq couldn't help but laugh as he watched Dalia frantically try to come up with a reason to delay seeing her parents. Finally she threw her hands up in the air and said, "Well, I guess we're going to Jordan."

As they started their walk back, Tariq wrestled with whether he was doing the right thing. *Even if they traced me to Cairo, there's no way they could have trailed me to Sharm. And it would be almost impossible to make the connection with Dalia and her family. We've got to go while we still can. Once we get to Jordan, I'll be back near my own neighborhood. Then Ramy and I can straighten all this mess out with the authorities, and we can start planning a wedding.*

47

THEY CROSSED THE STREET and reentered the crowded souks. Both were lost in their own thoughts. It seemed that the number of people in the market had doubled since they were there less than an hour ago. Keeping Dalia under his arm, Tariq used his size and determination to push his way through, always looking for the path of least resistance.

Ahead of them in the crowd, he spotted a European-looking man walking toward them. He reminded Tariq a bit of the two air marshals they had met at the Italian restaurant on Zamalek, except this one seemed like he was on a mission.

Tariq pretended to laugh, then nuzzled Dalia's neck.

"Dalia, I'm about to say something to you, and it is a matter of life and death that you show no emotion," he said with deadly earnest. "Now laugh and tell me whether you understand what I'm saying to you."

A choked chuckle burst forth from Dalia, and she croaked, "I understand."

"Do not look at him, but there is a tall man coming toward us. I believe he is here to kill me. I can't tell you why right now, but I promise I will explain everything later. There are things about me you don't know, Dalia, but you must trust me. Will you do exactly as I say?"

"Yes."

"When I push you, I want you to fall to your right all the way to the ground. Got it?"

"Yes."

Tariq gave her a quick kiss on the neck, then straightened up. He laughed and stroked her hair. Dalia laughed too, but he could see the fear in her eyes when she looked at him.

The man was close. *Please let this be a false alarm. Please let this be a false alarm.*

But Tariq knew it wasn't. The way the man was walking with only his left arm swinging told him that he had a weapon in his right.

The distance between them closed rapidly. Just before he reached them, Tariq pointed to something in a small purse shop and veered them that direction.

He pushed Dalia hard into the shop, then spun to meet his attacker. The man swung a long military knife up from his side. Tariq swung his left arm hard outward, deflecting the blow. Then, using his momentum, he angled a kick to his attacker's knee. The man's leg buckled. The European tried to keep his balance, and as he did, Tariq grabbed his right arm with both hands. One more kick and the man fell to the ground. Tariq followed him down, using all his force to direct the knife into the man's neck and through his windpipe.

Immediately Tariq turned toward the shop to check on Dalia. When he did, his heart sank. A second attacker was lifting her roughly to her feet. Tariq quickly reached his hand under the dying man's shirt and into the small of his back. He found what he hoped would be there.

Just as the second man stepped out of the shop and, with a grin, raised a gun to Dalia's temple, Tariq fired two shots, lifting off the back of the man's head. Dalia screamed, as did the shop owner.

Tariq stood and scanned the crowd for another gunman. He could see the fear in the eyes of the people as they cowered from him. Seeing no one else, he grabbed Dalia's hand and pulled her after him.

"Let's go," he yelled. "We've got to get out of here now."

He was grateful to feel no resistance from her. Soon they were running through the mass of shoppers, knocking people over left and right.

Once they cleared the souks, Tariq headed for the docks. Dusk was just beginning to fall. Many of the fishing and recreational boats were coming in, and the dinner cruises were just setting out. *Perfect,* Tariq thought. Their feet hit hard on the dock, then clomped on the wood as they made their way past the slips.

Tariq was looking for a boat, any boat. It just needed to look fast and be empty. Finally he found a six-meter ski boat at the end of the wooden pier that would do. He jumped on, then held out his arms to help Dalia in. She only hesitated for a moment before letting herself fall into his arms.

Tariq began searching under the seats and in the ski ropes and eventually found a key on a small floatie hanging on a hook in the engine compartment.

He quickly cast off, ran to the wheel, started up the boat, and eased her out of her slip. The boat slid into the inlet and got lost in the water traffic. It wasn't until ten minutes later, after he had cleared the rest of the boats and exited Naama Bay, that he opened the engines up and headed north toward the Gulf of Aqaba.

48

Half an hour later, after Tariq had navigated Tiran Island at the mouth of the Gulf of Aqaba, he throttled back the engines. Once the ski boat had slowed to a speed that wouldn't require his full attention, he swiveled his seat to look at Dalia.

She was huddled with her legs tucked under her on the seat behind him. There must have been a blanket stored under the rear bench, because she now had it wrapped around her.

"Dalia," Tariq said.

There was no response.

"Dalia," Tariq said again, this time getting up to move toward her.

"Stop! Don't," she commanded. She was looking at him, but in the half-light of the waning moon he struggled to make out her features.

Tariq sat and shut the engines all the way off. He leaned toward her but didn't leave his seat. The silence was broken only by the gentle lapping of the water against the sides of the boat.

Tariq waited. Time passed. At one point he could hear her crying. He wanted desperately to reach out to her, to comfort her. But since he was the source of her tears, he knew that, at least for now, he had no comfort to give.

A large yacht slid through the water about a hundred meters away. Music and laughter echoed across the open expanse, then slowly faded, leaving just the gentle rock of the boat's wake.

"Who are you?" Dalia asked, her voice barely a whisper.

"First, Dalia, let me say—"

"Stop. Just stop it. Before we can have a conversation, I need to know who I'm speaking with." Her voice was heavy with sorrow but still carried an edge of anger.

"My name is Marwan Accad. I own a private security company along with my brother, Ramy. Right now I am wanted by the police for crimes I did not commit—including the murder of my best friend."

Marwan let those words hang in the air, waiting for Dalia to absorb the information.

He heard her expel a breath, then say, "Is that who those men were back there? Were those policemen?"

"No, I don't know who they are, but I believe they were hired by the people who are trying to frame me for the murder. Those were bad guys."

"And you—the one who killed them both—you're supposed to be the good guy?" Dalia asked, bitterness in her voice.

"I used to think so," Marwan said softly. "Now, I don't know."

Again, silence filled the boat. Marwan put his head in his hands.

Suddenly Dalia's voice burst forth. "How am I supposed to deal with this? Am I supposed to say, 'Okay, Tariq or Marwan or whatever your name is today, it's fine that instead of working as a mild-mannered computer consultant, you kill people for a living'? Is that it? Oh yeah, 'And, my dear fiancé, if you happen to shoot someone in the head who's holding me hostage, that's okay. I'll just wash the blood and bits of him out of my hair and fix you a nice dinner.'" Her voice broke with the last of her words.

"Dalia, I'm so sorry. You should never have been in that situation. I went on autopilot trying to keep you safe and get us out of there. I totally forgot that . . . I should have . . . I'm just so sorry."

She was now sitting cross-legged on the bench. Her hands were moving, but Marwan wasn't sure what she was doing. Then it hit him—she was fidgeting with the ring, pulling it off, putting it on, spinning it around her finger. He watched her, mesmerized. His fate was in where that ring ended up. Would it be on her finger or at the bottom of the gulf? He felt like he was watching a roulette table back in Monte Carlo: *Round and round it goes; where it stops, nobody knows.*

The ring ended up in her right hand. Then, with a shake of her head, she slipped it back onto her finger. "I need to know everything! No more lies!"

"No more lies," Marwan repeated.

"I want to know from the time you were born up until today. If I'm going to marry you—which is a huge question mark right now—I need to know who it is I'm marrying. Nothing hidden."

"You'll know it all. I swear to you."

Marwan could see her shoulders begin to shake. He wanted to comfort her but knew he couldn't touch her until she invited him.

"Why didn't you just leave me? You know, all along I kept waiting for you to disappear on me. Now I almost wish you had."

Risking it, he touched her knee. "I couldn't leave you, Dalia. I fell in love with you the first time I saw you."

The shaking increased until finally she reached out her arms. Marwan leaped at the opening and held her tight.

"No more lies," he said into her neck. "I promise you, no more lies."

After a while, her sobbing slowed, then stopped. Leaning away from him, she said, "I'm ready to hear now."

"And I'm ready to tell."

Marwan helped Dalia into the front of the boat, then sat in the other seat, started the boat, and throttled her up.

Once they were moving again, Marwan began talking. He started with his childhood, his love for his parents, the devastation after their deaths, his responsibility for Ramy, his military service, his private sector work, and Accad & Associates.

He had held the truth of who he was from her all this time, it felt great to get it out—to at last let Dalia see who he truly was.

But he paused. *Can I really tell her everything about Ramsey? What about what happened to Kadeen? What will she think of me when she hears that? And all the dead bodies that have been left in my wake? Is it even possible she'll still love me when she hears what kind of man I really am?*

Off in the distance, he saw city lights on the shore. By his calculations, that was Dahab, the next step in their journey. He slowed the boat, then killed the engine. It was still the middle of the night. He wouldn't be able to do what needed to be done until morning.

No more lies. You promised her, no more lies.

Taking Dalia again by the hand, he led her back to the bench seat. He sat down and she leaned against him. The salt spray had kept him awake, but now that the boat had stopped, he was very tired.

"I have more to tell you, but honestly, I'm afraid of what you'll think of me when I do."

In response, Dalia took his hand and wrapped it around her.

"Okay," Marwan said, "it started in Monte Carlo. . . ."

By the time he was done, he was exhausted from trying to keep his emotions in check. He waited, wondering how she would respond.

After what seemed like an eternity, she raised his hand to her mouth, gently kissed it, then turned deeper into his chest and fell asleep.

Marwan's heart jumped into his throat. *Thank you, Dalia. And if there's a God out there, thank you, too.*

He leaned his head back with a smile but didn't close his eyes. He knew that he needed to stay awake and keep watch. He lasted another five minutes before he, too, became lost to the world.

49

Another city, another hotel, another night of pacing. It didn't take much to make Inspector Lemieux angry. However, it did take some effort to make him this angry.

I can't believe that idiot has put me on hold! Me! And without asking permission or even giving an apology or an "excuse me." I'm going to have to remind him who works for whom.

He walked back across the room, carefully avoiding the ceramic pieces of the lamp he had just shattered on the wall. He hated being in Cairo—the smells, the noise, the crowds. But the worst was the driving. How they fit eight lanes of traffic on a four-lane road, he'd never know. Then to top it off, they drove at insane rates of speed, weaving in and out of their makeshift tracks. He finally had to threaten his driver, a captain with the Cairo police, with a complaint to the police chief to get him to slow down.

I have surrounded myself with fools and incompetents! The only one with half a brain is Goddard, and he's the only one I want *to remain clueless.*

The line clicked over. "Inspector Lemieux?"

"Edgard, if you ever put me on hold again, I will make sure that you don't survive the year. Remember, I am the one who chooses the assignments. I am the one who has kept you safe in your comfortable office instead of in the field. I am the one! Do you understand me?"

"But, sir, I—"

"Do you understand me?" Lemieux roared.

"Yes, sir."

"Good. Now, what have you learned?"

"The two killed in Sharm el-Sheikh were definitely our men—confirmed by our other teams there."

"Why didn't they wait?" Lemieux yelled, grabbing another lamp, then putting it down. "The other teams were within—what—an hour or two? If they had waited as they had been ordered, Accad would be dead. Did you tell them to wait?"

"Yes, sir, just like you told me. But if you remember, the team was LeBlanc and DuCharme. They've always been good at what they did, but they had a history of doing their own thing. They must have thought they could take Accad down themselves."

Lemieux squeezed his eyes shut and rubbed his forehead. "Make it clear to everyone involved that no more independent actions will be tolerated. Let them know that if they act on their own, if Accad doesn't kill them, I will!"

"Yes, sir."

"What more can you tell me?"

"Apparently he is not alone anymore."

"Oh, great," Lemieux said, sitting on the bed. "Do we know who he is?"

"It's not a he; it's a she."

Lemieux jumped to his feet. "A woman? Is she one of their operatives?"

"Could be. When we first started looking for Accad, we had checked on any old girlfriends. There's nothing there."

"Interesting." If she was one of the Accad & Associates team, she could mean trouble for them. But if she was someone Accad had picked up along the way, she could mean a major weakness for him.

"Find out who she is. Fast!"

"Yes, sir. Also, we've discovered that he made his escape from Sharm el-Sheikh by boat."

"Boat? Which direction?"

"We don't know, sir. He was lost in the gulf traffic."

"What options would he have?"

"There are all sorts of places they could be going down the Red Sea—El Gouna, Soma Bay, Marsa Alam, all the resort areas along Egypt's coast. If they went up the Gulf of Aqaba, they would see Dahab, Taba, then up to Eilat and Aqaba. There's also Saudi Arabia, but I don't think that's a viable option."

Lemieux paced silently. *Where are you running to? Where would I go if I were you? Your greatest asset is your ability to blend in. The farther south you go into Africa, the more you'll stand out. But if you go north, you've got your home of Lebanon and, ultimately, Europe. That's got to be it. I'm onto you, Accad. You can run, but you cannot hide forever.*

"Edgard, keep an eye on the Red Sea coast, but I believe he's going north up the gulf. Watch the Egyptian coasts and Aqaba, Jordan."

"What about Eilat?"

Lemieux shook his head. "He'd be a fool to try. And we'd be fools to try anything if he did make it in. Is there anything else I need to know?"

"No, sir."

Lemieux hung up without another word.

Immediately the phone rang again.

"What now?" he answered.

"Inspector Lemieux?"

Goddard, Lemieux thought, wishing he had checked his caller ID before answering so that he could have let it go to voice mail.

"What is it, Goddard?"

"Have you heard of the activity in Sharm el-Sheikh? One man stabbed and another—"

"Of course I've heard of it! What does that have to do with us?"

"Well, it sounds very much like our man Accad, don't you think?"

"No, I don't think it does."

"What? How can you say that? Two, at least thus far, anonymous corpses. Both killed in a fairly professional way."

"And what about the woman?"

"The . . . uh . . . there was a woman?"

"Goddard, you fool! Get all the information before you start jumping to conclusions!" He needed to throw Goddard off this trail, and quickly. "Those two men in Sharm el-Sheikh were killed by a man and a woman—the man killed one in the street with a knife, and the woman shot the other in a shop. Unless you think Accad has suddenly become half of a new Bonnie and Clyde, I suggest you get yourself to Beirut and Ramy Accad, and have your men follow the actual lead of the rental car south from Cairo! Do I make myself clear?"

"Yes, sir."

Lemieux hung up. He stood breathing deeply to calm himself. At the desk, he called the hotel manager to complain about the cheap lamps that shatter when they are accidentally knocked off a table. After accepting the manager's apologies and promises of a cleanup and a replacement, he sat, poured himself a brandy, and began plotting how to bring Goddard down if he started getting too close.

50

A POUNDING on the boat startled Marwan.

"Hey, wake up! Hey, mister!"

"What? Who . . . ?" The words caught in Marwan's throat.

Next to him, he heard Dalia softly say, "Wow." Marwan soon followed suit.

It looked like the sea around them was alive with giant, colorful butterflies skimming across the waves. Once he was fully awake, he saw that the water surrounding them was filled with windsurfers riding boards of all colors and sizes.

The young man slapping the boat was wearing a blue and black wet suit and had his rig up against the starboard side of the ski boat. "Hey, mister, you're not allowed to have a boat in this lagoon."

Marwan looked beyond him and saw two other guys straddling their boards just a few meters off, glaring at him.

"Sorry, man, we were just out here partying last night, and I guess we got a little too wasted."

The guy laughed. "I don't know if there's such a thing as 'too wasted,' but I know what you mean. Anyway, only boarders out here riding the dawn patrol are allowed. You best clear out before the heat comes and starts asking you questions."

"Good call. Sorry about that."

With a shake of his head, the guy lifted his rig and skimmed off into the lagoon.

Marwan moved to the front seat and fired up the boat. He only put the throttle at a quarter so he could ease his way among all the sails. When he was clear, he pointed the boat toward shore.

"You never told me what you thought about what I said last night," he said once they were under way.

"I'm not sure what to say," Dalia replied, taking the other front seat. Even with her hair sticking every which way after spending the night drifting at sea, she still looked stunningly beautiful. "It's going to take me a while to digest everything. I can tell you that I understand why you lied. I can't say that I like it, but I do understand. I also know that despite what you think about yourself, I still feel that you are a good man, Marwan Accad—you know, it's going to take me a bit of time to get used to that name."

"Well, get ready for another," he said. "Here, take the wheel."

"What? What do you mean another?" Dalia asked as she traded seats.

Reaching into his pocket, he pulled out his wallet. It was a bit larger than the typical bifold, and Dalia had made fun of it more than once.

From his other pocket, he produced his pocketknife. Carefully, he cut the stitches that were holding the leather panels together. When one side was separated, he reached in and pulled out a British passport that was creased in the middle and wrapped in plastic. Then he slid a Visa credit card out from one side of the opening and an American Express from the other.

He handed the passport to Dalia, who opened it up. "Andrew Cooper?"

"At your service," Marwan said with a half bow. "I'm just down here honeymooning with my new wife, Helga, and I—"

"Helga?" Dalia said with a mortified look on her face.

"Gertrude?"

"Uh, no," she answered.

"Minnie?"

"Minnie? Very funny."

"So, my dear, what would you like your name to be?"

Dalia looked around and saw the sun coming up over the barren hills of Saudi Arabia on the far side of the gulf. "How about Dawn?"

"Dawn," Marwan said thoughtfully. "I like it. Dawn Cooper née Khoury—we have to account for your accent somehow. Switch back with me."

They traded seats again, and Marwan took the wheel.

"Oh yeah," he said, reaching into his waistband and pulling out the gun he had taken from his first victim last night. Holding his hand overboard, he let it drop into the gulf.

They were getting near the shore. Marwan spotted a small

dock with some open slips, and he pointed the boat that direction.

"What are we doing now?" Dalia asked.

"Getting new transportation. We're almost out of fuel."

"Then what?"

"I'm not sure. We could drive north to the Med, then make our way up to Lebanon. I've got tons of resources there. Or we could try to sneak into Israel through Eilat."

Dalia chuckled. "'Sneak into Israel.' That's almost funny."

"Yeah, I guess Israel's not known for easy border access."

"I say we keep going to my parents' house in Ma'an."

"No way," Marwan said, looking hard at Dalia. "I've already put you in danger. There is no chance I'm going to do the same to your parents."

"But they can help us. I know they can. Dad used to be in the military. He still has connections."

"It's Jordan; everyone used to be in the military. But it still isn't safe."

Leaning forward and grabbing his arm with both her hands, Dalia pleaded, "You yourself said that there was no way the people chasing you could know who I am. Please, Marwan, you know I'm right. And I really feel like I need to see them right now."

Marwan didn't say anything as he eased the boat into the slip and tied her off. *How can I say no to her after all I've put her through? She needs this. Besides, once you have a safe place to work from, you should be able to put this all to bed.*

"Okay, but you have to promise to follow my lead and do exactly as I say," Marwan said.

"Of course, honey," Dalia said with a wink. "After all, we're married. Isn't that the way it's supposed to be?"

Marwan couldn't help but smile as he shook his head. He had a feeling that in the years ahead, Dalia following his lead and doing exactly as he said would be the exception rather than the rule. *But with this girl, I really wouldn't want it any other way.*

51

Once they were onshore, they started walking north up the coastline. It felt good to be out of the boat and stretching their legs. The morning was already starting to get warm, but the sand was still cool on their feet. They mostly made small talk, and every now and then Dalia would kind of fade out for a few moments. Then, just as quickly, she'd be back in the conversation. Marwan figured she was processing the events of the previous night. He decided not to pursue it.

After about a mile, they came upon a market area. Marwan saw some boats piered, so he sent Dalia off to find provisions while he went to rent a boat.

His cover story of being a newlywed staying at the Sirtaki Hotel was accepted without a question in this tourist town, especially after the generous tip he added for the all-day rental.

He was a little disappointed when he saw where the owner was leading him. The boat was old and smelled like fish, but it was functional and had a healthy-sounding engine. By the time Dalia found him on the dock, he and the owner had it ready to go. After one final warning to watch for big cruise ships and to stay away from the Saudi Arabian shoreline, the man tossed off the lines and waved good-bye.

"How does the owner feel about you stealing his boat?" Dalia asked, only half-jokingly.

"Oh, he was perfectly fine with it. Says he has them stolen all the time," Marwan answered. "Besides, we're renting it just like we said. We're just going to return it to a different location. And trust me, there's enough money on that card number for him to cover whatever expenses he has getting the boat back, plus more."

"Well, I guess that makes it all right. Doesn't it, Mr. Cooper?"

Marwan turned to her. "Please, Dalia, I don't feel good about this either. This is not how I like to operate things. I pride myself in staying aboveboard and legal. This, however, is an unusual circumstance, and I'm forced to do things out of necessity that I wish I didn't have to do. Your comments are not making it any easier."

"You're right," Dalia said, moving behind him and draping her arms over his shoulders. She sighed heavily and leaned against him. "I guess I'm still having difficulty with the transition from bored flight attendant to international fugitive."

"It gets easier," Marwan laughed. Dalia gave him a light slap on the shoulder, then followed it with a quick kiss after she saw him wince. His shoulder was definitely getting better, but it was still a long way from healed. "So what did you find us in the market? I'm starving."

Dalia retrieved her bags and showed off her purchases. "We've got fruit—pears, figs, dates, and a few bananas. I found some cheese, a little dried fish, and some wonderful-smelling bread."

"Fantastic. I'll have a little—no, make that a lot—of everything."

They ate as they headed north up the gulf. Marwan had checked a map at the boat rental shop and estimated the distance to be a little over a hundred kilometers to Aqaba, Jordan. With this boat, that would mean about a three-and-a-half to four-hour trip. He actually wished it were longer. As long as they were out on this boat in the middle of this beautiful blue water, it felt like all their troubles were miles away. Here they were safe. Once they hit shore, who knew what would be waiting for them? They would be sneaking into another country under false identities with nothing but the clothes on their backs.

"Oh no," Marwan abruptly yelled out.

"What?" Dalia cried, dropping low.

Marwan saw the fear in Dalia's eyes. "It's nothing. It's just . . . I thought of something we left back in the hotel room."

Relief flooded Dalia's face as she lifted herself back onto the seat. "What, clean underwear?"

Marwan chuckled. "Yeah, that too. No, I just realized I left the Bible that Kadeen had given to me. It was his own personal study Bible, and it meant so much to him. I can't believe I lost it!"

"I'm sorry, sweetheart." Dalia tore another piece of bread, laid a piece of fish and some cheese on it, and handed it to Marwan.

He nodded his thanks and took a bite. "What do you think about the Bible? Do you really think it's the actual Word of God? Because Kadeen did. To him, that book was straight from the mouth of the Almighty."

"I think I do," Dalia answered. "I remember my dad preaching in the church, giving all these reasons about the truth of God's Word and the truth of who Jesus was. He called it 'evidence that demands a verdict' or something like that."

"Yeah, Kadeen told me about some of that stuff. He talked about all the copies that are out there of the New Testament and why we can trust the Bible we have today."

Dalia nodded as she bit deeply into a pear. The juices ran down her arm, and she scrambled to find something to wipe herself off with. "I remember my dad talking about those things, too," she said, using an old rag she found on the deck to mop up her arm. But then she smelled the rag and dropped it to the ground. "Yuck! What's stayed with me most, though, even after all these years, was when he talked about the disciples."

Marwan took another bite and asked through a half-filled mouth, "Those were the guys who hung out with Jesus, right? Like Matthew, Mark, Luke, John, Peter, Paul—all those guys?"

"Well, not all of them. I know Luke and Paul weren't disciples—they came later. And I don't think Mark was either. But anyway, yes, the disciples were the ones who were with Jesus. Do you know that every single one of them was killed for preaching about Jesus? No, wait, I take that back. John was only exiled to some island."

"You mean John the Baptist? the guy who ate grasshoppers and nasty stuff like that?" Marwan asked. A few of the stories about Israel he had read in in-flight magazines were coming back to his mind.

Dalia shook her head and laughed. "No, a different John. Sometimes the names get confusing. But anyway, all the rest were killed. I remember my dad saying that if you were about to be killed for something you knew to be a lie, don't you think you would admit it and save yourself?"

"I see what you're saying. Either these guys were caught up in some mass hysteria, were smoking some things they should not have been smoking, or they actually believed what it was they were preaching about."

"Exactly."

"See, I'm a pretty quick student when I put my mind to it," Marwan said, bouncing his eyebrows a few times. "But, Pastor Dalia, I don't see what that has to do with the Bible."

"First of all, don't call me that," she said, sounding serious. "I'm so far from deserving that title, I don't even want to think about it."

"Fair enough."

"To answer your question, most of the New Testament was written while these people were still alive. If any of the facts were wrong, they would have been challenged. I remember there's one point where Paul is talking about Jesus rising from the dead—where was it? I memorized it once for a scholarship to Bible camp. I know it was at the end of a long one like Romans or Corinthians. But anyway, in this section he actually comes out and challenges them to check his facts. He's like, 'Jesus died, he rose again, and he appeared to the disciples and five hundred or so other people, most of whom are still alive.' According to my dad, that was like a flat-out challenge."

"But with all that, you're still not convinced."

Dalia looked off into the sea. Then, without looking at Marwan, she said, "No, I think I'm convinced. My problem is that I keep trying to convince myself that I'm *not* convinced."

Marwan slouched back in the seat. Even though he still had the same salty spray cooling him down, the same wonderful smell of the sea, the same hot sun cleansing his pores, he no longer felt the same peace he had just minutes before. There was a restless feeling inside of him, a feeling he only got when he started thinking about this whole God thing.

It seemed that every time he turned around, more evidence was piling up about the Bible being what Kadeen said it was and Jesus being who he said he was too. *But that's still not for me. Why should I pick Christianity? Why not Islam or Hinduism or Buddhism? They've got just as many followers who are sure about their beliefs.*

But the more he tried to slam the door on God, the more it felt like someone's foot was blocking the way.

52

After so many miles of nothingness, it was both exciting and a little scary to see civilization ahead. At the top of the gulf, separated only by a narrow border, were the resort cities of Eilat, Israel, and Aqaba, Jordan.

Marwan veered right. Aqaba was Jordan's only seaport, and as such, it was crowded with boat traffic. He hoped to be able to blend in and get them ashore without any hassle from border agents.

"Who are you?" he asked Dalia.

She sat up straight in the seat next to Marwan and recited as if giving a test answer in school. "My name is Dawn Cooper née Khoury, recently married to the man of my dreams, Andrew Cooper, a computer consultant with Datalan Network Infrastructures. I was formerly a flight attendant for British

Airways until I met my future husband while he was on a quick business trip to Denver, Colorado, USA. By a stroke of luck, Mr. Cooper was on my flight back to London. The rest, as they say, is history."

"And what are you doing in Jordan, Mrs. Cooper?"

"I'm on my honeymoon. I have visited several places along the Red Sea, but Aqaba by far is the most scenic, romantic seaside city I have stepped foot in."

Marwan smiled. "Nice embellishment."

"We Jordanians appreciate the fine art of flattery."

Despite her humor, Marwan could hear the fear in Dalia's voice and see it in her eyes. *You've got to remember, she's never done this before. Who are you kidding? You've never done this before. But at least you're used to dangerous situations.*

Seeing a harbor area with a number of boats docked, he made his way that direction. However, as soon as he cleared the narrow area between two rock jetties, he knew he had made a mistake. Every one of the boats was far nicer than the one he was piloting, and a sign announced that they had just entered the Aqaba Yacht Club.

Unfortunately, it was too late to turn around now without attracting more attention.

"Did you mean to come in here?" Dalia asked.

"Yes and no. Yes, I meant to come in here. No, I obviously shouldn't have. We're going to stick out like a beggar in a luxury suite."

"It's okay," she said, sounding like she was trying to convince herself more than Marwan. "We'll get through this."

He smiled at her. Scanning the docks, he found an open slip and pulled the boat in. Quickly he tied it off, helped Dalia out of the boat, then started down the wooden dock with her hand in his.

When they had made it halfway to shore, a figure stepped out of the boathouse and onto the end of the pier. *Good, it's only the harbormaster. I can handle—*

Marwan stopped short as he watched the man point their way. Two uniformed officers appeared on either side of him and began walking toward them. Dalia's hand squeezed Marwan's hard. He gave two gentle squeezes back and began walking to meet the men.

"Officers," he said in a perfect British accent, "I think I may have committed a serious gaffe here. We were looking for a place to port, and—"

"Passports, please," the older of the two officers said.

"Really, if you could just direct me toward a public dock, I'd—"

"Passports," the officer interrupted again, holding out his hand.

Marwan pulled his passport out of his pocket and said, "You heard the chap, Dalia, hand him your passport."

They both handed their documents to the officer. He looked at them both, then passed them to the second man.

"Where are you from?" he asked Dalia in Arabic.

"Just a minute, that's not very sporting. Speak so I can understand you too," Marwan said, even though he understood every word.

The first officer put his finger on Marwan's chest. "You, be quiet," he said in English. Then, turning to Dalia, he again asked in Arabic, "Where are you from?"

"My family is from Ma'an, but I have lately been living in Cairo," she answered with surprising confidence.

That's the way, Marwan thought. *When you're in a bad situation, stick to the truth as much as is possible.*

"Where are you coming from?"

"We came from Dahab. I met Andrew on a flight—I'm a flight attendant with British Air. I met him on a flight, I had some time off, and he took me to Dahab. While we were there, I told him about how beautiful Aqaba was, so we decided to come here. Other than parking our boat in the wrong place, have we done anything wrong?"

Switching back to English, the officer asked a sulking Marwan, "Where are you coming from?"

"Dahab."

"How do you know Miss Nour?"

"I met her on an airplane. She's a stewardess—oh, excuse me," he said, turning to Dalia, "a flight attendant."

"What are you doing here with her?"

"Well, that's just a bit personal, don't you think?"

Once again, the finger went to Marwan's chest. "I do not find you amusing, Mr. Cooper. Nor do I have time for your games."

"Okay, okay. We were out on the beach in Dahab. I commented on how beautiful the water was. She said that it was much more beautiful up in Aqaba. I told her that I couldn't imagine it being so. She asked me if I wanted to bet. I told her yes. So we came here to settle our wager—the terms of which I am too much of a gentleman to share with you. Let's just say that I look forward to paying off my debt."

The officer stared at Marwan a moment longer before

quietly conferring with his partner. He nodded, then turned back to Marwan.

"If you say you were in Egypt, why is there no stamp in your passport?"

Marwan laughed. "I was wondering when you would get to that question. You see, I specifically requested that they not stamp it. Once I'm through with our little excursion, I'm expected in Israel for some consulting work in Tel Aviv. You know the hassle those Jews will give me if they see a recent passport stamp from an Arab country."

The two men held eye contact, both waiting to see if the other would flinch. Finally the officer said, "Mr. Cooper, I do not like your attitude, nor do I care for what you are doing to one of the fair flowers of our country. However, you have done nothing illegal. Talk to the harbormaster to see if you can work out terms to keep your boat here. I'm sure you will be able to come to an agreeable price."

Half of which will be going into your pocket, I'm sure, Marwan thought as the officers turned to go.

Waiting until the two men got a good head start, Marwan and Dalia silently followed. At the end of the pier, Marwan struck a deal with the yacht club's manager, paying what must have been close to a full month's slip rental for a two-night stay.

Once they were clear of the harbor and had crossed into the town, Dalia broke down in tears.

"I was horrible! I ruined the story, but I didn't know what else to do! I couldn't say I was your wife after he asked for my passport!"

Marwan put his arms around her. "You did perfectly—exactly

what I wanted you to do. That's why I called you by your real name. I was hoping you would get the hint."

"That's right, you did," she said, starting to calm down. "So I didn't mess things up?"

"On the contrary, my little lamb," Marwan answered, taking on the Andrew Cooper persona, "I'd say you put on a jolly good show."

After wiping her eyes on Marwan's shirt, Dalia said, "What do we do now?"

"The first thing we need to find is a bathroom. After that, it's transportation, and hopefully we'll be at your parents' in time for dinner."

53

It wasn't difficult finding a car that they could steal—something Dalia protested against but Marwan justified by necessity. She stopped pestering him after he wrote down the license number, promising to use it to track down the car's owner and send an appropriate amount of money in payment for the "borrowed" vehicle. After a quick stop to trade license plates with another car, they were on their way north to Ma'an.

Midway through the two-hour drive, Marwan blurted out, "I can't believe this place! It is utterly and completely barren. It's just miles and miles of nothing but sand and rock."

Dalia nodded. "When I was a kid, my dad piled me and a bunch of the other kids onto a bus and drove us down here for a field trip."

"Wow, lucky you. A picnic in the desert."

Dalia ignored his remark. "It was during a vacation Bible school, and the lessons had been about the Israelites wandering around the wilderness for years and years. I remember him telling us to look around. He said, 'How could all those people have trekked through this wasteland? Where would they have gotten their food? Where would they have gotten their water?'

"Before we came down, I heard the stories and thought, 'It couldn't really be that bad.' But once I was here and saw just how much of a wilderness it really is, I understood how it made sense that God had to give them food from heaven and water from rocks. Without his help, they wouldn't have survived a week."

Marwan snorted. "For someone who doesn't want to be called pastor, you sure like giving sermons." He was getting weary of talking about Dalia's God and hearing her Bible stories. It seemed like every conversation they had now ended up there.

A tense silence filled the car.

"What? Are you just not going to talk now?"

Dalia turned to him and there were tears in her eyes again. "That was a rude thing to say. I was just trying to tell you about me growing up."

Marwan sighed. "You're right. It was very rude, and I apologize. I'm really uptight and nervous and tired. I shouldn't have said that."

He looked at Dalia for some kind of response, but she gave none.

"Please, you were saying . . . ," he encouraged her.

"What if the story has God in it?"

"Whatever you have to say, I want to hear. Please, Dalia. Finish your story."

She paused a moment before continuing more quietly than before. "I remember thinking that there was no way they could have survived without God's help. But then my dad reminded us of the Israelites' complaining. You know, 'We want to go back to Egypt. Maybe we were slaves, but at least we had meat to eat'—that kind of stuff. And I remember wondering how anyone could be so ungrateful. Here they were seeing God at work every day giving them food and water, and they were saying it wasn't enough."

Marwan found himself nodding. "I know what you mean. I sometimes think that if only I could see some miracle from God—some wild, crazy thing that could only have been done by him—that's all it would take for me to really believe. Here these people had that every day."

"But that's just the thing, Marwan. Things like that do happen every day. Think about what a miracle it is that we are still alive."

"Funny, but I thought it was my finger on that trigger," Marwan said bitterly, the burden of having taken two more lives still heavy on his shoulders.

"But could you have done that without God's help?"

"Let me get this straight. You're saying that your God helped me to plunge a knife into one man's throat and then put two bullets into the head of another."

"I don't know! I can't tell you how it all works."

"And that's just the thing that I struggle with—and please don't get upset or take this wrong," Marwan said, trying desperately to avoid another quarrel. "It just seems to me that so many Christians overspiritualize things, putting God into places he never really was."

"But don't you think it's also possible—and please don't take this wrong," Dalia countered, "that you underspiritualize things, keeping God out of places where he actually was at work."

Marwan had to laugh. "My, my, my, Miss Nour. Whether you want to believe it or not, I do think you have some of your father in you."

But Dalia didn't join him in his laughter. "That's where you're wrong. I think I'm much more like those complaining Israelites. Even though I see the evidence of God all around me, I still can't bring myself to truly believe. Or maybe I do believe, but I just can't bring myself to surrender to God."

Dalia's words resonated with Marwan. *Which is it that I'm struggling with? Is it belief or surrender? Because honestly, neither one sounds all that appealing to me.*

Marwan reached over and took her hand in his. They drove on in silence, both lost in their own thoughts.

It was getting dark when they reached the outskirts of Ma'an. Marwan could tell that Dalia was becoming increasingly nervous. Her voice quavered as she gave him directions to her parents' house, and the little jokes he told to lighten the mood received no response.

Finally she pointed to a tall, white-plastered apartment building. Marwan parked the car out front.

"I don't really want this car sitting out here when morning comes."

"Later tonight, I'll ask my dad if you can park it around back," she said, making no move to get out of the car. "So who am I going to introduce you as? I'd rather not lie to my parents."

"I know, but let's stick with Tariq Jameel. It's safer for them, and it's safer for us. Who knows if Marwan Accad has hit the news channels here yet?"

The sound of her tense breathing filled the darkening silence of the front seat. He reached over and pulled her close to himself.

"We're going to get through this; I promise you. And once this crisis has passed and everything is explained, we'll begin our new life together as Mr. and Mrs. Accad. Okay?"

"Okay," she answered, but Marwan could hear the doubt in her voice.

He kissed her on the side of the head. Then, after letting himself out of the car and opening Dalia's side for her, he put his arm around her and walked her to the front door.

54

THEY ENTERED THE BUILDING, climbed the stairs to the fifth floor, and stopped in front of the door. Dalia's hands were trembling. Marwan used his fingers to wipe the beads of perspiration off her forehead and upper lip.

"I love you," he whispered.

Dalia looked into his eyes, searching for the reassurance she so desperately needed. And when she found it, she whispered back, "I love you, too."

Marwan smiled, took a deep breath, and knocked on the door.

"Naheem," a woman's voice shouted from inside the apartment, "there's someone at the door. Are you expecting anyone?"

"No, I'm not. But I'm on the phone, honey. Can you get it?"

"Sure. One moment, one moment, I'm coming."

"That's my mother," Dalia said as quietly as she could. "Rima."

"And your father's name is Naheem?"

"Right."

Dalia's grip tightened on Marwan's hand. He noticed she wasn't wearing the engagement ring he had given her. He was about to say something, but there wasn't time. Besides, she was probably right, anyway. It was too soon to spring that kind of news on her parents. First they just had to survive the introductions.

The door opened and there was Rima Nour, standing face-to-face with a daughter she had not seen in years. She was in her midfifties, graying a bit and gaining some weight, but she was still quite attractive, and Marwan could see Dalia in her eyes.

Rima gasped at the sight of her long-lost daughter. Her hand shot to her mouth. It was if she had seen a ghost, and she seemed too shocked to speak. But after a moment, after blinking a few times, she finally asked, "Dalia, is that really you?"

"It's me, Mama. I'm home."

"Oh, my baby," Rima cried as she threw her arms around her daughter's neck. "God bless you, my daughter; God bless you. I missed you so much."

"I love you, Mama. I'm sorry for staying away so long."

"I love you, too, baby; I love you, too."

They both hugged and kissed and eventually dissolved into tears. Marwan took a step down the hall to give the two women some room. He was moved by the obvious love and affection these two had for each other, and seeing them together again after so long reminded him of how much he missed his own parents, especially his mother.

But the emotion he felt quickly dissolved into nerves. He felt like an interloper—out of place and unwelcome. After all, how would Rima react to him when she came up for air and noticed him standing there? Had she even seen him at all? Maybe she thought he was the taxi driver or some other hired help, waiting to be paid. What would she say when Marwan explained who he was and why he was there? What's more, how would Dalia's father react to seeing them both? When it came down to it, he still barely knew Dalia, much less her parents. But there was no point speculating. He was about to find out for sure one way or the other.

"Mama," Dalia said, sniffling back the tears. "Mama, there's someone I want you to meet."

Marwan put his best smile on.

Rima looked startled all over again. "Oh, my. I didn't realize . . ."

"It's okay," Dalia said, taking Marwan's hand. "I want you to meet Tariq Jameel. He's the reason I had to come home and see you after all these years."

"Really?" Rima said. "Well, then, Tariq Jameel, you are an answer to my prayers. Please, please, come in. I will make us all some tea."

"Thank you, Mrs. Nour," Marwan said with a smile. "You're very kind. I can see where Dalia gets both her gracious spirit and her beauty."

They entered the apartment and were removing their shoes when Dalia's father came around the corner.

"Rima, what's all the commotion? I could barely—"

Upon seeing Dalia, he stopped midsentence. His jaw dropped. His eyes began to well up with tears. And then, without saying a word, he held out his arms. Dalia rushed into them, and the two began to hug and weep.

"My little girl has come home," he sobbed. "My Dalia has come home at last. Thank you, Jesus. Thank you. You truly are a prayer-hearing and a prayer-answering God. Blessed be your name!"

Marwan felt a lump forming in his throat. If he had let himself, he would have burst into tears as well. He had not yet been in this home a full minute, and already he could feel a depth of love he had never experienced in his entire life.

Dalia's father would not stop kissing and hugging his daughter. Nor would he stop praising the name of Jesus. It was as if their daughter had suddenly come back to them from the grave, and in some ways, Marwan guessed she had.

"Dalia," her mother said after a few moments.

"Yes, Mama?" Dalia wiped the tears from her eyes to see her more clearly.

Rima glanced at Marwan and raised her eyebrows.

"Oh, of course." Dalia turned back to her father, who was busy wiping his eyes with a now-soaked handkerchief. "Daddy, I want you to meet someone who has become very special to me. This is Tariq Jameel. He insisted that I come home and see you again. I wanted to, but I was a little . . . well . . . scared, I guess. I wasn't sure how you'd react at seeing me again. I guess I wasn't sure just how mad you are at me. But Tariq said that nothing is more important than family. He offered to escort me and make sure I got here safely."

Pastor Nour looked deep into Marwan's eyes. Marwan braced himself. But as he searched the older man's eyes, the anger and suspicion and condemnation he expected to see simply weren't there. Instead, he saw gratitude and love.

His surprise was compounded when the pastor stepped forward and wrapped him in a deep embrace. Marwan hadn't experienced an older man hugging him since his father died. Instantly, he was transported back to that final day of his dad's life, that final hug, that last "I love you." Tears began streaming down his face as he held tightly to this stranger.

"I do not yet know you, young man," the pastor said as he pulled away, holding Marwan's arms. "But I can see that you have a great heart. You have given me a great gift today. You have brought my daughter back to me at long last, and for that I am eternally grateful. May God richly bless you for that, my son. Now, please, you will eat with us tonight. You must stay with us also. Our home is your home. You are most welcome here."

"Thank you, sir," was all that Marwan could choke out. He turned to Dalia, who had a huge grin on her face. All in all, this couldn't possibly have gone any better. But at the same time he was smiling, he knew his problems were far from resolved. He was still wanted for murder, and there were still people out to kill him. And now he had brought that to these good people's house.

Smile while you can because there are still a lot of tears in your future. And not only in your future, but in the future of Dalia and her wonderful family.

55

Inspector Goddard sat across a small table from Ramy Accad in a nondescript interrogation room at the central police headquarters in downtown Beirut.

He smoked a cigarette but offered none to Ramy. He drank freshly brewed coffee but offered Ramy none of this, either. Instead, he waited as a technician hooked up the young man to a polygraph machine. *I have to get as much information out of this guy in as short a time as is humanly possible. And if he gives me any trouble, I have to be prepared to make his life miserable.*

When the technician was ready, Goddard pressed a button on an audio recorder.

"Once again, so there are no misunderstandings, you realize that you are under oath, do you not?" Goddard began.

Ramy shrugged.

"Yes or no answers, please—and speak clearly so your answers can be properly recorded."

"Fine—yes, I'm under oath."

"Very well. Let us begin. Is your name Ramy Accad?"

"You know it is."

"Yes or no."

"Then yes."

"Are you the co-owner of Accad & Associates?"

"Of course."

"Yes or no answers, Mr. Accad."

"Yep," Ramy said belligerently.

"Is this an executive security firm?"

"It isn't a beauty salon."

Goddard slammed his hand on the table. "Perhaps you do not appreciate the gravity of this situation, Mr. Accad. I can throw you in jail for refusing to answer my questions. And I can throw you in jail for lying to me. So a little less attitude and a lot more cooperation, you got it?"

Ramy shrugged again.

"Now, does your firm provide security to executives working in and around the Middle East?"

"Yes."

"Is your partner also your brother, Marwan Accad?"

"Yes."

"Was your brother hired by Rafeeq Ramsey to investigate the murder of his daughter and the kidnapping of his wife?"

"Yes."

"Was your firm paid an initial retainer of five hundred thousand euros, plus expenses, for this work?"

Ramy looked startled.

Gotcha, Goddard thought.

"How did you—?"

"Yes or no answers, Mr. Accad—and I remind you, you're under oath."

"Yes," Ramy said reluctantly.

"Was Marwan in any way involved in the murder or kidnapping of the Ramsey women?"

"Ridiculous!"

"Mr. Accad . . ."

"No!"

"Did he try to blackmail the Ramsey family?"

"No!"

"Is he currently trying to blackmail the Ramsey family?"

"No!"

"Really?" Goddard said, getting up and pacing about the room. "If that is true, then let me ask you this: did your brother know on the day of Rafeeq Ramsey's murder what country Claudette Ramsey was in?"

Ramy winced. Seconds passed, but he did not answer. He simply closed his eyes.

"Well?" Goddard pressed. "Did he?"

Again, Ramy said nothing.

Standing right behind Ramy, Goddard whispered in his ear, "Don't play games with me, Mr. Accad. Cooperate or go to prison—and we'll seize all your assets. It's that simple."

Then, stepping away, he said in a voice loud enough for the recorder to pick up, "I ask you again, on the day Mr. Ramsey was killed, did your brother know what country Mrs. Ramsey was in?"

"Yes."

"Was that country Brazil?"

Again Ramy looked startled by the information Goddard had compiled.

"Yes," he said hesitantly.

"Did he have a photo of Mrs. Ramsey in a bank in São Paulo?"

"Yes."

"Did he know the bank account that Mrs. Ramsey was accessing?"

"By that point he did, yes, but—"

"Just yes or no, Mr. Accad."

"It's not that simple!"

"I want a yes or no!"

"Then yes!"

"Do you currently have more than a dozen paid operatives of Accad & Associates in the mountains outside São Paulo, Brazil?"

Ramy said nothing. Goddard knew he had him rattled. His intel was good. His sources were right. He was about to crack Ramy like a piñata.

"I'm waiting, Mr. Accad."

"Yes, we do."

"Are these men carrying weapons?"

"Yes."

"Did these men call you this morning and ask you what you wanted done with Mrs. Ramsey?"

The look of shock on Ramy's face was priceless.

"You don't understand, I—"

"Is that what they said when they called you? 'What do you want us to do with her?'"

A look of realization appeared on Ramy's face. *You can almost see the lightbulb over his head,* Goddard thought with a smile.

"You tapped my phones."

"That is correct. Now, is that what they said?"

"Yes."

"And did you say, 'Nothing yet. It's complicated. I'll get back to you soon'?"

"Yes, I did."

"Mr. Accad, did you and your brother mastermind the kidnapping of Claudette Ramsey?"

"No," Ramy said emphatically.

"Did you do it on your own?"

"No."

"Really? But you know where she is?"

"Yes."

"And your men won't let her leave the house she's in, right?"

"True."

"And I'm supposed to believe that you and your brother are innocent of all this?"

"One hundred percent," Ramy answered with venom in his voice.

"That's getting very difficult to do, Mr. Accad," Goddard said, sitting down and pretending to leaf through some notes. "Let me ask you something else. Was your brother in Casablanca, Morocco, last week?"

"Yes."

"Did he visit a man named Kadeen al-Wadhi?"

"Yes."

"And is Mr. al-Wadhi now dead and his family missing?"

"Yes, but there's no way Marwan did that! He loved Kadeen! You've got the wrong—"

"Silence!" Goddard shouted. "You will answer my questions and follow my instructions or you will remain in jail until you are prepared to do so! Do you understand?"

Ramy stared hard at Goddard, hatred in his eyes.

"Is your brother still in Egypt?" Goddard asked.

Ramy sat there defiantly, saying nothing.

"Is your brother living in Cairo?" Goddard asked again.

Again Ramy said nothing.

"Did your brother go down to Alexandria?"

Silence.

"Has your brother left Egypt and gone to another country?" Goddard pressed.

But Ramy adamantly refused to answer.

Okay, I'm done with this! Time to pull out the big guns. Goddard threw down his notes and jumped up.

Leaning over so that his face was only inches from Ramy's, he said, "Your only brother is wanted for murder, Mr. Accad. And you know what? We're going to find him. And when we find him, it's very likely that we'll shoot him on sight. So if you've got information that might keep your brother alive, I suggest you cooperate with me. Until then, you're going to jail."

56

Naheem Nour was a large man with big eyes, big hands, and a big laugh. That laugh was helping Marwan to slowly relax.

While Rima disappeared out the front door to do some quick shopping for a now-expanded dinner menu, her husband showed Marwan around the small apartment. It was a simple, modest home with three bedrooms, a small kitchen, and a large combined living room and dining area with enough couches and chairs for at least fifteen to twenty guests. The walls were stacked from floor to ceiling with more books than Marwan had ever seen outside of a university library, and everywhere there were picture frames filled with snapshots of various family and church events over the years.

Naheem sat them down on one of the deep, comfortable couches and pulled out an album of photos of Dalia from when she was a baby up to her high school graduation. Some of the pictures caused shrieks of protest from her and laughter from the two men. But one thing was clear to Marwan as he watched Dalia grow. *This woman has been beautiful from the time she was born!*

A second album showed them pictures of Dalia's brother, Elias, who was now a fighter pilot currently receiving advanced training with the Royal Air Force in England. Marwan could feel Dalia's mood change as she began to realize just how much she had missed by being away.

"I'm sorry I was gone for so long, Daddy. I'm sorry I didn't answer your letters or e-mails. I don't know. . . . I just . . ." Dalia began to cry again. This time, though, it was not out of joy at being reunited with her parents. These tears came from a heart broken by her own guilt and sorrow.

Naheem put his thick arm around her and pulled her close to him. "That's all behind us," he said as she wept into his chest. "Do you remember the story of the Prodigal Son? Remember the joy of the father when he saw his boy coming down the road? What did he do?"

Between sniffles, Dalia answered, "Ran to him."

"And if I had known you were coming, you would have been amazed at how fast I could have gotten this old body to move. Coming home is not a time for sorrow and regrets. It's a time for forgiveness and feasting. You've already received the forgiveness, and as soon as your mother is home, the feasting will begin!"

Marwan began feeling out of place again and wanted to give this father and daughter a little privacy, so he said, "Pastor Nour, I know that this breaks all rules of hospitality, but I could really use some coffee. Would you mind if . . . ?"

Naheem began to get up. "My apologies! Let me get it."

But Marwan was up quicker. "Please, sir, allow me. This way you two can spend some time together, and I can impress you with what might potentially be the best cup of coffee you've ever tasted—apart from your wife's, of course."

The pastor laughed. "Okay, I'm convinced. Besides, I've already told you that my house is your house, so I suppose that extends to the kitchen, also."

"Thank you, sir," he said as Dalia mouthed a thank-you to him.

Marwan went to the kitchen and put a kettle of water on. It didn't take long for him to find the coffee, and he deeply inhaled the aroma of the beans. *It's not going to be too difficult to make good coffee out of this.*

As he prepared the beans, he thought through the last hour. He was amazed at the reaction of Dalia's parents. After so many years of neglect, still they instantly forgave and accepted their daughter back—no questions, no complaints, no I-told-you-sos.

Then he brings in that Prodigal Son story. He wasn't sure why he knew it—probably from another in-flight magazine or motivational book he had read over the years. And although the details were sketchy, he remembered a kid taking his dad's money, wasting it all on wine and women, and there was something about pigs; then he went home to his father, who welcomed him with open arms. The story was supposed to show the love of God and the power of forgiveness.

Well, that's great for him, but that son just wasted his dad's money, got drunk, and slept around a bit. I'm guilty of two out of those three. But what he didn't do was kill people. He never shot a man between the eyes. He never cut a man's throat. Some things are just beyond forgiveness, even for God.

He arranged cups on a tray and filled them with the thick, hot liquid. As he was walking to the living room, the front door opened, causing him to jump and almost spill the coffee. Rima, who was returning from her shopping, jumped too and dropped one of her bags.

"I'm so sorry," Marwan said, sticking his foot out to keep a cabbage from rolling away. He bent down to pick the vegetable up but realized he had no hands to lift it.

"Oh no," Rima answered with a laugh as she squatted down and retrieved the bag's contents. "It's my fault."

When she noticed what Marwan was carrying, a mortified look crossed her face. "Did my husband ask you to . . . ? Naheem Nour! How could you have—?"

"Please, Mrs. Nour. It's not like that," Marwan interrupted. "I asked to do it. I wanted to give them some time alone."

Rima looked at Marwan for a moment, then nodded, although she still seemed only half-satisfied with that answer. Leaving the groceries by the front door, she took the tray from his hands and shooed him back to the couch with the others.

A minute or two later, she reappeared with the cups nicely arranged on a much newer and bigger tray. Along with the coffee, she had also placed several small bowls with nuts and dried fruits. With a chastising look at her husband, she served her guests. After passing her hand softly along her daughter's cheek, she retreated to the kitchen.

"I didn't mean to get you in trouble," Marwan said to Naheem.

The older man just laughed.

Marwan leaned forward to grab a handful of nuts, while the other two sipped their coffee. He realized that it had been hours since he and Dalia had eaten, and he was famished.

"Well, you were only wrong about one thing." Naheem held his cup toward Marwan and said in a conspiratorial whisper, "This coffee might actually be better than Rima's."

Now it was Marwan's turn to laugh.

Naheem took another sip, then put down his cup and slapped his hand on Marwan's thigh. "Well, Mr. Tariq Jameel, my daughter has been telling me a little about who you are and how you met. I have to admit, though, I'm still not totally getting what it is you do, possibly because it seems that Dalia is not even sure."

Oh, great, here it comes. The Grand Inquisition.

"I'm a computer consultant, sir," he offered.

"And this computer consulting takes you all over the world—Europe, Egypt, Lebanon, the Far East?

"Yes, sir. You see, I help banks and insurance companies and other multinationals develop security systems to safeguard their mainframes from hackers, viruses, Trojan horses, that kind of thing."

Dalia's father laughed out loud. "Well, God bless you, Tariq. I have no idea what you just said. But at least it sounds like something that provides a decent living."

"It does indeed, sir."

"You may be more of a godsend to me than you know. Every time I start up my computer, it seems to be taking longer and longer. When it does come up, I get all these different things popping up on my screen for programs I never remember purchasing."

Thankfully, the conversation seemed to be going in a direction that would keep him away from questions along the lines of *"What are your intentions with my daughter?"* Marwan said, "A lot of that has to do with things that have attached themselves to your computer when you download something. Do you want me to take a look at it?" He began to stand.

But Naheem caught his shoulder with a surprisingly strong hand and sat him back down. "We have plenty of time for that later. You sound like you've got a bit of a Lebanese accent. Were you born in Beirut?"

Internally Marwan flinched. *How much can I tell him about my past without putting him and Mrs. Nour in danger? It seems that the less they know about me the better. But it's getting harder and harder to lie to these good people.*

Marwan knew he'd made a mistake coming here. If the people looking for him were able to trace him to Kadeen, they certainly would be able to track him to the Nours. *What an amateur mistake! I let my heart overrule my brain!*

But then he saw Dalia, sitting under her father's arm with her hand laid gently on his side. That's when he knew there had been no other choice. This was meant to be. It was almost as if the force drawing them had simply been too powerful to resist.

Let's just hope that same power can protect them if the bullets start flying.

57

When Marwan began speaking, he was almost surprised that what came out was the truth. "Yes, sir. I grew up in Beirut in the eighties. It was kind of a scary time to be a kid, as you can imagine, with the civil war and all. Everybody, Christians and Muslims, killed each other in the name of religion, each claiming God was on their side. And I hope this won't offend you, sir, but the whole thing kind of soured me on religion. In my neighborhood, people who called themselves Christians were constantly blowing people up and destroying everything in sight. They weren't the only ones, of course, but it all left a bad taste in my mouth."

Dalia's head lifted up from her dad's chest, and Marwan could see a concerned look in her eyes. But he kept going.

"Because I grew up in a 'Christian' home," Marwan said,

air-quoting the word *Christian*, "I pretty much had to sympathize with the Christian fighters. But I kept away from the fighting. To be honest, I hated them all—Christians and Muslims alike. Which side do you choose when they are both equally evil?"

"That's an impossible choice for a young man to make," Naheem said.

"Then, when I was a teenager, I watched as a car bomb took my parents from my brother and me—a bomb placed by a Christian," he said angrily. He didn't know why he was working himself up so much, pouring his heart out to someone who, until an hour ago, was a total stranger. "So you can see where I'm coming from when I tell you with the utmost respect, sir, that although I greatly respect you as a person, I have no use for your beliefs."

Dalia stared at him with horror. Marwan wondered if she was seeing all her hopes for a happy extended family flying out the window. He gave her a look intended to say, *What can I tell you? I have to be honest!*

"I'm going to go see if I can help Mom," Dalia said, getting up. Apparently her stress at the conversation was getting to be too much.

But for all the shock Dalia was feeling, Naheem just smiled a sad smile. "I'm so sorry for your loss, son. No child should see their parents taken like that. No child should *have* their parents taken like that. But please believe me when I tell you that those people who did that to your mother and father were not Christians."

"Well, that would be news to them."

"Yes, I'm sure it would be. But just because someone calls

himself a Christian, it doesn't necessarily make it true." He leaned forward, plucked a nut out of one of the bowls on the table, and held it up to Marwan. "If I told you I was a pistachio, what would you say?"

"You're crazy."

"Why? What if I really believed myself to be a pistachio? What right do you have to say I'm not?"

"Well, because it's obvious you're not a nut—although it would be quite possible that you're nuts," he said with a laugh. "But I guess I would just say that you and a pistachio are so completely different that it would be absurd if you called yourself one."

"Precisely! Jesus said that if we were truly his followers—true Christians—we would obey him. And what were the two things he told us to do? Love God and love others. Now, when you think about what those people did to your parents, how is it any more absurd for me to call myself a pistachio than it is for them to call themselves Christians?" And with that, Naheem peeled back the shell and popped the nut into his smiling mouth.

"Fair enough. It just seems like in all of history, religion and violence have gone hand in hand. That's why I decided long ago I wanted nothing to do with religion."

"How interesting. I remember making that very same decision."

"What made you decide to come back to it?"

Naheem gave him a surprised look. "Back to it? Why would I ever want to go back to it?"

"But . . . I mean . . . well, aren't you the pastor of a church?"

"Yes, I am," Naheem said, taking a bite of a dried apricot. "But at my church, we don't practice religion. Instead, we rejoice in a relationship. We don't preach Christianity; we preach and worship Christ. And trust me, son, there's a huge difference."

Marwan sat silently, trying to process what the pastor had said and wondering at the feelings welling up inside him. This man was single-handedly breaking down all the walls he had built against the church. He was redefining what it meant to be a follower of Christ.

"Tell you what," Naheem said, rising to his feet with two audible pops of his knees, "you look like you've got a little bit you need to consider. In the meantime, why don't I show you that computer?"

Marwan gratefully followed him down the hall to one of the bedrooms that doubled as an office, happy to finally be facing a situation he felt he could actually handle.

58

GODDARD WAS SITTING in a small coffee shop in downtown Beirut when his phone rang. He checked the caller ID, then answered it anyway.

"Any progress with Accad's brother?" the Skeleton demanded without so much as a greeting.

"Some," Goddard said, pushing away the plate with the small pastry. Talking with Lemieux always made him lose his appetite.

"Did he break?"

"No."

"He didn't tell you where Marwan Accad is?" Lemieux pressed.

"No."

"What did he give you?"

"Very little. So I threw him in jail."

"You did *what*?"

"I threw him in jail. What did you expect me to do?" Goddard shot back, pushing away from his table and walking outside to avoid listening ears. The night was well lit by streetlights and signs, the air just beginning to cool.

"Make him give us his brother, you fool," Lemieux retorted.

"That's why I put him in jail. I don't think a man like Ramy Accad is going to want to spend much time in a Beirut prison."

"And I don't think you give these Accad brothers enough credit. They're smart, they're dangerous, and they're fiercely loyal to each other. If you want any information from Ramy, you're going to have to be more forceful with him."

Goddard wasn't sure he was really hearing what he thought he was hearing. A car with its stereo's bass thumping enough to shake its windows was slowly driving by. He waited until it passed before he said quietly, "Are you telling me to torture him?"

"No, you idiot! How dare you accuse me of that! What I am saying is that you are in Beirut of all places, where the rules of interrogation are different. If things happened to get physical, no one would ever know."

"So you are telling me to torture him."

"No! I'm telling you to get from him the information that we need. And if you are too squeamish to provide the proper encouragement, I'm sure you can find someone around there who is not."

The city was noisy with horns honking and people talking

and laughing, but an icy silence filled the line as Goddard worked through Lemieux's words.

Finally the inspector spoke. "You said you made some progress, but it sounds like you've got nothing. Which is it?"

"I did make some progress," Goddard answered, trying to put aside his rapidly growing disgust for his superior.

"Let's hear it."

"We tapped Ramy's satellite phone account."

"At last, an intelligent move. What did you discover?"

Ignoring the slight, Goddard continued, "It turns out he's got a dozen armed men in the mountains outside of São Paulo. Guess who they're holding?"

The line was silent.

"Inspector, did you hear what I just said?"

But Lemieux said nothing.

"It's Mrs. Ramsey. They've got Claudette Ramsey," Goddard said, dropping his bombshell and waiting for the reaction.

But there was none. The line was still silent.

"I've just dispatched one of my teams there to arrest them all and help rescue Mrs. Ramsey," Goddard continued. "They're coordinating with the Brazilian authorities even as we speak."

Goddard waited for something—anything—but Lemieux said nothing.

"Are you still there, Inspector?" he asked.

"Yes, I'm here."

"Do you understand what I'm saying? This could prove the Accads' involvement in the kidnapping. Forty-eight hours from now, Mrs. Ramsey will be safely back in Monte Carlo, and I'll be able to debrief her about everything. We have

Marwan Accad dead to rights. So let me congratulate you, sir, on being right about him all along. Can I expect you to join us in Monte Carlo?"

"I'll have to get back to you on that," Lemieux said absently. Then the phone went dead.

Goddard stood on the street trying to figure out what had just happened. That conversation had definitely gone in a direction he hadn't planned. He didn't know what exactly it meant, but he did know that the alarm bells that had been ringing for a long time about Lemieux were rapidly increasing in volume.

59

For the next hour, Marwan deleted files and restructured the computer's start-up.

"Please be more careful about the programs you download, Pastor Nour," he said. "If you didn't have such good antivirus software, your whole computer would be compromised by now. Also, I've installed an anti-spyware program to keep out all that extra stuff that finds its way onto your hard drive without you even knowing it."

"Thank you." Naheem patted Marwan on the back. "You have blessed me greatly, but you may have blessed my computer even more."

Rima's voice rang through the apartment, calling them to dinner. It was all Marwan could do to not run to the table.

The smells had been gradually filling the home, and now the whole place smelled like an Arab spice market.

Marwan pulled out the chair for Rima, then did the same for Dalia, all the while noticing the amused look on Naheem's face. Then Dalia's father held out his hands, and everyone else followed suit, Marwan only slightly belatedly. Once everyone was linked together, Naheem prayed.

"Our Lord, you have blessed us today in a way we could never have imagined. You brought our daughter home. You truly are a God who answers prayer. Thank you for watching over her while she was gone. Thank you for never letting her out of your strong, loving grasp. Thank you . . ."

As Naheem prayed, Marwan couldn't help but notice the difference between the two hands he was holding—Rima, with her soft, cool fingers; and Naheem, with his calloused, scratchy palms. *Pastoring isn't the only thing this man has ever done. His hands didn't get that way sitting in an office reading the Bible.*

Marwan chanced a look around and was surprised to see Dalia with her eyes closed, nodding agreement to her father's words. It amazed him how natural it looked on her. *I guess it's not that strange that she's praying; it's just that I've never seen her do it before.* Still, he couldn't help but feel a bit of a distance growing between them as he watched her connecting with a God he had never truly met.

Finally, and mercifully for Marwan's raging appetite, the prayer ended. Instantly Rima was out of her seat to begin running dishes of food to and from the kitchen. The food turned out to be as good as it smelled, and over the course of the next hour, Marwan partook of everything set before him—and a lot of it.

The dinner conversation revolved mostly around Dalia catching up on family and on the happenings in the town of Ma'an. Her brother, Elias, was excelling in the Air Force and was about to be promoted to captain. He was interested in an English girl and was apparently considering bringing her to meet his parents on his next leave. Naheem said he wasn't too sure about the morals of those English girls, and he received a chastising glare from Rima in response.

Dalia asked about friends and neighbors and church members. She was sad when she heard of the deaths. She was amazed at the marriages. She oohed and aahed when she heard of the births. As Marwan watched her, he could tell that she was back home where she belonged.

What does that mean for me? How does that affect our future together? He shook his head. *And why am I worrying about a year or five years or ten years down the road, when I don't even know if I'll survive into next week?*

Already feeling he had divulged a bit too much about himself earlier, Marwan deflected most questions addressed to him by asking about Dalia's childhood or Naheem's church, subjects both parents were all too eager to talk about.

By the time the dishes started to be cleared away, everyone was full and Marwan, particularly, was exhausted. Feeling unable to keep his eyes open another minute, he asked if he could be excused to bed. Dalia led him to her brother's room, which happened to be the same one he was in earlier with the computer.

"So what do you think?" Dalia asked.

"About . . . ?"

"About my parents, of course."

"I'm wondering why you ever left this place."

Dalia sat on the bed. "I've been spending the evening wondering that too. I mean, I know why I left. But all my reasons now seem so juvenile, so petty. It was a stupid decision to run off and a stupid decision to stay away."

"Why *did* you stay away so long?" Marwan asked, sitting next to her on the bed.

"I don't know. I think that after a while—you know, after so many ignored messages and screened calls and deleted e-mails—I guess I couldn't face them again. I knew I was in the wrong, and I figured they would hate me as much as I hated myself."

Marwan nodded as he took her hand. Then, rubbing her finger where the cheap Egyptian ring had sat, he asked, "Are you regretting any other decisions?"

"Not at all," she answered, giving him a long kiss on his cheek. "It's just . . . I don't think I'm quite ready to tell yet. I mean, it's obvious they know about 'us.' They just don't know how 'us' we are."

"I can understand that. You let me know when it's time, and I'll talk to your father. Is that a deal?"

"It's a deal." Dalia got up from the bed. "I'm going to go help my mom clean up. She said you're welcome to any of my brother's clothes. He's a little bigger than you are, but they should work."

"By the way, how did you explain us arriving without any bags?"

Dalia smiled. "I told her how terrible it is to fly anyone other than British Air. Those idiots at Royal Jordanian lost our bags." Her smile faded. "I guess that's just one more lie I'm going to have to answer to them for."

Marwan got up and put his arms around her. As he held her tightly, he said, "You're a good woman, Dalia Nour. Never forget that. Sure, you've made mistakes, but your parents have forgiven you, and . . . and you know that God has forgiven you too."

Dalia's smile returned as she looked at Marwan. "Look which one of us is becoming the pastor," she said before kissing him.

"I love you, Dalia."

"I love you, too."

When they'd separated for the night, Marwan raided Elias's closet and found a pair of shorts and a shirt to sleep in. Then, after washing up, he climbed into bed.

Although he was so tired, he knew there was no way he would be able to sleep. There were too many dangers to prepare for, too many contingencies to plan against. Somehow he had to find a way to keep these good people safe, to direct the hunt for him away from them. Things like that were too important to put off until the following morning.

The next thing he knew, he awoke with a start, looked at the bedside clock, and saw that it was six in the morning.

60

THE DREAM had been similar to the one Marwan had been having since leaving Kadeen's house, except this time Naheem was the one who was killed backing him up, and Dalia and Rima were the ones leaning against the door.

Only one day, he thought as he climbed out of bed. *One day to figure out my next steps, and then I'm gone.*

He listened at the bedroom door but didn't hear any movement in the apartment. Putting on a pair of Elias's running shoes, he crept from the bedroom and out of the apartment. Once downstairs, he set off on a jog around the town. The sun was just coming up, and people were beginning to emerge from their homes. Smoke from early-morning cooking fires hung in the cool air and reminded him of walking to school in Beirut when the power was out due to the fighting.

He wound his way through the streets, sometimes getting a wave from people he passed, sometimes having to speed up to avoid an overzealous stray dog. By the time he arrived back at the apartment forty-five minutes later, he was feeling refreshed and ready to face the day.

Quietly, he opened the door, then tiptoed to Elias's room. When he arrived, he saw that Naheem was already there working on the computer.

"Oh, excuse me, sir," he said, trying to back out. "Don't let me disturb you."

"No, come in, come in," Naheem said, turning off the monitor. "Please, have a seat."

Marwan obeyed, planting himself on the stool that the pastor had motioned to.

"How was your run?"

"It felt great."

"I'm envious. I may not look it now, but I used to be quite the runner when I was younger. Then my knees went out on me, and that part of my life ended. It's not a fun thing getting old."

Marwan nodded.

Naheem leaned forward and stared at him for a long while—right in the face, barely blinking. After several uncomfortable seconds, he sat back in his chair. "Can you tell me what you are doing here with my daughter, Mr. Accad?"

"I . . ." But that's as far as Marwan got. *Mr. Accad?* He felt like he had been hit in the solar plexus. He tried to breathe in, but it felt like his body was frozen.

"I hope you don't mind me calling you Mr. Accad. *Marwan* seems so informal, seeing as I hardly know you." Naheem's gaze was hard.

"How . . . how long have you known?" Marwan managed to stammer.

"Pretty much since you first arrived. We don't have a television here at the apartment—Rima hates the things—but I do keep a little one hidden in my office at the church. Since yesterday, your face has been spread all over the news channels. And then, while you were gone, I read this." Naheem turned the computer monitor on. There, on the front page of the Al Jazeera Web page, was Marwan's face with a caption stating that he was wanted for numerous murders, including the recent slaying of billionaire Rafeeq Ramsey.

Marwan put his head in his hands. *I've done it! I've brought my problems to this family! My nightmare is going to come true—again!*

"I never meant to bring you and your wife into this," he said.

"You do realize how empty those words sound as you sit here in my apartment."

Marwan linked his hands behind his head. "Yes, sir, I do. I came against my better judgment," he said to the ground, not able to look Naheem in the eye. "It's just that it was so obvious that Dalia needed to see you and her mother again. I was willing to risk anything to make that happen."

"Including our lives?"

Marwan didn't answer. He just kept staring at the ground.

Then he felt a hand rest on his shoulder. For being so big, it was surprisingly light. "Marwan, son, look at me."

Slowly Marwan raised his head.

"You did the right thing," Naheem said with a soft smile. "To have my daughter back in our home, I would have given my life ten times over. And to have seen her late last night on her knees recommitting herself to God, I would have given a hundred lives."

Naheem shifted his hand from Marwan's shoulder to the back of his head and gave it a gentle shake to emphasize his words. "You will, of course, explain everything, and I will listen. But first, I want to say thank you, my son, for giving me back my daughter. You have given me the most wonderful gift. And if a little trouble should follow you—so be it."

61

Goddard got up early. Although it had been only a few hours since he had fallen asleep, he knew that there was no chance he would get any more rest. Questions filled his mind, and he needed answers. He quickly grabbed some bread and cheese and coffee from the complimentary breakfast adjacent the lobby, then began walking the six blocks to Beirut's central police station. As he traveled the already-busy streets, his mind raced.

What if Marwan Accad isn't guilty of trying to blackmail Rafeeq Ramsey? What if instead of kidnapping Claudette Ramsey, Accad and his brother were just trying to find her, as they claimed? What if Claudette Ramsey wasn't ever really a hostage to begin with? Is it possible she engineered the whole thing and was hiding out in Brazil? And what if Accad uncovered evidence of this—and of her plot against her fabulously wealthy husband, who showed no signs of a convenient imminent death—and was helping Rafeeq Ramsey crack the case? And what if Claudette and her accomplices, whoever they were, found out what Accad knew and decided to strike first?

This scenario, far-fetched though it seemed, could explain the way events had played out. And every other possibility seemed to fall apart as soon as any serious examination took place.

Even the accepted scenario of Marwan Accad acting alone or Marwan and Ramy Accad together planning the kidnapping had more logical holes than the Swiss cheese he was currently eating on the heel of a baguette. *But this is Lemieux's theory and, as such, is officially the gospel truth. Why is he holding on to Accad's guilt so tightly?*

The scenario of Claudette's being involved could certainly explain Ramsey's assassination. It would also explain the car bombing and the assassins at Le Méridien and in Saint Michel. But how would it explain why Accad was on the run instead of cooperating with the authorities? How would it explain the murder of Kadeen al-Wadhi?

The Lebanese police were preparing Ramy for the polygraph when Goddard entered the interrogation room, but he waved them off. Ramy glared at him as he walked in, looking like he would just as soon put a knife in him as answer his questions. *Two can play at this game,* Goddard thought as he stared back. By the time he sat across from Ramy, the pair looked like two prizefighters giving each other the stare down as they listened to the ring instructions.

"No wires this time?" Ramy asked.

"Not necessary. I hope you've thought about our previous conversation," Goddard began.

"Nothing but."

"May I assume, then, that you've decided to help save your brother's life and tell me where he is?"

"No. Instead, what you may assume is that hell will freeze over before I help you in any way to find Marwan."

Goddard's cell phone rang. He quickly silenced it.

"So you're content for some other country's police, who will not show the same kind of restraint as we will, to put a bullet in your brother's head."

Ramy let out a derisive laugh. "No, you imbecile. I'm trying to prevent any information that I give to you from getting to the people who are trying to kill him. I hate to break it to you, Monsieur Detective, but you've got leaks in your department big enough to flood this whole city!"

"What do you know about my department? I will not have an accessory to murder impugning the name of . . ." Goddard stopped as he saw the satisfied smile spread across Ramy's face. He had reacted exactly as the man had hoped he would.

His cell phone went off again.

"Phone's ringing, Detective. Maybe it's the mole calling to pump you for more information."

Goddard stood from the table with such force that his chair clattered over backward. *Another amateur move,* he chastised himself as he pulled the phone from his pocket.

When he saw that it was DuVall, he answered. "I told you not to disturb me while I'm—What?"

He paced the room as he listened for a while, then said,

"And where was he? . . . How did he know her? . . . Okay. . . . Okay. . . . This isn't a game show! Just tell me!"

Goddard suddenly stopped. He picked up the chair he had tipped over and sat in it with the phone in one hand and his head in the other. "I knew it! That makes perfect sense. And when exactly was it sent? . . . Send me copies of everything over my phone. And great work, Colette."

Goddard hung up the phone and waited for DuVall's message to come through. His mind was going a mile a minute as he processed his new information. *Could this really be true? If it is, we've got a long and dangerous road ahead of us!*

62

Marwan shook his head. "Pastor Nour, you need to understand that it could be more than just a little bit of trouble. One of my closest friends took me in, and now Kadeen is dead because he helped me."

"I'm sorry for that," Naheem said. "But understand, that was back when you were fighting this battle alone. You're not alone anymore."

Marwan was having a hard time grasping this all. This man's attitude was totally foreign to any experience he'd had in the past. "But why . . . ? What makes you think I'm worth risking your life for? I mean, come on, you don't even know me. How do you know that I didn't do all the things that the police are accusing me of? How do you know that I won't be the one to harm you and your family?"

Naheem laughed. "Listen, my daughter isn't always a great judge of character, but she's not that bad. Besides, I always have this." He pulled a SIG Sauer P226 from the small of his back and placed it on the desk.

Once the shock at seeing the weapon wore off, Marwan couldn't help but join in the older man's laughter. "Dalia said you were ex-military. I should have expected you'd have a weapon or two lying around here."

"Unfortunately, there's just the one. But she's a beauty, eh?"

"That she is," Marwan said appreciatively. "And I suppose you setting it on the desk between us is designed to show that you trust me not to harm you."

Naheem gave a sideways nod of his head.

"Well, thank you, sir. I do appreciate the confidence. Although, I do have to admit that the message loses a bit of its power when it's made with an unloaded gun."

Naheem looked at Marwan with surprise on his face. Then his whole body started shaking, his face broke into a huge smile, and like lava from an exploding volcano, his laughter burst forth and filled the entire apartment. Soon they both were in hysterics.

Dalia, who looked like she'd been woken up by the sound, burst through the open door. Her jaw dropped open as she saw her father and her fiancé doubled over, laughing, with a gun sitting on a desk between them.

Finally starting to calm down, Naheem managed to say, "Go, please, Dalia. Everything is okay. And close the door behind you."

Dalia looked at Marwan for guidance, and he nodded his

agreement. Visibly frustrated at being left out, she turned and closed the door hard behind her, which started the two men laughing all over again.

When he could, Naheem asked, "How did you know, O wise one?"

"It's the sound. To the trained ear, a loaded SIG sounds very different from an empty one."

Naheem nodded appreciatively. "Then I suppose I owe you an apology and an explanation."

"Please—you owe me neither. I would have done the same thing."

"But I feel I must explain. What happens to me—" he shrugged—"do to me what you will. However, when it comes to my wife and daughter, that's where I feel I must use all means of defense."

"You draw a fine line, Pastor Nour."

"Sometimes that's all the line you need."

"But isn't killing killing? Doesn't the Bible say not to kill? It seems contradictory to me that a man of God such as yourself should resort to harming others rather than just trusting God to protect you and your family."

"First of all, the Bible says 'Do not murder,' not 'Do not kill,'" Naheem said. As he talked, he pulled a loaded clip out of his pants pocket. He expertly ejected the empty one from the pistol, slid the full one in, and chambered a round before placing the gun back on the desk with the grip facing Marwan. "I believe I am fully justified in using force to protect those that God has placed under my care."

Marwan took the gun, ensured that the safety was on, then

tucked it into his waistband. "If that's the case, let's talk about how we're going to protect all of our lives."

"Son, first I'd like to talk about how we can protect your soul."

63

Ramy shifted impatiently, but Goddard ignored him. He needed to see this confirmation before he acted on it in any way.

Finally his phone beeped. He opened the message and read the attached documents. All showed exactly what DuVall had said they would. Closing his phone, he turned to Ramy.

"Your brother's using the alias of Tariq Jameel, correct?"

The stunned look on Ramy's face was confirmation enough.

"He was staying in an apartment just outside of Cairo in Heliopolis, near the airport, right?"

Ramy hesitated and then slowly nodded.

"What can you tell me about Dalia Nour?"

"Never heard of her."

Goddard brought his hand down on the table. "Come on!

Whether you believe it or not, I'm trying to help your brother! Tell me about Dalia Nour."

"I'm telling you, I don't know who she is!"

Goddard stared at Ramy. *He's telling the truth. Looks like big brother is withholding information from little brother.*

He closed his eyes for a moment to calm down. When he opened them, he said, "Your brother thinks someone inside this investigation is framing him, right?"

Again, Ramy nodded cautiously.

"And you sent your people to Brazil to find Claudette Ramsey because you and your brother believed she was blackmailing her husband, right?" Goddard pressed.

"That's right."

"And his plan has been to stay on the run until you found Mrs. Ramsey and figured out who was trying to kill him?"

"Yes," Ramy confirmed.

"But the problem was that when your guys found Mrs. Ramsey, you weren't sure whom to turn her over to—you didn't know whom you could trust down there or who was compromised, right? So you told your men to wait for further instructions."

"Yes, sir."

"But you're stuck in jail and Inspector Lemieux is on the verge of tracking down your brother and throwing him into jail too—if he doesn't kill him first, right?"

"'If he doesn't . . .' What's your point, Inspector?" Ramy asked. "Are you offering me a deal or something?"

"Mr. Accad," Goddard replied, "I have become convinced that your brother is innocent."

Ramy threw his hands up as he dropped back in the chair. "That's what I've been telling you from the beginning."

"Well, now I believe you. I also believe you when you say there is a mole in our investigation."

Ramy's eyes grew wide. "Who is it?"

"Marcel Lemieux."

Ramy gasped. "The lead investigator? You're sure?"

"I am now," Goddard said. "When I received the court order to tap all of your phone calls, I also gained access to your e-mails." He could see Ramy's anger at that revelation, but he pressed on. "In searching through your e-mails, my assistant, Colette DuVall, discovered one from a high-ranking official in French intelligence. Do you know of whom I am speaking?"

"That's Pierre Bessette. We've known each other for years. He's clean as a whistle. There's no way you can convince me he's in league with Lemieux," Ramy said defensively.

"Stay with me. I'm not trying to tell you that. Do you remember the e-mail he sent you a few days ago while you were in Baghdad—the one where he said that Lemieux had asked French intelligence for copies of their files on Marwan Accad?"

"Sure, but what does that prove? Wouldn't you expect Lemieux to track down everything he could about his prime suspect in a high-profile murder?"

"Of course he would," Goddard agreed. "However, DuVall tracked down that original e-mail from Lemieux to French intelligence. That one, my dear sir, was dated three days before Ramsey's murder in Monte Carlo."

"Three days *before* the shooting? I don't understand. That would mean . . ."

". . . that Lemieux knew Accad was onto Claudette Ramsey's scheme. Lemieux has to be the one working with her. He planned the hit on Rafeeq Ramsey and your brother to protect both her and, more importantly, himself, because if Claudette was ever found out, it wouldn't take much to run the trail back to him."

"And he's in a race against you to try to find Marwan."

"Right. And if he finds him first, your brother's a dead man."

"How close is Lemieux to finding Marwan?" Ramy asked, his face showing his rising anxiety.

"I've got to think he's very close, Ramy," Goddard admitted. "He's always seemed to be one step ahead of us. Which is why I need your help. Tell me where your brother is, and let me get him into protective custody until I can bring charges against Lemieux and get him arrested."

"I'd help you if I could, Inspector Goddard," Ramy said. "But I honestly don't know where Marwan is right now. The only way I can reach him is on my satellite phone. That's the sole number he'll accept a call from."

"Okay, your sat phone is in my hotel room," Goddard said. "I've been monitoring it in case your brother called. We've got to try another call to warn him. I need to know if I can trust you to work with me on this."

Ramy reached his hand across the table, and Goddard took it. "One hundred percent, Detective. You're the only other one around here besides me who seems to be interested in saving Marwan's life."

Goddard signed all the paperwork necessary to release Ramy Accad. Then the two hurried out of the police station, jumped into a cab, and raced to the hotel.

64

Marwan rubbed his hands over his face, feeling the slight scratch of the dried sweat from his earlier run. Then he stood and walked to the window. *This is the last thing I want to be talking about right now.*

He drummed his fingers on the sill. *However, doesn't he at least deserve a hearing? He's opened up his home to me, demonstrated his trust in me—he's even gone so far as to arm me! He at least deserves enough respect from me to hear what he has to say. Then, when he's got it out of his system, we'll start planning how to protect the family.*

Reluctantly he returned to his stool. "Okay, give it your best shot."

"Ah, a challenge! I like that. I'll tell you what," Naheem said with a smile. "I'll ask you one question, and I'm done. Unless, that is, you ask me for more. Fair enough?"

Marwan nodded.

"Let's say one of those bullets finds you tomorrow or the next day," Naheem said, shooting his fingers at Marwan's forehead. "Suddenly you're standing before God and he asks you, 'Marwan, why should I let you into my heaven?' What would you say?"

Marwan thought for a moment before responding. "There's nothing I could say. I don't deserve to be in heaven—I know it and God knows it. He knows what I've done in my life. He wouldn't even bother asking the question."

"Interesting. Are you happy with that answer?"

"No. But it is what it is."

The two sat silently. Marwan stared at the ground, but he could feel Naheem's eyes on him. He looked up. "Is that it? Are you done?"

Naheem shrugged. "I already broke my promise by asking you two questions instead of just one."

"You're a crafty old man," Marwan said with a bitter smile. "With all due respect, of course."

"Of course."

Just let it go! Move on! There's no time to deal with this stuff. You can work it through after you have a plan or maybe even after this whole thing blows over. Now is not the time.

But part of him would not, could not, let it go. "Okay, you win. Go on," he said.

"As you wish," Naheem said with a twinkle in his eye. "You said it wouldn't matter what you said because of all the things you've done. But I'll tell you that it's those very same things that you've done that actually don't matter."

Marwan dismissed the statement with a wave of his hand. "You don't know what I've done."

"You're right. But God does, and still he wants you to be part of his family. You see, there's nothing you can do that will move you any closer to God or any farther away from him. All of us have sinned and become separated from him. And the only way back is through taking his free gift of salvation."

Marwan nodded. "'Salvation is a gift, not a payment.'"

Naheem looked surprised. "Yes."

"Dalia told me you used to say that a lot."

The older man smiled. "I did. And I still do. Because it's true. And here's something else that's true. You told me about your friend Kadeen, who was killed after he helped you. He proved his love for you by putting his life on the line to save yours. But you need to know that you've got another friend who also sacrificed himself for you—and he did it not to protect your life but to protect your death."

Marwan shook his head. "You're losing me, Pastor."

"Let me put it this way. This life is just a blip in our eternity. We are put here on earth for a short time with the purpose of serving God and loving others. Once this short life is over, eternity begins, and you will either spend it with God or apart from God.

"Jesus died so that you can know, beyond a shadow of a doubt, that your eternity is safe in God's hands. But as we've both said, there's nothing you can do to earn that precious gift. All you can do is receive it."

"But that's the frustrating thing," Marwan said, getting up to look out the window again. This conversation was making him extremely uncomfortable, but for some reason he just couldn't break away. "Everyone talks about 'receiving the gift' and 'accepting his sacrifice' and 'being born again.' You may know what you're saying, but to someone like me, I have no clue what you're talking about. Yes, I want to receive the gift," he said, holding out his hands. When nothing magically appeared, he threw them up. "Do you see what I mean? They're meaningless words."

"You want to know the difficult, soul-wrenching, spiritually-exhausting process of receiving the gift of salvation?"

Marwan held out his hands again. "I'm ready," he said, half-mocking.

"Just say yes."

Marwan dropped his hands. "Just say yes?"

"Exactly. Just say yes. Yes to Christ. Yes, Jesus, I believe you are who you said you are—the Son of God. Yes, I believe you died for my sins. Yes, I want your forgiveness for all I've done. Yes, I want to live for you."

"Yes, huh? That's it?"

"That's it. The Bible calls it believing and receiving. Believing means you accept it with your head as truth. Receiving means you accept it with your heart as the principle on which you are going to base your life. Believing and receiving—yes, Jesus, I believe in you; yes, Jesus, I receive you as my Lord."

Marwan didn't know what to feel. It was as if all the years of running from God, all the reasons and excuses he'd been harboring for turning his back on Jesus' gift, came crashing to the ground in that moment. *I'm done, God. I'm tired of saying no. I'm ready to say yes.* "Would you . . . ?"

"Of course."

They both bowed their heads, and Naheem led Marwan in a prayer, using words very similar to what he had already said.

When they were done, Naheem put his hand on Marwan's shoulder and said, "God is good! The second prodigal in two days has returned home."

65

"HE'S NOT ANSWERING." Ramy threw the satellite phone down on the bed in Goddard's hotel room.

"What?" Goddard looked up from the laptop he was working on.

"Marwan's not answering."

"Try again," Goddard said, turning back to his work.

"I've tried four times!"

"Okay. So what does that mean?"

Ramy ticked off the answers on his fingers. "It means either the phone is off, he doesn't have it with him, or . . ."

The room went silent. Ramy snatched the phone off the bed and dialed again.

"Don't worry," Goddard insisted as the phone rang and rang in Ramy's ear. "We'll find him." *I just hope he's still alive when we do.*

Goddard's own phone rang. It was DuVall. He answered immediately. "What have you got, Colette?"

"A message from the Skeleton," DuVall answered bitterly.

"Let me guess. Lemieux's information has led him to believe that Marwan Accad is hiding out in Tehran or Kathmandu or Ulaanbaatar, and we better get there quick."

"Right idea, wrong location. He said that they were able to track a boat leaving Sharm el-Sheikh and heading south down the Red Sea to Soma Bay. There are witnesses there who saw Accad and a woman walking through town and entering the Sheraton."

"And you, my lead investigator, find yourself doubting the veracity of his statements?"

"Most definitely. Especially since I think I know where he is."

Goddard leaped to his feet. "You know where he is?"

Ramy threw the phone onto the bed and ran over to Goddard.

"We've been able to locate the boat that was stolen in Sharm. It was moored in Dahab. And about an hour ago a complaint was lodged with the police in Dahab about a rental boat that was never returned. They showed a picture of Accad, and—"

"He was the one who rented the boat."

"Exactly, but as an Englishman named Andrew Cooper."

"Where is the boat now?"

"We haven't found it yet, but I can almost guarantee it is in Aqaba, Jordan."

"Where is he?" Ramy demanded of Goddard, who waved him quiet.

To Duvall, Goddard said, "That makes logical sense, but why are you so sure?"

"The girl with Accad—Dalia Nour—"

"Yes, yes."

"She's from Jordan—grew up in Ma'an."

Goddard turned to Ramy and said, "They're in Ma'an, Jordan!"

"Ma'an?" Ramy echoed, not at all expecting that answer.

"Where's Lemieux?" Goddard asked, knowing the answer he was going to get.

"I don't know. He's pulled one of the disappearing acts that he's so famous for before breaking open a case. Everyone here is abuzz thinking he must be following a hot lead and that an arrest is imminent. I agree with them—all except for the arrest part."

Goddard felt his stomach tighten. "Have the Jordanian authorities been alerted that Lemieux is coming?"

"Not that I can tell, sir."

Not good, not good, Goddard thought. *That means he's taking his own men. We've got to get some help on this! But how do we break through Lemieux's reputation?*

"Colette, can we prove yet that Lemieux is crooked?"

"No, sir. I don't believe so."

"What's it going to take? What do you need?"

"Time. We just need more time."

Frustrated, Goddard shouted, "We don't have more time! If Lemieux finds Marwan Accad, he'll kill him!"

"Should I call the Jordanian authorities and have them arrest Lemieux?"

"No," Goddard said. "They're not going to take down the

great inspector unless they have a whole lot more evidence than we have at the moment."

"Then what are you going to do, sir?"

"The only thing I can, Colette. I'm going to take down the Skeleton myself."

66

Marwan expected to feel totally different, but there really wasn't much of a change. He was still wanted for murder. There were still people who wanted to kill him. Dalia's family was still in serious danger.

But something *had* changed. The feeling of guilt that had been weighing him down was gone. The anger that he felt at his situation had been replaced by a strange sense of peace. The fear he felt for Dalia and her family had been overtaken by trust in God's will and God's power.

"Thank you," he said to Naheem.

"Don't thank me. I haven't done anything except point the way."

"Even so, thank you."

Naheem nodded, then stood with a loud grunt. Marwan followed.

Before they left the room, Naheem asked, "Would you be willing to do me one favor?"

"Of course. Anything."

Naheem paused, as if trying to weigh whether or not to say what he wanted to say. Finally he made his decision. "Don't tell Rima about who you really are—at least not yet. You said you think that we have another day or two before things might get dangerous. Let Rima have a day with her daughter; then tonight I'll tell her the truth. I'll probably pay for it, but I think it'll be worth it."

Marwan wanted to say, *"No, it's too dangerous. We're already on thin ice."* But he was finding it very difficult to give a negative response to anyone in this family.

"Okay. But tomorrow you follow my lead so that I can get all of us to safety."

"It's a deal," Naheem said, shaking Marwan's hand with his big paw. "Now, let's go out and tell the women about what's happened in here this morning."

The news of Marwan's conversion was received with screams and laughter and tears and hugs. Dalia, especially, held on to Marwan, whispering in his ear, "Let's start over, you and I. This time we'll do it God's way."

"If you'll show me how, that's what I want too," he whispered back.

Once things calmed down, plans for the day were made. When Marwan heard that Rima and Dalia wanted all of them to go to Petra—Jordan's most famous archaeological site, only a few kilometers from Ma'an—he protested at first.

But again, contrary to his better judgment, he found himself saying yes.

After taking a quick shower to wash off the residue from the morning's run, he decided against shaving. His three-day beard gave him a shadow on his face that just might help him achieve the look he wanted. Borrowing an old pair of aviator sunglasses and a large cotton safari hat from Elias's closet, he checked himself in the mirror and decided he did indeed look just ridiculous enough to blend in well with all the American and European tour groups that were bound to be there.

After Marwan endured some razzing from Naheem and Dalia, they all piled into Naheem's car. Along the way to the site, Dalia, who sat in back with Marwan, pointed out different places to Marwan—her elementary school, the first site of her dad's church, the church's new location, the small community theater where she first held a boy's hand.

Marwan smiled and made small comments during Dalia's tour, but the whole time he was thinking what a bad idea this was. At least he had the gun, in case things fell apart. But would it be enough?

When they arrived, Rima asked if she could hire a donkey cart to carry her through the one-mile Siq. Dalia offered to go with her, while Naheem and Marwan walked.

As they trudged down the narrow gorge between the sandstone cliffs, Naheem told Marwan about growing up near Petra half a century ago. Born just two years after the creation of the state of Israel, his childhood was filled with memories of Palestinian refugees and poverty.

The day after his seventeenth birthday, his father left the family to fight against Israel in the Six-Day War. When he returned, minus a leg and the lower half of his right arm, he wasn't the same. He lasted three months before he hung himself.

Devastated, Naheem vowed revenge, and on his eighteenth birthday he enlisted in the Jordanian army. Knowing he'd have a far better chance for action in the special forces, he signed up right after boot camp, training hard and pushing his body beyond what he thought he could do. But in his mind it was all worth it, because when the time came to push Israel into the sea, he'd be on the front lines.

As it turned out, his first action was not against the Israelis after all. It was against fellow Arabs. In September 1970, the militant elements of the Palestinian refugees were getting too strong, and King Hussein was afraid they were going to try to set up their own separate state along the Jordan River. So he sent in his military to push the *fedayeen* guerrillas out of the country. Well over three thousand Palestinians were killed by Jordanian ammunition—five by bullets fired from Naheem's own rifle.

Anger and guilt plagued Naheem, and the first opportunity he had to get out of the army, he did. Without a job and without a future, he seriously considered joining the Palestinian Liberation Organization, which was reorganizing itself in Lebanon. But misgivings about leaving his mother alone kept him at home.

That's when the man from Amman came to town. His name was Samir Toukan, and from the day he arrived, he made it clear that his whole reason for coming to town was to build a church and win souls for Christ.

Naheem didn't care about Christianity one way or the

other, but he did see a chance for work. Soon he was hired on to help construct the church's building. The one requirement Pastor Toukan set down for working there, however, was to participate in a lunchtime Bible study once a week—a small price, in Naheem's mind, for a paying job.

It took only three studies before Naheem was on his knees saying the same words Marwan had prayed earlier in the day. And in that moment, all his anger against Israel was gone, all his bitterness at his dad's suicide ended, and all his guilt from killing fellow Arabs was washed clean. For the first time in his life, he truly experienced peace, hope, and joy. Naheem started working at the church, and two years later when Pastor Toukan went back to Amman, he took over as pastor.

"So, you see, Marwan, I too know what it means to feel the power of God's great forgiveness," Naheem concluded as he walked.

But Marwan was no longer listening.

He stood rooted in his tracks, eyes wide. They had just about reached the end of the Siq, and Marwan was looking through the Eye of the Needle to the astonishing rock facade of the Treasury—a view made famous to the world when Indiana Jones rode through it while on his last crusade.

Slowly he moved forward, and with each step he took, the view expanded until he was able to take in the whole rock carving at once. He stopped and shook his head in wonder.

Marwan felt he could stand there all day taking in the view—until Dalia asked him if he wanted to look inside. Then he was off in a flash.

67

Marwan ran up through the front entrance, ready to tour the depths of the caves inside, but was stopped short by the rear wall. He looked around for the passage that would take him beyond the twelve-square-meter room.

"Surprise," Dalia said, bouncing up next to him. "Welcome to Hollywood magic!"

"You mean this is it? No tunnels, no deep crevasses, no ancient crusaders?"

"Nope, just a tomb for two-thousand-year-old rich guys!"

"Really, that's it?"

"That's it," Dalia answered with an I-know-something-you-don't-know smile on her face.

I can't believe all that hype for one big—albeit amazingly beautiful—rock carving, Marwan thought as he walked back out into the sunlight. That's when he saw the facades carved in the rock faces across the way, and his jaw dropped a second time. He had been so fixated on the Treasury that he hadn't noticed there was anything else.

Again Dalia appeared beside him.

"You mean there's more?" he asked.

"Surprise a second time!"

She led him to the middle of the Treasury's courtyard and pointed him left. All along the walls for as far as he could see, there were carvings—some big, some small, some plain, some unbelievably ornate.

"Care to walk with me awhile?" Dalia asked with a grin, slipping her arm in Marwan's.

"Lead on, my beautiful tour guide."

For the next three hours, they wandered the ancient Nabataean city. They explored cliffs and caves. They listened to a string quartet from stone bleachers in an amphitheater carved from the cliffs. They lunched at a busy café. They almost took a camel ride, but for once Marwan insisted on saying no—partly to avoid being up high and in the open, but mostly to steer clear of the horrible stench of the beasts. He'd learned his lesson riding through the Egyptian dunes with Dalia.

When it was time to head back, everyone's legs were tired and their feet were sore. But it had been an amazing day. Marwan had seen things he never imagined existed, wonders of human skill, discipline, and dedication. It was a day he'd never forget.

They were just passing the amphitheater again when a gunshot echoed through the canyon, and Marwan dropped to the ground, clutching his leg.

Dalia screamed. Naheem whipped around to see where the shot had come from, then tried to cover the women with his body.

Another gunshot rang out. This time the bullet ricocheted off the stone theater benches to their right, sending shards of rock and dust through the air.

"Get down," Marwan shouted through gritted teeth. "Over there, behind the pillars!"

He had Naheem's SIG in his hand and was scanning the cliffs. He did a quick check of the wound in his leg. It felt like razor blades were embedded in it, but at least he could move it. Still looking up, he shuffled over to where Naheem lay across his wife and daughter.

Slapping him hard on the back, Marwan said, "Get them behind the pillars now!"

Naheem responded quickly, nestling Rima and Dalia under his arms. Two more shots kicked up dirt at Marwan's feet as he hustled the threesome backward. Spotting a long stone wall, he redirected them that way.

By the time he got them there, bullets were hitting all around them. People were screaming and running in panic. A passing camel grunted and fell to the ground, trapping its rider underneath.

As Marwan tried to figure out what to do next, the horror of last night's dream flashed behind his eyes. *I will not let that happen! No matter what, that will not happen!*

God, protect this family. Don't let them die because of me. Take me; I'm ready to go. But please watch over these three.

Marwan peeked over the stone wall and got an eyeful of dust from a near miss. Abruptly he dropped back down. Rima was crying, and Dalia was trembling with fear as Naheem held the two of them close.

"These people are after me. I'm going to draw them away," he said to Naheem, putting his hand on the big man's shoulder. When he did, he felt that it was wet. He quickly pulled his hand away and saw that it was red with blood.

"I'm fine," Naheem said with a determined look.

"But—"

"Go! Deal with the threat, soldier! I'll watch over my family. You just be sure to take care of yourself."

"Don't you worry about that," Marwan said with a fierce glint in his eyes. "I've got to survive. I'm planning on marrying your daughter."

A savage smile spread across Naheem's face as he pointed with his head for Marwan to go up the theater's steps. Just before he turned to go, Marwan's eyes caught Dalia's. The look that passed between them said all that needed to be said. Then Marwan was off.

68

Marwan raced up the steps, zigzagging as he went. Bullets ricocheted all around him. *How many of them are there?* he wondered as he dove into the entrance of a small tomb. *There's got to be at least four or five, probably more.*

The darkness of the tomb and its elevation allowed him to survey the scene. He could see the Nours crawling into another access tunnel. *Excellent move, old man. Now just lie low.*

It was mayhem down both sides of the canyon as people fled, but below him empty space had opened up.

He saw three men with machine guns running across the open area, heading for the theater. They were firing short bursts at him, keeping him pinned down. He managed to get three shots off in their direction. One of them connected.

Marwan hated being trapped, and he looked for an exit.

There was nothing to his left, but to his right there was a small shaft of light. He chanced another look out. What he saw was not good. The two remaining gunmen were rapidly approaching, and two more were on their way, coming from the other direction.

I've got to get them away from Dalia's family! I've got to keep moving! The pain in his leg was growing steadily worse, and he knew he was losing blood. *Come on, make the most of the time you have left!*

He ducked back into the cave and moved toward the light. As he drew close, he found a small opening. Beyond the gap was a narrow path that led to other caves and tombs that dotted the mountainside.

Wedging himself through, he stood up on the other side and immediately pressed himself against the stone. The path was little more than a ledge. One slip would plunge him seventy feet to the rocks below. He hugged the rock face and worked his way forward as quickly and carefully as he could, leaving a streak of red to mark his progress.

Somehow, Marwan managed to get to the next cave. He hunkered down there for a moment, trying to catch his breath and steady his nerves. *Think! What now? Those guys are moving twice as fast as you. You don't have time to—*

Suddenly a shadow blocked the entrance to the cave, quickly followed by gunfire. Surprised, Marwan began firing and didn't stop until he saw the shadow fall backward off the cliff.

Before he could catch his breath, the barrel of an automatic assault weapon nosed around the corner. Bullets ricocheted off the cave walls, and the air filled with smoke. Marwan felt one round clip his arm and another take a chunk out of his ear.

He dropped flat and tucked himself into a corner to ride out the assault. When the firing stopped, Marwan pointed his gun toward the light and waited.

Patience, patience.

Eventually, way down low, the gunman poked just enough of his head around the corner for a bullet to send him down the cliff after his buddy.

Crawling to the front of the cave, Marwan looked both ways along the ledge. For the moment, it was clear. He jumped to his feet and had a moment of vertigo. Too much blood was pouring out of his leg for him to keep this going much longer.

Got to keep moving! There's got to be safety somewhere! You stay here, eventually you'll run out of either ammo or luck.

Marwan edged himself onto the ledge and worked his way farther down the cliff face. His head was spinning and he was having trouble keeping his balance. Shouts from below echoed up the rock wall. He'd been spotted, and now he was a sitting duck.

As he prepared to be picked off, the wall suddenly gave way to an old rock stairway leading to the top of the mountain. He hurried up the steps as fast as his wounded leg would let him.

Something slammed into his back. As he stumbled forward, he heard the distinctive report of a sniper rifle. He started gasping for breath even before he hit the ground, and he knew that one of his lungs was collapsing.

Got to keep moving, he thought as he pulled himself along the dirt. *Got to keep . . .*

69

WHEN MARWAN CAME TO, he saw a tall, gaunt man standing over him. He was flanked by two other men, and they all had murder in their eyes.

"Well, well," the man in the center said, "if it isn't the great Marwan Accad."

Marwan said nothing.

"Allow me to finally introduce myself. I am Inspector Marcel Lemieux. Perhaps you've heard of me."

Marwan's breath was coming in short gasps, but he managed to say, "My brother . . . knows everything. . . . He's got men . . . in Brazil . . . hunting Claudette Ramsey."

"Claudette is in hiding," Lemieux said with a sad shake of his head. "And Ramy is in jail. But don't worry, I'll take care of him next."

"I don't believe—"

"Enough! I don't care what you believe! You've caused me enough trouble, and now your time is at an end."

As Marwan watched Lemieux point the gun at his head, he was amazed at the peace he felt. Rather than facing death alone, he was going to meet his God. And when he did, he'd have the right answer to that question Naheem asked him earlier.

He closed his eyes.

An enormous roar filled the air, and a violent rush of wind stirred up a thick cloud of dust on the mountaintop. Had Lemieux pulled the trigger already? Marwan opened his eyes again, only to see a helicopter rising quickly above the cliff's edge. The aircraft hovered near the group of men.

"Put your weapons down, Lemieux!" a voice said over the chopper's loudspeaker. *"All of you, don't make it worse for yourselves! Claudette Ramsey has confessed to everything in São Paulo. It's over! Put your weapons down, drop to your knees, and put your hands behind your heads!"*

Lemieux's men did what they were told. But Lemieux himself refused to be taken that easily. He fired through the dust at the helicopter—round after round. The pilot banked left, then right, then circled the entire mountaintop, trying to stay out of Lemieux's line of fire. When the inspector's gun was empty, he quickly dropped the clip out and reached into his pocket for another.

Marwan saw his chance. He pushed himself to his feet and fell onto Lemieux. The gun dropped from Lemieux's hands and went skittering across the rocks. Lemieux swung and kicked, trying to get Marwan's deadweight off his back.

Marwan saw one of Lemieux's men reach for his gun, but three shots rang out and the man slumped to the ground. Knowing he couldn't hold on much longer, he began working his hands up Lemieux's shoulders. When he reached the man's long neck, he closed them tight.

Lemieux reached up to pull Marwan's fingers away, but his grip was too strong. He held for Kadeen; he held for Rania and the girls; he held for Rafeeq Ramsey and his twelve-year-old daughter. Tighter and tighter he squeezed, until Lemieux dropped to his knees. Using his own weight, Marwan pulled him backward until they were both facing the sky with Lemieux stretched out on top of him. The inspector was flailing now, and Marwan felt things begin to pop in the man's neck.

"Marwan, no! Don't do it—please!"

He was stunned. It was Dalia's voice.

Her eyes red with tears, she was walking toward him. Naheem and Rima were following behind, and just beyond them, Marwan could see the helicopter touching down.

"Marwan, please, it's not right," she cried. "Don't become like him."

Slowly Marwan released his grip. Lemieux rolled off of him, coughing and gasping for air. A moment later, Naheem was on top of the man, keeping him down with a knee to his back.

Dalia dropped next to Marwan and cradled his head in her lap. Rima came up behind her and stood praying.

"I know you wanted us to stay put," Dalia said as she held him close, "but we saw the helicopter and we had to come. I'm so sorry."

With his breathing so shallow, Marwan was unable to get any more words out, so he simply mouthed "I love you" to Dalia.

"I love you, too," she said through her tears. "So very much."

Everything was getting hazy for Marwan, and he bounced in and out of consciousness. The second time he came to, Ramy was there helping to lift him onto a makeshift stretcher.

"We got you now, Big Brother! We're getting you out of here."

Marwan tried to smile but wasn't certain if he was successful or not. So he blinked instead, but when he opened his eyes, he saw he was being loaded onto the helicopter.

Just beyond the crowd surrounding him, two uniformed deputies were handcuffing the last of Lemieux's men. Lemieux himself was also cuffed and was being held tightly by a European-looking man in a dark blue suit.

Marwan's body was jostled around as his stretcher was strapped to the floor. He knew that it should hurt, but he really wasn't feeling much of anything anymore. Ramy climbed in and sat at his feet; then Dalia followed and sat by his head.

Through the encroaching blackness, Marwan saw Dalia's face and felt her cool hand stroking his cheek and forehead. In her eyes was so much life, so much love. *There's no way I'm letting this take me away from her. Forget it. We've got a whole life to spend together.*

Marwan fought to keep consciousness, but it was a losing battle. The last thing he saw before the peaceful blackness enveloped him was a cheap, already-peeling Egyptian ring sitting firmly on the third finger of Dalia's left hand.

About the Author

Josh McDowell received a master's degree in theology from Talbot Theological Seminary in California. In 1961, he joined the staff of Campus Crusade for Christ International. Not long after, he started the Josh McDowell Ministry to reach young people worldwide with the truth and love of Jesus.

Josh has spoken to more than ten million young people in eighty-four countries, including more than seven hundred university and college campuses. He has authored or coauthored more than seventy books and workbooks and has sold more than 51 million copies worldwide. Josh's most popular works are *More Than a Carpenter*, which has been translated into over eighty-five languages and sold more than 15 million copies, and *The New Evidence That Demands a Verdict*, recognized by *World* magazine as one of the twentieth century's top forty books. Josh continues to travel throughout the United States and countries around the world, helping young people and adults bolster their faith and scriptural beliefs.

Josh has been married to Dottie for more than thirty years and has four children. Josh and Dottie live in Dallas, Texas. Visit his Web site at www. josh.org.